LOVE DETOUR

ALLIE MCDERMID

Copyright © 2022 by Allie McDermid

All rights reserved.

The right of Allie McDermid to be identified as the author of this work has been asserted by her in accordance with the Copyright, Designs and Patents Act 1988.

No part of this book may be reproduced in any form or by any electronic or mechanical means, including information storage and retrieval systems, without written permission from the author, except for the use of brief quotations in a book review.

All characters and events in the publication are fictitious and any resemblance to real persons, living or dead, is purely coincidental.

ALSO BY ALLIE MCDERMID

Love Charade

Love Detour

Love Magnet

Long Time Coming

1

Kirsty Hamilton slammed her head into her pillow, letting out a loud groan of frustration.

'This is fucking ridiculous.'

Four searches of her bedside drawers had proved unfruitful on the mission to find her earplugs but she was happy to add a fifth, just in case. She swished her hand around the contents – there wasn't much to move: passport, loose change, loyalty cards, her vibrator, and a few other things – but they were still nowhere to be found. If Dani had borrowed them without returning the box she was really going to hit the roof.

Little sisters: who would have 'em?

Certainly not Kirsty. Especially when said little sister was having absurdly loud sex with her latest conquest.

Hours this had been going on. Hours. Surely they would run out of stamina soon?

Banging on the wall had done nothing. Shouting through the door had only earned laughter and a lacklustre apology. Naturally, all texts were being ignored.

The only saving grace was that the noise wasn't being made by Dani, just her faceless guest.

Most likely Kirsty would never get to meet the girl, thank God. There was nothing worse than enduring the racket from one of Dani's dates only to have awkward chat in the morning while she made a coffee. At least Dani was a one-and-done type girl: Kirsty never had to endure the same squeeze twice. It made small talk easy – she could recycle it should the worst happen.

'Fuck's sake, Dani,' Kirsty yelled as a loud bang reverberated through the wall.

She'd purposely refused the offer to go out with her and Dani's pals last night, intent on having an early evening and being fresh-faced in the morning. Mum wanted her to do some stupid matchmaking event to help promote the café and although it was way out of her comfort zone she'd agreed, happy to help her mother in any way. Now though, the thought of going on little sleep was even less appealing. Everything had been carefully planned and now that plan was out the window.

Maybe Dani could go instead.

Her mum had already ruled that out. Tonight's activities being case in point.

Had Dani done this on purpose? Acting out because Kirsty had a chance to actually meet someone?

It was impossible to know. To look at they were chalk and cheese. Dani, at the grand old age of thirty-three, always dressed like she'd grabbed what she could from the sports department. Her trademark item was a backwards baseball hat or beanie. She'd dressed like that forever, way before the lesbians of TikTok made it cool. The newfound popularity of the style only inflated Dani's ego.

Kirsty on the other hand . . . well, she wasn't hyper-feminine, but she'd never be caught dead in a snapback.

On the surface, all that connected them was their wavy brown hair, chestnut eyes, and the fact they shared their Dad's smile.

But it was deeper than that. Yes, she could be a little brat at times – Kirsty picked up a shoe from the floor and chucked it at their dividing wall – but Dani was her best friend as well as her sister. There was no one else in the world she loved more.

But FUCKING HELL would she ever Shut. The. Fuck. Up?

Silence descended in the flat, as if the universe could read her very thoughts. She raised herself on her forearms and listened.

They were quiet. They were actually quiet.

Kirsty looked at her phone: just shy of four. If she got to sleep now she could get a few hours before her shift in the café.

She settled back in bed, rearranging her pillow, hugging it tighter.

Peace at last.

She closed her eyes, ready to drift off.

Then the banging started again.

2

Rhona Devi smiled, trying in earnest to take everything in, but the sheer deluge of information her newest client was throwing at her wasn't making the task easy.

She scribbled another point in her notebook: *don't mingle, just observe.* 'So, how many people do you think will be there tonight?'

Annie blew through her teeth: the petite woman's black bob bounced as she gently shook her head. 'Good question. Response has been great online. I'd expect at least double what we got last year. It will be busy but manageable.'

Not a concrete answer, but she could work with that. 'So, I'm a little like a referee? Skirt around the attendees but don't interfere with what's going on?'

'Exactly. So a little different to your usual gigs; I don't want you to give any direction at all.'

'Got it.' A little different was an understatement. Rhona was used to high-end wedding photography and a little arty architectural stuff to satisfy her own creative itch. This was a whole other ball game. She needed cash, though, and if it

Love Detour 5

meant covering paternity leave for a local business investment group she was all in.

From what she could gather this was now a yearly thing. The event had launched last year with much success, so was being rolled out again. A month of matchmaking events in the up-and-coming Glasgow suburb of Shawlands, spanning the entirety of August. All the businesses in the area got involved, hosting events and donating prizes. All inviting publicity for the area. Tonight's singles event kicked off the celebration and five lucky couples would be selected, treated to a month of free dates, and then one lucky duo would be publicly voted the winner, earning themselves a tidy five grand.

Rhona almost wished she could compete herself.

She liked Shawlands: it had a trendy vibe without feeling pretentious. She'd only discovered it through the job listing, having chosen to live in the West End when she'd moved through, but she was fast falling in love with the place. Shame she wasn't planning on sticking around. Maybe if she eventually settled in Glasgow. God knows when that would be, though.

'So, if you come at six-thirty you can run through the list of shots I need.'

'Yep,' Rhona said, putting on her best smile.

'Did I already say that?'

'Yeah.' Rhona bit her bottom lip, not wanting Annie to think she was winding her up. The poor woman was stressed, that was all. She'd dealt with brides that were a thousand times worse. This was nothing.

'Sorry – it's just so weird not having Isaac here. You forget how in sync you are with someone when you've worked together so long. It's odd having to explain stuff.'

'Honestly, don't worry about it. It's good to be certain we're both on the same page.'

It wasn't the first time Isaac had been brought up. Annie clearly missed the guy. Spectacularly bad planning for him to have a baby over their biggest marketing month.

'When will you be able to get the photos to me?' Annie asked, pacing the floor by the pub's table. She'd chosen to meet where the event was being held, a venue called Cal's, and Rhona was glad to get a feel for the establishment without punters. The place was like a labyrinth.

'If all goes to plan, tomorrow lunchtime. These are candid shots, so I take it you won't want them heavily edited?'

'No, no,' Annie replied, a hand stroking her chin. 'They're just to get a flavour of the event, show people what they missed out on.'

'Brilliant. Well, yeah, I'll get up early tomorrow and have them done ASAP.' She wouldn't usually be so appeasable, but this was a gig that paid good money. If she played her cards right now maybe she would get a repeat performance for other campaigns.

'You're an angel.' Annie ran a finger down her open notebook on the table. 'I think I've covered everything. Do you have any questions?'

Rhona shook her head. 'I'll probably hang around here instead of going home, though. Anywhere you think I should grab some food?'

ON ANNIE'S ADVICE, she'd scoped out Shawlands' best brunch spot, Cafella. It had a cult-like Instagram following and if the photos were anything to go by Rhona wouldn't be leaving disappointed.

Shawlands was like a café Mecca. Rhona had never seen so many in such a small area and not a big brand name to be seen, either. She almost felt bad for going somewhere so busy when plenty of other cafés were queue-free, but when in Rome. She couldn't visit and not try out one of the area's hottest spots.

She joined the short queue and pulled out her phone, checking her emails. Nothing. Good: that meant that Amber was happy with last weekend's shoot.

A toddler screamed to high heaven a few spots further up the queue. Hopefully, he would be calm by the time Rhona got seated. Or at least be far enough away to not make her ears ache.

Babies were fast becoming the theme of the moment. She'd been more than a little surprised to hear from Amber a few months ago, having not been the best at keeping in touch once they left uni. It was hardly her fault, though: times changed, people grew up. They were no longer carefree twenty-somethings whose only responsibility was getting to photography class on time. Now they had babies, businesses, and mortgages to worry about. Well. Amber did. Rhona most certainly did not.

Amber had recently completed the hat-trick, which was where Rhona came in. She'd been looking for freelance work so when Amber had got in touch trying to flesh out her maternity plans, Rhona had jumped at the chance.

Two photography jobs covering maternity and paternity leave. What were the chances of that? It had to be a sign. Of what, she had no idea. That her life was changing? Full of pregnant possibility? She could run with that.

It was fun working for Amber. They'd always got on

well, so it was easy to pick up where they left off. Plus, she had amazing clients and Rhona was excited to be getting paid to travel around Scotland. Now Amber was slowly returning to work, she got the Glasgow gigs and Rhona got the ones further afield. They were a dream team.

The queue moved forward. Across the road, the deli and neighbouring cocktail shop were also queued out. Maybe she could pick up some cocktails to take back to the flat, build bridges with her flatmate, Niall.

He was a weird guy and barely ever in. He valued his social life more than getting to know who he lived with, which suited Rhona fine to a degree, but she did miss having someone to speak to in the evening. Someone to unwind with. That's what you get when you find a flat online on a whim. But everything was temporary; she could easily change that if she wanted to.

Not like she'd be here long, though. A few more months could easily be tolerated.

'Sitting in or taking away?' a cheery woman with short red hair asked, kitted out in Cafella's trendy uniform: a black T-shirt emblazoned with their stylish logo. 'Sitting in,' Rhona replied with a smile. 'But happy to take away if you're too busy.'

'Don't you worry: won't be long.' She went to move down the line but did a double take before she could get going. 'Are you the new photographer?'

'Hmm?' The question caught her off guard.

'Are you Annie's new photographer?'

'Oh, yeah. That's me.' She extended a hand. 'Rhona.'

'Beth. I own this place,' she replied, giving Rhona's hand a shake. 'I don't suppose Annie's mentioned the Christmas shoot to you yet?'

'Oh no, just Lovefest.'

Beth pursed her lips as her eyes narrowed. 'She promised us a date for the Christmas shoot soon. My guys want to take holidays, but she usually shoots it in September; I want the whole team in it if I can.'

'She's not mentioned it, sorry.' A Christmas shoot? Would Isaac be back by next month? Hopefully not. That could be another good wedge of cash.

'Can you do me a favour? Would you ask her? She's got that much going on, sometimes getting answers can be tough via email.'

'I'll do my best.'

'Thank you! Lifesaver. And if you do get info, your next lunch is on me.'

'Sounds like a deal.'

'And have a coffee on me in the meantime, keep your energy levels up for tonight.'

Rhona could get used to working in Shawlands.

3

Kirsty didn't say a word as Dani walked through the kitchen doors, intent on taking up her usual position behind the counter, making coffees.

Instead, she shot daggers and smacked the baseball cap right off her sister's head as soon as she was within reach.

'Hey, what was that for?' Dani asked, playing the victim, hamming up her distress for the customers in the queue.

Kirsty couldn't give a rat's tooter who was watching. 'You know exactly what that's for,' she growled out of the side of her mouth.

Dani retrieved her cap from the floor, smoothing her hair back before repositioning it. She pulled a face that could melt butter. 'Sorry. Got a bit carried away.'

'A bit? A bit? You know how many hours sleep I got? Two, if I'm lucky. Two!'

Dani looked sheepish. 'I'll make it up to you.' She considered her options, her eyes lighting up as she settled on one. 'Why don't you finish early? Go home and have a nap.'

'It's too busy,' Kirsty replied, monotone. She tipped a

double espresso into a cup before reaching for the milk. 'Lovefest properly starts tonight – we've been rammed all day.'

'Is that tonight? Fuck.'

Kirsty tipped her head to the side, her eyes unblinking. 'You knew fine well that was tonight. That's why I didn't go out with you.'

Dani swallowed hard. 'Shit.' She surveyed the queue: there was no denying how busy they were. 'Busy enough to rival Cafella today, sis.'

Kirsty was done with small talk. She batted at the checks pinned with magnets to the shelf above the coffee machine. 'Table two need three lattes. One oat, two cow.'

Dani pulled the doe eyes again, bumping her hip into her sister's. 'I really did forget, honest.'

'Three lattes. Now.'

Dani huffed and set to work. Flat white done, Kirsty popped the final drink on the tray and hit the bell, letting her cousin Tara know it was ready to go out.

She liked working with so many family members – in a team of twelve, only two weren't related by blood. Yes, she was pissed at Dani, but anger never lingered. Family meant unconditional love. Forgive and forget. Life's too short to stay mad. By tonight she'd be flopped on the sofa with her, telling her how dreadful this Lovefest event had been.

Her stomach lurched at the thought.

She really, really didn't want to have to do it.

Mum had been sympathetic this morning and listened to her moan about Dani and her latest misdemeanours, but at the end of the day, there was no going back on her promise.

Mum's friends Catherine and Harry owned a deli round the corner and their sales had gone through the roof when their daughter was selected as part of a lucky couple last year.

Of course she wanted to help her mum and the café, but this was so far out of her comfort zone it might as well be in a different galaxy. The thought of it made her feel sick and her palms sweaty.

Café Odyssey was a little over a hundred years old and currently on its fourth generation of owners. Her great-great-grandad had started it, just shy of Queen Victoria, and it had been going strong ever since. Well. Strong was maybe generous these days, with so many new and trendy cafés popping up in Shawlands, but it was going nonetheless.

One day it would be Kirsty's and the pressure scared her shitless.

The queue was thinning out, with the initial lunchtime rush being sated by Dani's capable hands. Kirsty could moan all she wanted, but Dani was a damn fine barista and they made a good team. There was a reason Mum had put them on the front counter together. She'd always preferred it to working in the kitchen. Waiting tables she could take or leave, but the kitchen? No thanks: too hot, too much stress. Out here you got to chat to customers, get to know them, be the face of the café. Chat came easy to Kirsty. When she wasn't going on two hours sleep, anyway.

But, like all seasoned professionals, her smile never wavered and her demeanour never faltered. Customers were none the wiser.

An hour later she'd thawed enough to talk to Dani. 'So, what did I miss last night?'

Dani shrugged, her own lack of sleep catching up on her. 'Not much. Izzy still has her tits in a twist over Carly. Trip was surprisingly quiet. Kim continues to be perpetually single.'

Kirsty waited for the final member of their gang to be listed. Nothing came. 'And Ashley?' she prompted.

Dani shook her head, confusion ghosting her features. 'No Ashley. She was boring, like you.'

'Unlike her.'

'Something to do with her mum.'

'She okay?'

Dani shrugged.

That was weird. Usually where Dani was, Ashley wasn't far behind. Kirsty didn't have the energy for follow-up questions. Whatever it was would sort itself out.

'Pals, I need a triple shot.'

Kirsty turned to find her best friend Izzy lolling over the cake fridge.

'And Dani, this is free. It's your fault I need it,' Izzy groaned.

She was dressed up, make-up perfectly done, her blonde hair braided in a pretty updo, and a denim jacket styled with smart casual clothes. She was here to work, not socialise.

'I didn't make you stay out, Iz,' Dani said with a smirk.

'You know I can't say no to tequila.' Izzy turned to Kirsty. 'Do I look okay? Can you tell I'm dying inside?'

Kirsty had known Izzy for the best part of a decade, having met her when she got a job as a barista to pay the bills in uni. It was fair to say her new job paid significantly better than Café Odyssey did. 'I think he'll cope,' Kirsty replied with a quiet laugh. At her best, Izzy was a stone-cold ten. Today, she could still run circles round most women. Some people just had it. 'When's he due?'

'Ten minutes. So, better make me a flat white too. Make him think I'm a civilised woman,' she said, checking her phone as she spoke. 'Please. Sorry. My mind isn't working.'

Kirsty couldn't help but laugh. 'That better not be Carly's Insta you're checking.'

Izzy stuffed the phone back in her handbag. 'Shut up. Dani says you're out tonight?'

If looks could kill, Dani would be on the floor. 'So you did remember?'

Dani shot Izzy an equally brutal look. 'At the time. Yes, I must have remembered to impart that information before forgetting.'

Kirsty raised an eyebrow. 'Whatever. Yes, Izzy, I am out tonight. I don't suppose you fancy chumming me? I really don't want to go alone.'

'No can do. Even the thought of smelling booze makes me want to vom.' She held a hand to mouth for good measure. 'Keith and I have a date with the sofa and a Chinese delivery.'

Keith the cat had a better life than Kirsty at times. 'Please, Iz.'

'No, honestly. I can't stress how hungover I am. It's rotten. Take Dani.'

Kirsty snorted. 'Mum's said never in a million years.'

Izzy didn't protest. She'd fallen prey to Dani's charms many, many years ago, only to become a notch on her bedpost. They were much better suited as friends and that dalliance was all but forgotten. Kirsty did like to bring it up now and again, when Izzy claimed she had good taste in women. Carly was the latest terrible choice.

'I'm not ready to mingle again, or I would,' Izzy said, trying hard to look sympathetic. In her hungover state, it looked like even facial expressions hurt.

'It's been a month, Iz,' Dani interjected. 'You need to get on Tinder.'

'Aye, and I saw where that got you last night.'

'Yes – sex,' Dani replied matter-of-factly as she placed the cup of espresso shots in front of Izzy.

'I don't do one-night stands.'

'Right, guys, listen,' Kirsty interjected. 'Izzy, have you heard from Ashley? Do you think she'll go with me?'

'You're not taking Ashley,' Dani said, flipping a towel over her shoulder after wiping down the bar.

'Why not?' Kirsty asked, knowing fine well she wouldn't get an honest answer.

'Because she's got this thing with her mum.'

'I thought that was last night?'

'No,' Dani huffed. 'She couldn't go out last night because she wanted to be fresh for today.'

'Shit, he's early,' Izzy said, spying a well-manicured man walking past the window.

'Handsome,' Kirsty said.

Izzy winked. 'Cappuccino when you're ready, ladies.'

'Thought it was a flat white?'

'I don't pissing care,' Izzy called over her shoulder, rushing to get a seat and look nonchalant.

Dani turned to her sister. 'Just tell Mum you went but you didn't get picked.'

'I think Mum's got some deal going with Annie.'

'What, really? She's pimped you out?'

Kirsty rolled her eyes. 'I really don't want to do this. What if no one matches with me?'

'Well, at least you've double the average person's choice.'

That earned another exasperated look. 'Yeah, and look how well that's gone so far.'

4

Annie was on cloud nine, her expectations for the evening exceeded by far.

Cal's layout made it hard to gauge actual numbers – the place was massive, with no definable sections despite housing a cocktail bar, pub, and club. They all just kinda merged into one. But Rhona estimated there were nearly a hundred people attending the Lovefest opener.

The event was like speed dating but with a few twists. Each attendee got a name sticker with a coloured band – yellow if you were seeking a woman, green if you were seeking a man, orange if you were looking for either – and then you were just expected to mingle. No bells or buzzers and hopping from seat to seat. Just a big free-for-all. Annie had an icebreaker game which seemed to be going down well. Everyone got part of a well-known phrase and your mission for the night was to find the other half. Genius, really.

A few awkward people lingered on the sidelines, but on the whole people seemed to be having a good time getting stuck in.

Rhona was surprised how many lesbians were here. If she happened to be in Glasgow this time next year she'd definitely be swinging by.

'Is it okay if I take your picture?' Rhona asked a blonde woman who was chatting with a lady covered in gorgeous tattoos.

They exchanged glances. 'I mean, yeah, if it's okay with you?' the blonde asked the tattooed brunette.

'Yeah, why not?'

Rhona didn't believe in love at first sight, but these two had hit it off straight away. She'd spied a few definite couples in the hour since the night started. One man and woman had already exchanged a kiss. No guesses where their night was likely going.

'Right, Ashley,' Rhona said, reading their name badges. 'Stand next to Hazel and act natural.'

Annie had been clear with her 'no directions' rule but she figured a little discretion was necessary when taking couple shots. Crowds and groups she could snap with reckless abandon, but one on one? It was only polite to ask.

Hazel took the lead and swooped an arm around Ashley, leaning closer together. The grin that spread across Ashley's face was genuine and Rhona already knew these were going to be great photos. You couldn't fake that kind of connection.

'Thanks, guys,' Rhona said, checking the camera's screen as she left them to get on with their night. As predicted, they were cracking pictures.

She wandered back to her station at the rear of the stage and surveyed the room. A glass of water would be great, but so much of tonight involved wandering that she didn't want to get one only to leave it unattended.

God, it was hot.

Rhona pawed at her brow. She should have known better than to wear her hair down tonight. Stuffy didn't cover it. The air was so humid it could have been a pool party.

A cute brunette locked eyes with her and Rhona couldn't help but smile. It was too crowded to see her sticker but she was chatting to a guy, so likely playing for a different team. *Here to work*, she reminded herself.

She snapped a few wide shots of the crowd.

It had been a while since her last relationship and she was in no rush to couple up any time soon.

She'd met June in art school and it hadn't taken long for Rhona to up sticks and move to Manchester to be with her. They'd built a business together. In hindsight, that had probably been the issue. Too much time together. Roles got blurred.

When Rhona discovered June had drained the business bank account and done a runner, it was a surprise to find little could be done. She'd been too trusting and had forgotten to get anything on paper. With no contracts, she couldn't prove anything. The money was gone and so was her fiancée.

The ordeal would have probably broken most people, but Rhona firmly believed everything happened for a reason. Okay. She had been broken for a while. But time was a great healer. She was exactly where she was meant to be. Without June's arseholery she wouldn't have taken the job with Amber. Manchester was good, but Rhona was made to travel. It made her soul sing. Now she got paid to do it.

Yeah, her wallet was lighter, but whatever. Karma would sort June out in time.

Rhona was surprised to snag the brunette's gaze again when she lowered her camera. A room with nearly a hundred people, and now she was aware of this single woman she couldn't help but be drawn to her. The smile playing on her admirer's lips told her she was thinking similarly.

Rhona winked.

Even from a distance, she could see a blush bloom on the brunette's cheeks.

'Getting on okay?' Annie asked as she appeared from nowhere. Rhona jumped.

'Yeah, just getting some wide shots.' She looked back to the crowd: the woman was lost in the sea of faces.

'Seems to be going well,' Annie said, almost to herself more than Rhona.

'I'll say. Lots of couples pairing up already. I don't suppose you have a hairband, do you? I thought I had some in my bag but I can't find them.' Long shot. Annie's bob didn't look long enough to be tied up.

'I don't, but I'll ask if any bar staff do.'

'Thank you. It's bloody boiling here.'

'It's all the sexual tension,' Annie said with a wry smile.

Rhona couldn't tell if she was joking or not, so laughed anyway. 'Better crack on, but if you find a hairband I'll be around here.'

'On it.'

She was surprised to find the brunette hanging on her own when she descended the stairs from the stage. She was leaning against the raised platform, scrolling on her phone, looking at social media. Not exactly the actions of someone having a good time.

'Taking a breather?' Rhona asked, cradling the camera in her hands. She gave the woman a quick once-over. God, she was cute. A little shorter than her, with long brown wavy hair, just the right amount of curves, and brown eyes so delicious they should come with a lifeguard; you could just dive right in and get lost.

She clocked her sticker. *Kirsty*. Orange band on the top. Rhona's heart skipped a beat.

Here to work.

'Something like that,' Kirsty replied, slipping her phone away. 'So you're the new Isaac?' She followed it up when Rhona didn't reply straight away. 'My mum owns a café, so we're often involved in board stuff.'

Rhona laughed quietly. 'I guess I am, yeah. Big boots to fill though. I think Annie is happy with me so far.'

Kirsty didn't even try to hide the way her eyes swept over Rhona's body. She shivered as if she'd run a finger over her skin.

'Looks like you're doing a good job to me.'

Brazen. Rhona liked that.

'I'd better get back to work before Annie accuses me of slacking.'

'Have fun,' Kirsty replied with a wink.

5

All Kirsty wanted was her bed. Alcohol had only made her more sleepy, so she'd switched to an energy drink. She still couldn't wake up.

She sighed as she scanned the crowd, searching for anyone that might be her type. Like yeah, there were plenty of good-looking people, but so far no one had grabbed her full attention.

Well. Maybe the photographer.

She was an absolute fox.

But she wasn't going to help when it came to finding a match for Lovefest.

Harmless flirting was fun. She loved flirting. She gave herself a subtle shake. *Come on, wake up. Just go out and have fun. Make a game of this.*

A surge of new energy washed over her. A few more conversations, then she could happily say she'd done her best. Mum couldn't argue with that.

Just two more minutes of peace though. She still was recovering from her last conversation. Ross. The guy was perfectly handsome – bit of stubble, nice smile, a decent amount taller than her – but the spark wasn't there. Maybe he was nervous, but their chat hadn't gelled. He was, and she felt bad for thinking it, bless him . . . boring. He was an architect over in the West End. Which seemed nice. He liked walking holidays. Again, nice. And camping. He loved camping. Not as nice. She'd never actually slept in a tent. The notion always felt a little too rustic.

She'd encountered two of Dani's exes. And no doubt there would be more hidden among the lesbians. And some of the greens and oranges too.

Fun times.

A good-looking masc girl had been okay but seemed a little too much of a player, like she was only looking to add to her tally. For a one-night stand, yeah, maybe. To spend four weeks with while she did this stupid Lovefest competition? No. Kirsty needed someone she could have a laugh with.

Time to get back out there.

She took two steps before stopping in her tracks.

Hanging at the edge of the crowd was Ashley, involved in some serious flirty touching with a super cute woman.

Time to investigate.

'Ash?'

You'd think Kirsty had just let off an air horn in her ear. The colour drained from Ashley's face, her hand dropping from her date's arm. 'Kirsty, hey, hi, how are you?'

Kirsty ran her tongue along the inside of her teeth, suppressing a laugh. 'I'm good. Didn't expect to see you here.'

'Nor you. You at the Lovefest event, or did you get lost?'

'Mum made me do it.' Kirsty turned to Ashley's current company, giving her name badge a quick scan. She couldn't be more different from Dani. Tall, with short brown hair, cute dimples and absolutely killer tats. She was covered. Not just her arms: right up her neck, too. A highly detailed lion stared out from under her ear. 'Hazel, hi. I'm Kirsty.'

'I've been friends with her little sister since I was thirteen,' Ashley offered. Her eyes were still wide like Kirsty had caught her doing something truly terrible. 'Can you give us a second?' she asked Hazel.

In a second Ashley had Kirsty pulled over by the stage. 'Dani said you were doing something with your mum,' Kirsty said, pulling a playful *what-the-hell* face.

'She told you.'

'Course she told me. Why weren't you honest with her?'

'Cause she would have talked me out of coming.' Accurate. Dani and Ashley had a somewhat complicated relationship. Even a blind man could see they were in love with each other and had been since they were kids. For reasons known only to Dani, things had never gone further despite them living in each other's pockets 24/7. This was an interesting development. 'Please don't tell her you saw me here.'

'Ash. I'm not going to lie to her.'

'Kirsty, please. It's not a lie, it's just an omission.'

Kirsty rolled her eyes, taking a second to consider it. 'Why not just be honest?'

Ashley's mouth hung slack as she pondered the best way to answer. She dropped her voice low, her face so close Kirsty could smell the booze on her. 'I'm sick of waiting, Kirsty. I'm thirty-three. I've wasted enough time. I want to be loved, I want to have kids. I can't play Dani's games anymore.'

Fuck. Well, that was raw honesty she wasn't expecting. They'd had plenty of lovelorn drunken chats in the past, but nothing like that. Kirsty wished she'd kept going with the wine; maybe she'd know what to say right now. She swallowed hard before attempting to assemble a sentence. 'You deserve to be happy, Ash. And she's super cute.'

Her face lit up. 'I know, right? And she's so easy to talk to.' She looked over her shoulder, flashing Hazel a full-beam smile.

Dani was going to be crushed. But maybe this was just what she needed to actually get a fire under her bum. 'I won't tell Dani. But you need to. Soon.'

'I will. Promise. You having a good time?'

'Not really,' Kirsty replied with a laugh.

'Your mum will appreciate you making the effort, though.'

'Aye, well, she'd better. Some of the chat I've had to endure today. You get back to your girl, she looks lonely without you.'

'I'll tell Dani tomorrow. Honest,' Ashley said.

'Just be gentle with her, yeah?'

'Always.'

Kirsty forced a half smile before watching Ash walk away. *FUCK.* Ashley was like a sister to her: talk about being put in an awkward position. Her stomach did a weird flip when Hazel placed a hand on Ashley's hip. Seeing Ashley with someone else just felt *so* wrong. But she was right. She couldn't wait for Dani her whole life.

Dani and Kirsty could share anything; nothing was off-limits – they'd been through so much together that Kirsty couldn't hide anything from Dani if she wanted to – but she'd kept her reasons for withholding her feelings for Ashley under wraps. It was to do with their dad, that much Kirsty knew. They'd shared plenty of heart-to-hearts on that. But get Dani started on the specifics of her and Ashley and she quickly found a way to change the topic.

She couldn't be hard on her. Kirsty was no better. She just didn't have an Ashley in tow. Not that she hadn't left her own wake of broken hearts. Until recently, being in a relationship hadn't even been a blip on her radar. But turning thirty-five had flipped a switch and now it was like there was a ticking time bomb inside her.

Even after a lifetime of tests and getting a full house of all-clears, she couldn't shake the countdown that loomed over her.

It wasn't a new feeling, but being so close to the age Dad had been when he died made it a thousand times worse. Sometimes it felt like the walls were closing in and she'd run out of time.

She wanted the same as Ashley. Well, minus the kids. She could happily go without them. But someone to love and be loved in return: that was somehow now top of the list. She didn't want to die without finding someone special. What was the relationship version of a biological clock? A connection alarm? Marriage watch? Whatever it was, something had nudged hers awake and now it wouldn't bloody shut up.

Maybe it was seeing her littlest sister, Kat, get engaged, and suddenly realising she might never experience that. The way Kat lit up around Andy . . . she'd never had a connection like that. Not even close.

She let out a ragged sigh. This wasn't the time or the place for spiralling.

'Penny for your thoughts?' asked the hot photographer, leaning beside Kirsty on the edge of the stage.

She forced a smile. 'Just wondering how much longer I need to stay for.'

'No matches?'

'Not yet.' She was stunning. She'd tied her long black

hair up since Kirsty last saw her, revealing a stylish undercut at the base of her hairline. Kirsty tried and failed not to drink her in. She sported a nose ring and more piercings in her ears than Kirsty could count. Dreamy dark eyes. A few subtle tattoos. Her loose white sleeveless top showed off her toned arms. Kirsty's heart picked up pace.

'You're bi, yeah?'

She couldn't help but laugh quietly. Lesbians always wanted to talk about her sexuality. Not that she was assuming this woman was gay, but the way she'd raked her eyes over Kirsty was hardly shrewd. 'Sticker gave me away, eh? I don't really like labels. I just like who I like.'

'Sorry, that was a personal question. I just want to help you find someone to chat to.'

'Honestly, I think I've done enough to keep my mum happy. I'm going to bounce soon.'

A smile pulled at the photographer's lips. 'Your mum made you come? She worried about you being single?'

Heat flushed Kirsty's cheeks. 'She owns a place called Café Odyssey. It's for publicity. It's a lot to explain.'

'Café Odyssey. I'll need to remember that. I'm new here so I'm still getting to know the area. I checked out Cafella today.'

'And?'

'Decent, yeah.'

'Not the rave review I was expecting.'

The photographer shrugged. 'I'd like to find somewhere I can sit and work one day. The food was good but I would feel bad staying – the queue was never-ending.'

Kirsty had heard similar reviews before. The problem was, Cafella only had a dozen tables, if that. Not like Odyssey. They had two full levels to play with and twenty-three tables, to be exact. 'You should check us out then. We make the best scones in Glasgow.'

The photographer nodded, her lips dragging in a way that said she understood how big a claim that was. 'I'll need to pop in some time, then. You work there?'

'Five days a week.'

'And the other two?'

'I do shit like this. Wha—'

'I'd better go. I can feel Annie's eyes on me.'

She was going to ask her name, but the moment was lost as the crowd enveloped her.

A lone guy made nervous eye contact. One more conversation wouldn't hurt. Plus, you never know. Maybe this would be the conversation that changed her life.

6

Rhona's fingers finally found her phone, slamming her alarm off. God, it was early.

She rolled onto her back, rubbing her eyes. She couldn't risk falling back asleep. She stared at the ceiling through bleary eyes and traced the hazy lines of the room's cornicing.

It wasn't a bad flat. High ceilings. No damp. Kitchen could do with an update, but when you rented that was often the compromise you had to endure.

Much like flatmates. Niall had been noisy last night. The longer she stayed, the more he pushed boundaries. Yes, she liked the freedom his desire to sleep all day brought, but when he came home and played music, boshing about the living room in the wee small hours? She could do without that.

Not to mention the strangers she inevitably found every morning.

She raised herself on to her forearms, repositioning the pillows so she could sit up in bed and check her socials.

Her room sparked zero creativity. She knew she'd be

here around six months at least but the months passed in a flash. There was no point putting her mark on it now. The more shit she had, the more she had to box up. And Mum and Dad would only store so much. She was at her limit already with them.

Still, she couldn't help but imagine bringing someone back here and how confused they would be, probably labelling her a sociopath or a weirdo. A suitcase stood in the corner. More clothes were stowed in the dresser. A few perfume bottles littered the desk. Throw in a photography journal by the bed and that was it. The room was pretty much devoid of Rhona.

Her flat with June had been an explosion of personality. She loved mixing textures and materials, sourcing unusual decorative items. Quirky patterns and fabrics. Decor should be as tactile as it is visual.

She missed that. Life just now was a bookmark. Keeping place until she could get going again.

Whatever the new 'get going' was. She still had another four years before the bankruptcy would disappear from her credit file. It wasn't like she could buy a place, even if she wanted to settle.

But travelling was the aim of the game for now.

She'd always loved travelling. It wasn't just the thrill of seeing new places. Travelling was a luxury some never got, whether through time, money, or restrictions. Her brother would love to see the world but it just wasn't practical. She would never take it for granted.

It felt like a lifetime ago she was standing in her beautiful kitchen looking at the ever-mounting bills, tears smeared on her cheeks. She'd told herself that if she got through this, if she got out the other side, she'd treat herself to a once in a lifetime trip. She'd earned this.

The two years had flown by.

And the last few months had gone the quickest. She was starting to feel like her old self. She had Amber's job to thank for that. Taking the leap and moving out of her parents' house was when it really kicked up a gear. She'd returned from Manchester a shell of who she was, but her parents had been great: they knew it wasn't her fault.

Rhona sighed.

She tried not to think about it much because it really fucked up her whole 'stay positive' vibe.

But today, she'd woken up thinking of June.

The crappy practical stuff was fine; she was over that, shit happened. It always came back to the same memory: waking up to find June gone, then discovering her note in the kitchen. *I can't do this any more.* That was it. She hadn't seen hide nor hair of her since. That's what drove Rhona crazy. What had she done that was so bad, June had to drain the bank accounts and disappear into the night? She was a good girlfriend. Or so she thought. She bought her flowers, she left silly little notes in with her sandwiches, she sent her sappy voicemails when they were apart. She listened to her. She gave her space. They had amazing sex.

On paper, they were perfect. They'd even booked a wedding venue and signed off on vendors.

But no, she left. Leaving Rhona to deal with the fallout.

Why not just leave? Why did she have to steal, too?

Every time the going got tough – closing the business, using her savings to pay off wedding stuff, losing her flat, moving back home – Rhona promised herself she'd add on another destination to her Big Trip. Now she could finally reap her rewards.

But six months of high-intensity wedding season had flown by and she still didn't feel quite ready to take the leap.

Something was holding her in place. Like a final thread that wasn't ready to break.

She couldn't be away over the Christmas season; it was too important to be with family. So she was here for a few more months at least.

Maybe she *could* get a new lamp. They were small enough, at least. A wee injection of colour.

What was the point, though? She got home late and went out early. A lamp wasn't going to fill the gap in her chest.

She closed Facebook, having not really looked at it, and skipped to Instagram.

Babies. Babies. Babies. To be fair, anyone in their thirties was going to have a similar feed. But she'd never fully noticed it until now.

Rhona googled what babies symbolised. The future. Interesting.

She'd only discovered spiritualism and the law of attraction after June. Something had just clicked: suddenly everything made perfect sense. To Rhona, it went hand in hand with what she already believed: trust in the universe and everything will turn out fine.

She was on the right path. This was a sign she was working towards the right end goal.

Rhona didn't often talk about her beliefs out loud. Tell anyone, and they either glazed over or looked at you like you were an absolute nutter.

It didn't matter what anyone else thought. Only what she believed in.

And where was the harm in being an optimist? The world could do with a bit more positivity.

She dumped her phone and looked at her work bag at the end of her bed. She'd packed it the night before, intent on getting a quick start to the day: all she had to do was get up and wash.

But there was a melancholy tug in her bones.

She'd felt it last night when she was looking at the shots before bed. A little jerk of absence.

She'd dissociated from weddings long ago. Focus on what could have been, and she wouldn't get any work done. A year. She should have been married a year. Talk about dodging a bullet.

But last night was different. It triggered something else. It had been all about the delicious moment you meet for the first time. Complete unknowns. Would there be a spark, or was it purely superficial? Not that going by looks alone was a bad thing. She'd had her fair share of lustful, sex-led relationships.

Getting to know someone was exhilarating. And if there was physical attraction too? Wow. Nothing beat the build-up.

It had been a while.

But now wasn't the time or the place. She wanted to travel, never mind that she had no roots in Glasgow.

One final job before she meditated: check the freelance listings. She grabbed her phone and pulled the site up.

Working with Amber was a dream come true. She was getting paid to travel around Scotland and do what she was best at: photograph weddings. But she needed as much moolah as she could get, so side gigs were necessary as Amber's jobs dried up. She'd done family portraits, animal adoptions, christenings, and PR for local ad agencies. Not to mention all the strange and wonderful things in-between. She'd even shot a pregnancy announcement for a dog.

There was a listing for an engagement shoot. She put in her details and fired off a reply.

She put her phone on the bedside table before running her hands down the length of her face.

She was flat. Totally deflated.

Time to focus on the positives. Last night was successful. There were more than a few hopeful couples, and she was lucky enough to have been part of it.

She'd likely photographed the evening someone met their soulmate. That was pretty cool.

She'd get that again. When the time was right.

Everything happens for a reason and I'm exactly where I'm meant to be.

She stretched before heading to the bathroom to pee.

It was an absolute tip. Towels on the floor. Something dubious by the toilet.

She cringed and tried her best to ignore it.

The kitchen was no better. *Fuck's sake.* She'd cleaned it the other day. Now the worktops were littered with empty cans, crumbs, and a half-eaten pizza.

She pouted.

In another life she would be turning on her top-of-the-range coffee machine and loading it with fresh beans, ready to start the day with a home-made cappuccino.

Instead, the Rhona of now, who was definitely on the right track for something bigger and better than spotless marble worktops, thank you very much, located a clean glass and filled it with tap water.

She stole a look into the living room before going back to her room. It was a bomb site. And a random man lay sleeping on the sofa, nothing on but his dirty boxers.

It was no wonder June was on her mind. It didn't seem fair. Rhona was living here and she was probably swanning it up in some high-spec flat, enjoying the spoils of Rhona's hard work.

Everything happens for a reason and I'm exactly where I'm meant to be.

Another sigh. She needed to shake this mood, fast.

Meditation would help.

She rolled out her mat at the side of her bed and got comfy.

A few deep breaths and she was in the zone.

Everything was working out. She just needed faith; she was in good hands.

Soon she'd be on the plane, starting her trip across India.

Everything else would fall into place. One step at a time.

June was a detour in the right direction.

She was stronger for it.

And she was meant to be here.

Amber needed her. Yeah, it was only temporary, but sometimes that was all it needed to be.

It was all stepping stones.

Maybe she'd meet someone else travelling through India and fall for her.

Maybe she'd strike up conversation on the plane and get a job in London.

Maybe she'd go to the corner shop tomorrow and buy a winning scratch card.

Anything was possible. She just had to trust she was on the right path.

All she wanted was to be happy.

How that happened she didn't really care.

She emptied her mind and focused on her breathing.

Ten minutes later she was finally centred again.

She sat, enjoying the peace.

She couldn't work in the flat today. Not with some random bloke taking up residence in the living room. And there was no way she was cleaning the kitchen. She'd need to find a café.

The desire for a scone floated to the front of her mind. Plenty of decent cafés in the West End, but now the pull to go south was strong. Never one to say no to intuition, Rhona sprung into action and rolled her mat away.

Time to check out Café Odyssey.

7

Kirsty felt like a normal human today. Amazing what a night of actual sleep could do for you.

Being on the later shift had even afforded her a lie in. Dani greeted her with a goofy look as Kirsty entered the café.

'What's that look for?' Kirsty negotiated the queue, not bothering to wait for a reply as she slipped through the back. She dumped her bag and coat in the office and tied her pinny in place.

The queue wasn't too bad so she took the scenic route to the counter, cutting through the kitchen to see her mum. She gave her a kiss on the cheek. You could count on stability with Mum. She always wore one of three loose sweatshirts she had on rotation, her wavy honey-blonde hair up in a scrappy ponytail, her cheeks flushed red from working in the kitchen. It wasn't massive by any means, but big enough that their team of three cooks didn't get in each other's way. 'Morning.'

'Morning,' Mum echoed. 'How did last night go?'

Kirsty shrugged. 'I did my best.'

'Not hopelessly in love today, then?'

'Only with my bed. I think I could have stayed in it all day.'

'Aye, well, living with your sister will do that.'

'Speaking of which: you heard from Kat? Did she get the place settings signed off?' Katherine, or Kat as everyone called her, was getting married soon and as chief bridesmaid, the last-minute details were falling on Kirsty's shoulders. No change there.

'Nothing yet. But I'm sure it's all fine.'

'I know, but if they're to be done in time she needs to confirm ASAP. They're hand-lettered.'

A smile pulled at Mum's lips as she edged her spatula around a frying egg. 'Don't you fret.'

'I'm not fretting, it's just . . .' Kirsty groaned with frustration. No one seemed to ever take anything seriously. 'It's a two-minute job and she could easily have ticked it off by now.'

'I'll let her know it's a priority.' Mum's eyes turned sympathetic. 'Now, go help your sister. It's been non-stop today.'

'Aye, well, she could do with a little comeuppance for yesterday.'

'Play nice, you two.'

She didn't need told twice and pushed through the swinging saloon door to the back of the counter. Dani's face split into a grin.

'You're in a weird mood. What's going on? Did you talk to Ashley?'

Confusion muddled Dani's features. 'What? No. Why would you jump to that conclusion?'

Shit. 'Sorry. Meandering train of thought. I just wondered how her mum was.'

Dani didn't look convinced. If her eyes narrowed any further they'd be closed. 'I've not heard from her. And I don't think Irene was sick, or whatever. She was just doing something with her.'

Kirsty took the next person's order before turning her attention back to Dani as they made coffees side by side. 'So, why the weird mood?'

'Not a weird mood. Just excited.'

'Excited?'

'Your bird's upstairs.'

Kirsty nearly dropped the group head she was holding, despite having no idea who Dani was referring to. Knowing her, it could be any one of Kirsty's ex-partners. Surely not Lara? She'd been a thorn in Kirsty's side for months last year. Forever turning up, despite Kirsty making it painfully obvious she wanted nothing more than sex from their relationship. She scrunched her eyes up at the thought.

'Not Lara,' Dani said as if reading her mind. 'Her from last night.'

Kirsty's face was as blank as a piece of paper. 'You're going to have to elaborate.'

Dani held her bottom lip between her teeth, a devilish glint shining in her eyes. 'The photographer.'

If Kirsty had still been holding anything she would have actually dropped it this time. Her heart stumbled into action, rattling against her ribs. Why was she suddenly so nervous?

'No she's not,' Kirsty said, fighting to keep composure. 'You're winding me up.'

She'd relayed the evening to Dani when she got home, sparing no details.

'Swear on my life. I got Robbie to sit her upstairs, give her peace to work.'

Kirsty turned, as if she might have developed superpowers to see through two sets of walls and the mezzanine's balcony. 'No she's not.'

'Why not?'

'Because.' Kirsty finished off the takeaway latte she was making. It was a surprise her hands weren't shaking. She wasn't usually one to get flustered, but when she'd suggested the photographer come visit she hadn't expected it to happen so quickly.

'She's hot.'

'Right. You shut that down right now,' Kirsty retorted with a laugh.

Dani smirked. 'You know I'm not like that.' To give Dani her due, if she knew Kirsty was interested in someone she would never go there in a million years. She placed a cup by Kirsty. A flat white, by the look of it. 'Go take her a fresh drink. She's been here an hour, she'll need one. My treat.'

Kirsty looked at the queue. It wasn't too bad. Not even half a dozen people. Dani could cope for fifteen minutes.

'This isn't a wind-up?'

'I swear. Go upstairs and see for yourself.'

With a final look at the queue, Kirsty picked up the drink. 'I won't be long.'

Dani replied in a singsongy voice: 'Take as long as you need.'

She pushed through the doors to the kitchen, beelining for the door on the opposite wall, the main one from the kitchen to the café floor. It was only a few metres but she barely made it two steps before Mum's voice piped up, 'Everything okay?'

'Yeah, yeah, just lending a hand.'

It was a terrible excuse: she never did this – that's what

her cousins were for – and she could feel Mum's eyes boring a hole in the back of her head. She ignored it.

The stairs felt like Everest. Although, part of her still thought this was a prank. She'd go upstairs and find it empty.

But it wasn't. Engrossed in her laptop's screen was the photographer.

Fuck.

Kirsty's breath caught in her throat. She was even more stunning today than last night.

Her hair was up in a messy bun, exposing the sexy undercut that Kirsty was dying to run her fingers over.

She was so focused on work she'd still not clocked Kirsty was en route.

Nearly at the top of the stairs, Kirsty took a second to appreciate this woman in all her glory. A simple grey T-shirt looked like a masterpiece on her. Which was silly. But the way she'd rolled the sleeves up slightly and coupled it with a few gold chains? *Urgh*. Not to mention the way it fell from her shoulders, accentuating her soft curves. Kirsty swallowed hard. Her insides were garbled.

Words. She was going to have to use words pretty soon. Her mouth was dry.

Shit. She'd seen her.

Oh Jesus. That smile.

Her teeth were perfect. Of course they were.

Kirsty put the cup on the table, suddenly aware she was yet to speak.

'Hey,' the photographer said, her brown eyes smiling just as much as her perfect mouth.

'Hi.'

Silence hung for a beat.

Wow.

'Thought you could do with a fresh coffee,' Kirsty finally managed. It was a surprise she hadn't melted. Her cheeks were burning warmer than Mum's hot plate.

'You must be a mind reader – I was just going to pop down for one.'

Kirsty spied the empty cup by her side and reached for it, realising halfway through the manoeuvre she was pretty much shoving her boobs in this poor woman's face. At least she didn't protest.

Cup cradled in her hands and with a normal, acceptable distance created, Kirsty found her voice again. 'Are they the Lovefest photos?'

'Certainly are. Do you want to see?' She pulled the closest seat nearer.

How could you say no? Kirsty sat down, leaning closer to the laptop. A sweaty man filled the screen.

'Not my best work,' the photographer said, the hint of a blush on her cheeks.

'What's your name?' Kirsty blurted but it came out sounding okay, despite being totally off-topic.

The blush on the woman's cheeks deepened. Was she as flustered as Kirsty? She didn't usually get like this around women. Perhaps her sudden appearance had thrown Kirsty off-kilter. 'Rhona. Rhona Devi.' She held out a hand before retracting it. 'Sorry, force of habit. I'm more used to business meetings than—' she paused for a moment, looking for the right word, 'This.'

'And do you remember my name? Or did you talk to a lot of girls last night?' With her heart rate returning to normal, Kirsty was starting to feel like her old self. Where had that awkwardness sprung from?

Rhona held her gaze for a moment, a playful smile

quirking her lips upward. 'I might have spoken to a few, in a strictly professional capacity of course.'

'Of course. So I'll take that as a no, you don't remember my name,' she joked.

Another smouldering look snagged Kirsty's. In a blink she was clicking at her laptop, bringing another picture up. This one was good: lighting was on point, composition excellent. Rhona zoomed in on the crowd. Her and bore-off Ross. 'Kirsty. The woman who doesn't like labels.'

'Impressive. And my full title, no less.'

'Well, I cheated a little. It's written there,' Rhona said, pointing to the sticker in plain view. 'The first bit, anyway.'

Kirsty held a hand over Ross. It wasn't a bad picture of her. She'd never had a professional do any shots before; Rhona had done a good job. The heat of Kirsty's arm over Rhona's was immense. She hadn't meant to lean over her like this. Twice in as many minutes. Invading personal space wasn't her usual forté.

'You not keen on him?' Rhona asked, interrupting Kirsty's thoughts.

Kirsty snapped her hand back, shoving it between her thighs, just in case her body made an attempt at invasion number three. 'He was painfully dull.'

Rhona made a face like she was holding something back. 'Dull but bearable?'

Weird question. 'For the evening.'

'For four dates?'

Why did that feel like a loaded question? Oh God, did Rhona know something Kirsty didn't? 'Please tell me Annie hasn't told you the pairs already.'

Rhona rubbed at her chin, hiding a sly smile.

'Rhona,' Kirsty said as she raised an eyebrow, willing her

to spill. The name felt nice to say; familiar, even though she'd never met a Rhona before.

With a few swift stabs at her phone, Rhona swirled it to show Kirsty an email.

Sure enough, there it was in black and white: Kirsty and Ross. *Fucking hell.* Mum was really going to owe her for this. Like, really owe her. *Fuckity fuck fuck fuck.*

She couldn't help but notice the next two names on the list. Ashley and Hazel.

Could this day get any worse?

'Sorry to be the bearer of bad news.'

'To be fair, there wasn't much choice.'

'No one at all caught your eye last night?' A smile threatened to spill from her lips. God, this woman oozed sexy confidence.

She was fishing, no doubt about it. Kirsty had put yesterday down to alcohol but it would seem Rhona was just as assured after coffee. Not that Rhona would have been drinking last night, come to think of it. But you never know.

It was nice to finally meet her match: in Kirsty's experience women were rarely so bold.

'No one with a handy label telling me their name and sexual preference,' Kirsty replied.

'Ah, so you do like labels?'

'They would certainly make picking up women easier.' Oof, that didn't come out as planned. What was meant to be a joke sounded sleazy. *Oops.*

Rhona worried her bottom lip with her teeth for a hot second. 'I didn't have you down as a player.' She sounded mischievous: good. Kirsty refrained from breathing a sigh of relief.

'Not my style. I just meant it would save trying to guess if a woman was into me. I'm very shy.' The jokey tone landed well this time. *Phew.*

Rhona snorted. 'I guess we'd better hope Ross isn't the shy type too, then.'

Kirsty scrunched up her face. 'Please. Don't. Is there no way Annie can rematch me?'

'Anyone you want me to suggest?'

Kirsty pulled a face dripping with pity as she pretended to quietly weep. 'I dunno, a rock? Or this table? Anyone with better conversation skills.'

'He wasn't that bad, was he?'

'I'm being harsh. He just wasn't what I was looking for, I guess.'

'And what would that be?'

The way Rhona's eyes had dipped from Kirsty's eyes to her lips wasn't lost. Was this really happening, in her mother's café, no less? 'Someone that can hold a conversation, for a start.'

Rhona fiddled with the lower hoop in her right ear. 'Bit of a low bar.'

'You prefer a challenge, then?'

The sound of her cousin Robbie calling her name cut through Kirsty like nails on a blackboard.

'Sounds like someone needs you.'

'Always.' Kirsty stood, smoothing her bar apron out. 'See you about.'

'Yeah, looks like I'll be spending August with you and Ross,' Rhona replied, a wicked glint in her eye. 'See you soon, Kirsty.'

Kirsty's face ached from grinning as she walked down the stairs.

8

Day one of dates, and Annie was considerably less fraught than at the opening event.

First up were Ashley and Hazel. And holy smokes, they were just too cute. Today's date was sponsored by a local bakery, meaning the girls got to make their own bread and pastries.

'Right, ladies,' Annie said, signature bulging notebook and folder cradled to her chest. 'If we can get a few shots of you guys kneading the dough together, then we'll be off.'

The bakery was tiny: so small, in fact, that the owner had to wait outside while they did the photos, but it was obviously super popular. Trolleys taller than Rhona lined one side of the room, with space for dozens and dozens of trays. She could see they were well used, and going by the moreish smell of the place it had been a busy and productive day.

'Hi guys, I'm Rhona. Don't worry: this will be quick and painless. Now, first up, pronouns? What's your preference?'

The couple exchanged looks. A lot of people weren't used to being asked, but Rhona liked to make a point of it; in her experience, the little things made the biggest differences.

'She/her,' Hazel said with a shrug as Ashley echoed her answer.

'Brill. Let's get cracking.' Rhona slid round to the other side of the counter, searching for the best angle. She adjusted her settings as the women got into position. It was obvious there was a mutual attraction, but neither seemed to be brave enough to actually touch the other.

Whoever coined the phrase *opposites attract* must have been thinking of Ashley and Hazel. Hazel was taller and obviously worked out, her sculpted arms hinting that all might not be what it seemed under her loose cotton tee. Her short hair was styled in a stylish quiff today. Whereas Ashley was nearer the short end of the spectrum and, well, it was tough to tell what her shape was: she had on a blue jumper over a denim shirt, and her long blonde hair was scooped up in a ponytail. Rhona would put bets on the fact Ashley had never even glanced at a tattoo parlour, never mind set foot in one. There was a timidness to her demeanour, but Rhona had caught a sparkle in her eye that hinted she was anything but, in the right company.

Hazel smiled at Ashley with a look that could light up the room. Rhona needn't have brought her reflectors today.

She couldn't help but wonder how Kirsty would be in this situation. She'd see her and Ross later today, but it wasn't Ross she wanted to think about.

Since their little chat in Café Odyssey Kirsty had never been far from Rhona's mind.

She wasn't out to meet anyone before heading off on her travels, but if a connection was there, why not have a little fun, see what happened?

There was no harm in chasing what felt good.

Chatting to women had always come easily to her, but it wasn't often she met someone equally as confident. But there was a casual composure to Kirsty. She hadn't asked for Rhona's number or been pushy. She didn't strike her as someone on the play. She'd given Rhona just enough to hook her, and now she wanted to know more. Very sneaky, and Rhona liked it. A lot.

Her mind wandered to how it might feel to put her hands on Kirsty's hips, but she grabbed the thought like a wild animal and stuffed it back into its box. Not the time or the place.

She rolled her neck, still stiff from sitting at her laptop for the last two days. 'Just a little closer together, please.'

They closed the gap by a millimetre. Adorable.

'Okay, now get kneading. And try to look at each other, be in love or whatever.' Rhona hid her smile behind the camera as she started snapping.

Ashley and Hazel shared a look of comfortable awkwardness and the giggles that erupted instantly defused the atmosphere of the room. Rhona lapped it up, snapping away like nobody's business. Even professional models couldn't fake the sparks they were giving off. Rhona needed a welding mask.

She paused, wanting to adjust her shutter speed, go for some action shots. 'Did you have a good time at the opening event?' Rhona asked, her attention fixed on her camera.

'Yeah, it was great,' Ashley said, sharing a coy smile with Hazel.

'It looked fun. I'm new here so still trying to get the lay of the land, find out where's good. Cal's looked decent.' She fanned her hand to the left, lining up a shot. 'Guys, if you could scoot over, I'll get you on the diagonal.'

'Yeah, Cal's is awesome,' Hazel agreed, shuffling into position.

'And The Stables. Have you been there?' Ashley offered.

Rhona clicked her tongue to the roof of her mouth. 'That's just up from Cal's, isn't it? Not been, but I'll add it to the list. Right, smile. And really lean into it, girls. Work those triceps.'

Hazel was surprisingly into it and Rhona could have sworn Ashley's mouth hung slack for a second as she watched in awe.

'Nice.' Rhona encouraged them as she checked out the viewfinder, reviewing the last few shots. She surveyed the room, looking for inspiration. Nothing was dynamic enough. There had to be something to give this a wee bit of pep. She stalled, still scanning her surroundings. 'And what about gay places? I've noticed a distinct lack of rainbow flags in Shawlands,' Rhona joked.

Ashley snorted quietly. 'Yep, distinct lack of gay places in the South. Which is why Lovefest is so popular, I guess. But Bar Orama is good. You heard of there?'

Rhona shook her head, photographic inspiration striking. 'Nope. I'll need to look it up. Annie, can you ask Yaroslav if he could get me a little flour, please?'

'Yeah, sure, right on it.'

Conversation was easing the couple closer to being relaxed, so Rhona searched her mind for further chat. 'So, are you going anywhere after this, or leaving it at baked goods?'

'Erm, yeah, I think we'll go for a drink. I'd like to, anyway. Although it's up to you,' Ashley said, combing Hazel's face for hints of agreement.

'Sounds good to me,' Hazel said with a grin and Ashley's shoulders straightened. 'I've got a PT sesh quite early so I can't be out late, but I'd be up for one or two.' Her hand skirted Ashley's and Rhona got the distinct feeling they wished their third wheel would vanish. The feeling was mutual – how long did it take to find flour in a bakery?

'You giving or receiving?' Rhona asked and quickly backed the sentence up. Hazel's cheeks already burned crimson. 'The PT sesh, I mean.'

She gulped before answering, her dimples pulling at the smile she was hiding. 'Giving. I'm a personal trainer at the gym up the road.'

With that killer smile and her top to toe tats she was probably queued for days with women wanting an hour with her.

In Rhona's experience, tattoos were a good icebreaker with women, and by God, they certainly loved to touch them given the chance. Hers were a lot more subtle than Hazel's full sleeves and neck artwork, but Rhona liked what she had: each one had been chosen with great care and attention. The symbol below her ear was a favourite for partners to kiss. She liked to inform them it was the Viking symbol for manifesting your own destiny, but always failed to let on that she'd later found out that was a load of crap and it was little more than two lines depicting arrowheads stacked on top of each other, the supposed meaning nothing but drivel some wee toad had made up online. Didn't matter. It had meaning to her. And it was minimalistic enough to pass under the radar.

Rhona blinked, realising she'd let silence hang in the air. 'You'd think flour would be easy to find in a place like this.' That earned a chuckle. 'We'll be done soon, don't worry. I've got another date to go to after this.'

'Kirsty's next, isn't she?' Ashley said, giving the sagging dough a poke.

Rhona perked up, her eyes gaining a sparkle. 'Yeah, you know her?'

'I've been pals with her little sister since I was thirteen.'

'Small world.'

'Always is in Shawlands,' Hazel interjected. 'It's like a village here.'

'Ladies, your flour,' Annie said, her voice as bouncy as ever.

'Fantastic,' Rhona said, springing into action. 'Right, find somewhere for your folder. I need you to be prop master.'

Annie looked elated at her sudden promotion and quickly found a clear surface for her work stuff. She held the paper bag of flour aloft. 'Where do you want me?'

Rhona got into position, squatting almost level with the table, the lens aimed at the dough. 'Girls, you do what you did before. Hazel, push that dough, Ashley, you link—' She carefully placed Hazel's hand where she wanted it. 'You link your hand under here. Yep, get close. Nice.'

She checked the frame, the women looking stiffer as their proximity was increased. It was a nice stiffness, though. Rhona longed for that feeling. The fledgling flutters of desire. The uncertainty. God, it had been a while.

'Annie, you shuffle in behind Hazel, and when I say "go" you chuck a bit of flour in the air, over their hands, yeah?'

Annie took direction like a pro, going exactly where Rhona needed her. She double checked that only the couple were in frame and squatted back into position. It looked good.

'Okay, we ready?' Nods all round. 'Right, on three: Hazel, you knead, Annie you throw, Ashley, you stay where you are, look at Hazel. Provide some sultry moral support.'

'Gotcha,' Hazel said, looking serious. Clearly a woman out to impress, and Rhona loved it.

'One, two, three!' Annie chucked the flour in the air and Rhona sliced the camera forward. It was over in a flash, but a little post-production tonight and it would look like the best bread-based date Shawlands had ever seen. Boring photos be gone: Ashley's smile looked genuine and Hazel had nailed the smouldering goof Rhona was hoping she'd provide. Local lesbians were going to eat this up.

Hopefully she could bring a little pizazz to every date.

Kirsty and Ross next. Yoga with a local instructor. Rhona would be lying if she said her heart hadn't skipped a little at the thought of Kirsty in yoga pants. That was assuming she had any. She might be fitnessphobic and turn up in denim shorts. Still, it was a good shout for Kirsty. Not much emphasis on talking.

Rhona patted down her shirt, trying in vain to rid it of rogue flour. Hazard of the job. She'd purposely worn her favourite short-sleeved black shirt, the one with the subtle leaf pattern. She always felt good in it; the fit was nice, comfy to wear, and it showed off her tattoos. The golden trifecta.

'Annie, you happy to leave these two lovebirds to it or do you want some more shots?' Rhona asked, still swiping at the white patch on her belly.

'I think we're good. We've got twenty minutes until the next date – you can show me the photos while we wait in the park.'

'Say hi to Kirsty for me,' Ashley said with a smile, as if she knew something Rhona didn't.

9
___

The only thing making this bearable was the thought of seeing Rhona.

Kirsty trudged up Langside Avenue towards one of the side gates to Queen's Park. They were to meet at the noticeboard, then she was being treated to an hour of yoga.

Company aside, she was quite looking forward to it. She wasn't much of a sporty person but she did enjoy yoga in the confines of her own flat. Even a little meditation, if Dani wasn't in.

She was by no means advanced but her balance had slowly gotten better and her muscles thanked her for the stretching. Frothing milk all day wreaked havoc with your shoulders.

It would be good to get some professional tips, iron out bad habits. Although she worried Ross would make her self-conscious. Hopefully he was as on board as she was.

Rhona would be a good icebreaker, help them ease into a few poses. Ashley had already texted to say how much she enjoyed the photography session, which was good news. Ash had been stressing about it when she popped by yesterday. Kirsty didn't particularly like getting her photo taken either, but it was part of the parcel. She had to endure this charade for Mum.

Kirsty sighed, replaying last night in her head. Dani had taken Ashley's news like a pro, her face dropping only the tiniest fraction, but once Ash had left? Mother of God, she was grumpy. Then again at work today. She wanted to head to Bar Orama tonight and Kirsty would probably give in and play the role of the dutiful sister, but her gut told her alcohol wasn't the answer. She should be talking to Ashley, not venting about her problems to Kirsty.

But Dani's love life was none of her concern. She would do what she liked regardless of Kirsty's thoughts. Not that she could offer any decent advice. She'd joined Tinder to shut Dani up. She could see the appeal, given Dani's approach to hooking up, but she was over casual sex. Kirsty wanted more. And chatting to someone online wasn't providing the connection she desperately craved. You couldn't get a feel for someone over text. Little nuances were lost, along with physical interaction.

Her time with Rhona ticked all the right boxes.

She couldn't fall for the first woman to cross her path, though. Thirty-five years of avoiding anything more than a hook-up and she jumps ship for the first woman to show her attention? That wouldn't float.

The gate to Queen's Park loomed closer. Three dates. One evening of getting drunk and standing about on stage. She could do this.

Plus, there was always the possibility of winning five grand. If she and Ross looked cute enough in the pictures it could be a real option.

She and Dani could go on an all-inclusive holiday. Somewhere hot. Somewhere far away from here.

The noticeboard came into view as she neared the zebra crossing. No sign of anyone else. She *was* ten minutes early. No harm in standing about the park for a bit, checking out the squirrels.

Queen's Park was a Southside hub. The massive park marked the centre of its main suburbs: Strathbungo, Govanhill, Battlefield, Shawlands, and technically Crosshill if you really wanted to get pedantic about things. But if you lived in Crosshill you might as well say Govanhill, in Kirsty's opinion. The area had a bad rep for being run down but it had changed in recent years: the shops were a little more interesting, the space a lot cleaner, and the cafés welcoming. Not that Kirsty even ventured to the other side of the park. Shawlands had nearly everything she needed. The only thing it lacked was good clothes shops, but that's what the internet was for.

Kirsty pulled at her tank top as she rounded the corner into the park. Definitely no one else here. Nothing else to do but hang by the sign and scroll on her phone. She fished it out from her bag and leaned against the metal pole of the noticeboard.

Did Rhona have social media for her business? Surely she must. Everyone did these days. Mum had even got it for the café. She'd tried to rope Kirsty and Dani into helping, but do it once and it would soon be their full time responsibility. Plus, Mum's complete and utter ineptness was entertaining the masses. She still didn't know you had to type # and not just write out 'hashtag'. And last week she'd managed to do a post just saying 'Thank you Brenda'. The people of Shawlands loved it. Added a human side to the café. It set them aside from Cafella and their professional photos, each one worthy of a thousand likes.

Saying that, maybe Rhona could be cajoled into doing

some publicity shots of the café. Bolster Mum's content fodder.

As if her thoughts had come to life, Kirsty looked up from her phone to find Rhona entering the park.

It only took a second for Rhona's face to split with a grin and Kirsty happily returned it, her eyes taking in her monotone ensemble: black patterned shirt, black skinny jeans, and black-and-white trainers. What looked suspiciously like flour smudged her left thigh.

Kirsty felt Rhona's gaze travel her length and she mentally congratulated herself on choosing a winning outfit. It was all for her: Ross could run and jump. She swung her rucksack over her shoulder, giving Rhona a better view of her leggings and vest. The glint in her eye said she appreciated the gesture.

'Early,' Rhona said, coming to halt just a few feet away.

'Makes it easier to be on time and punctual is always better than late,' Kirsty replied, trying to sound blasé. But really, nothing annoyed her more than poor timekeeping. 'Where's your boss?'

'She's popped into the shop on the corner,' Rhona said, looking over her shoulder despite the thick wall of trees obscuring the road. 'The owner needed to chat to her about something.'

Kirsty closed the gap, dropping her voice to a near whisper. 'Will we just go? There's a good pub up the road; they'll never find us.'

Rhona smiled and for a brief second it looked like she was actually considering it. 'I can't quite afford to get sacked just yet, but maybe another time, when I'm not on the clock.'

'Kinda takes the fun out of it though, if you go just whenever. Loses the thrill.'

Rhona stood her ground, the space between them mere inches. 'So you're a thrill seeker? And there was me thinking you only craved conversation.'

'That's just one of the few things I crave.'

Rhona's eyes flicked from Kirsty's eyes to her mouth before darting back. *Jesus.* The chemistry here was off the charts. Why the fuck was she here to meet Ross? Screw jokes; she really did want to ditch the yoga.

Time to dial things back before Kirsty lost control.

Rhona had other plans. 'You can fill me in when we go for a drink.'

Kirsty gulped, searching her mind for a way to turn this conversation around while still keeping her cool. All her brain could imagine was pulling Rhona into the bushes and running a finger up those buttons, pinging them open.

Not helpful.

She remembered the phone in her hand and gave it a gentle waggle. 'Where can I find you, then? I take it your business has a page online?'

Rhona scooted to her side, pushing her camera and its strap under her arm so she could edge a little closer. She knew what she was doing. She absolutely had Kirsty played; if she was a fiddle her strings would be close to snapping, the tension between them almost tangible.

'It's Rhona Devi Photography, but—' She hovered an open hand around Kirsty's, the air between them charged. 'It's probably easier if I just give you my number.'

Did Kirsty want this? Her body gave her no choice: before she'd even had a chance to contemplate a comeback her hand had turned the phone over.

'I'm pretty busy this week with Lovefest shoots, but maybe next week. If Ross doesn't mind sharing?' She bit her bottom lip, side-eying Kirsty as she suppressed a wicked grin.

'Been playing at baking, I see?' Kirsty said, running a finger over Rhona's floury shirt. She couldn't help herself. Her body was working of its own accord. There was nothing to do but play along.

Rhona passed her phone back. 'Sometimes I get carried away and I get a little dirty.' Her tone was playful; however, her eyes were anything but.

Kirsty's centre had its own pulse and she was hyper-aware of her breathing, each heave of her chest feeling a few heartbeats long. This woman had her in a tailspin. She'd never met anyone like her.

'Happens to the best of us,' she replied, her voice low. It was a relief to see Annie in her peripheral vision. Any longer with this beautiful woman and Kirsty wouldn't be held accountable for her actions.

'Hi, Annie,' Rhona called, casually taking a step to create a normal, platonic distance with Kirsty.

She'd had plenty of encounters with flirty women in her time, but that was usually in bars; this was something else. Was Rhona like this with everyone? It was fun, but Kirsty couldn't keep the red flags from waving in her face.

'Ladies, hello!' Annie called, her cheeks red from power walking to the park. 'How are you, Kirsty? Ready for yoga?'

'Looking forward to it. I've been doing it at home for a few years. Will be fun to get some tips off an instructor.'

'Flexible, then?' Rhona said with a smirk. Was she really going to carry this on in front of Annie? Kirsty blushed. 'I'll make sure Elaine gives you some hard poses – will make for some interesting photos.'

The only answers that came to mind weren't quite PC and she didn't have the balls to say them in front of Annie.

Kirsty composed herself with a quiet cough. She was saved by the arrival of Elaine, the yoga instructor.

'Hi, guys.' She wrung her hands together. She was laden with three yoga mats but it wasn't just sweat glistening on her brow: nerves dripped from her pores too. 'You must be Kirsty.' She offered a meek wave.

'The one and only.'

'Just Ross to go, then,' Rhona stated, shooting Kirsty a look. She looked at the chunky watch on her wrist. 'He's late.'

'Only just,' Annie said, jovially jumping to his defence.

'Where we doing this? Over there?' Rhona asked, pointing to the area of open grass to their right.

'Yeah, probably,' Elaine said with a curt nod.

'He'll see us. Kirsty, why don't you and Elaine come with me, warm up, and I can get some practice shots?'

Something told Kirsty she had ulterior motives but no harm, no foul. 'Sounds good,' she said with a quick shrug.

'I'll hang back, wait for Ross,' Annie said, whipping her phone out, obviously wanting to fit in a few emails while she had the chance.

Elaine escaped the pack first, trudging on without another word.

Rhona kept close and dropped her voice when Annie was a safe distance away. 'Time to see how flexible you are.'

'I keep my best moves for the privacy of my own home, thank you very much,' she retorted, catching up to Elaine with a little skip.

'Excited for this?' Kirsty asked the instructor, aiming to appease her nerves a little. This was just a bit of fun – Elaine didn't need to be skittish.

'I'm more used to working with big groups, but yeah, should be good.' She forced a half smile. 'Funny how I can talk to a class of twenty but make me do one on one and I'm nervous.'

'I'll behave, promise,' Kirsty said, placing a hand on her heart.

Elaine made light work of putting the mats out and Kirsty rid herself of her trainers while Rhona fiddled with her camera.

'Don't fancy a spot of yoga yourself?' Kirsty asked the photographer. 'There's a mat going spare and I don't think a professional like you really needs to warm up.'

'This is a couple's event,' Elaine said, her voice cracking as she barrelled the words together. 'The moves I've devised are meant for couples to do. Together.' She tacked the last word on like it was the most heinous thing in the word. It wasn't homophobia driving her words, more an anxious reaction to the unknown.

Rhona perked up. 'If it helps you loosen up, why not?' She placed her camera on the grass and kicked her shoes and socks off, revealing black-painted toenails. 'Jeans might make it interesting, but we'll see how it goes.'

In a flash her left foot was to her right knee, hands held in prayer at her chest. *Tree position, nice.* And not a wobble in sight.

Kirsty was about to congratulate her but Rhona wasn't done.

In a swift motion she flowed into another asana, this time a standing bow: balanced on one leg, the other extended behind her, bent above the height of her head, her foot grasped by her hand. She extended her other arm out and wobbled a fraction, but it was impressive nonetheless. A difficult move at the best of the times, never mind in skinny jeans.

'That all you've got?' Kirsty said with a smirk. Was

Rhona like this with all women? This arrogant, peacock attitude? Half of Kirsty was intrigued, the other half was screaming that this woman was a player and too big for her boots. She was standing right on the edge; it was going to go one way or the other, and Kirsty would bet her savings on Rhona being the latter. Shame, because she was pretty, but Kirsty didn't have time to be dicked about, no matter how good the sex would be.

The heat between Kirsty's legs faded.

'You practice yoga?' Elaine asked.

Rhona nodded enthusiastically. 'When I can.'

Elaine turned to Kirsty. 'Since you're both advanced, maybe we can try the couple's bow. Just for fun.'

Now she'd gotten used to the idea, Elaine was loosening up. Thank God. It was already going to be tedious enough with Ross, never mind if her instructor was a ball of jitters.

'You up for that?' Rhona asked, a smile plastered on her face as she stood hands on hips.

Kirsty could give as good as she got. 'Sure, if it's not too easy for you.'

'Right, one mat, both of you scoot the back of your feet to the opposite edges. Then come into standing bow; you'll link hands in the middle.'

'Put it like that and you make it sound easy,' Kirsty joked.

It didn't take long for Rhona to get into position. Kirsty let her hold it for a beat. If she was going to be cocky, why not let her show off? Or better still, topple over. Kirsty smirked, unable to hide how funny the mental image was.

'Don't leave me hanging,' Rhona said, as if reading her mind.

'It's been a while, so don't laugh,' Kirsty replied, her knee shaking before she'd even brought her other leg up. She clenched her stomach, engaging her muscles.

A little wobble and she was in standing bow, looking every bit as good as Rhona. She reached out and linked hands with the photographer, surprised to find the slightest hint of sweat on her palm. Maybe she wasn't as cool and collected as Kirsty thought.

They locked eyes and Kirsty desperately wanted to make a joke about Rhona's hotshot attitude, but was all too aware of Elaine's gaze boring into them.

'You two are naturals,' she beamed.

Kirsty chuckled, hiding the fact that her muscles were already aching. This wasn't an easy pose to hold, never mind with the counterbalance of another person wanting to pull you over.

Rhona locked eyes with Kirsty and she noted the way her jaw muscles were tensing. A smile threatened, but it was obvious she was having to concentrate to keep balanced. Kirsty gave her hand a quick squeeze. The flicker of something, but not enough to cause issues. She was about to give her hand a gentle yank when Ross's voice boomed across the lawn.

'Kirsty, hi, sorry I'm late.'

She dropped Rhona's hand and stood straight, her legs instantly breathing a sigh of relief and the pain that had been building in her thighs subsiding.

Before she knew it Ross was by her side. What was the etiquette here? Okay, he was going for a kiss on the cheek, his hand on her waist. Straight in there. Fantastic.

He didn't look the yoga type: his baggy shorts said more ill-fitting holiday attire, but at least his T-shirt was clean.

'You ready for this?' Kirsty asked, giving her hands a wipe down her tank top. Ross's eyes drifted to her cleavage and regret flooded her bones. She should have gone for a comfy hoodie.

She clocked herself, aware she was being internally grumpy with everyone. Maybe he'd be different this time around. And there was no harm looking at boobs: she did it herself.

'Right guys, a few shots, then I'll be off,' Rhona said, camera at the ready. 'Before I start, just a quick pronoun check: what do you guys prefer?'

Very progressive. 'She/her,' Kirsty said, rolling her neck, getting ready for the next hour.

Ross looked like you'd just asked him the meaning of life. His face wasn't so much blank: even a plain sheet of paper had more expression. He was completely void, utterly baffled.

'Ross? What pronouns do you prefer? He/him? They/them?' Rhona asked with a friendly waggle of the head.

'Well, the male ones, obviously,' he said indignantly, although confusion still reigned supreme.

Rhona took it in her stride. 'Fantastic. Right, Elaine, you get them into an easy pose and I'll take some photos.'

'Okay,' Elaine said with a wee clap as she jumped into action. 'Bring these mats together, then you two get to the ground in a cross-legged position.' She joined them on the floor. Ross looked reluctant even to sit, but did eventually. 'Fantastic, now, back-to-back, and bring your arms out.' Elaine stretched her arms to full wingspan. 'Okay, great. Now Kirsty, you bring your arms under Ross's, and take hold of his wrists.'

At least she didn't have to face him for this. Although his cologne was nice: earthy.

Rhona worked her magic, ducking and diving, getting shots from different angles, giving direction when needed.

'Do we have to hold this much longer?' Ross asked.

'Two mins,' Rhona replied, her mind elsewhere.

When the camera was only facing Kirsty, Rhona took a shot face on and Kirsty jumped on the opportunity to cross her eyes. Rhona snorted.

'Sorry, bug,' she offered, a grin still obvious below her camera.

Given the choice, Kirsty knew exactly who she would rather be doing this with, player or not.

∼

'I'M JUST SAYING,' Dani said, a slight slur edging its way into her speech. 'Why didn't she tell me?'

'Because you would have been an arse about it,' Trip said, taking a swig of her beer.

As predicted, Kirsty had given in and gone to Bar Orama, the Southside's unofficial gay bar in the suburb of Mount Florida.

It wasn't big by any means, but it had a decent amount of tables and even a stage. And it certainly wasn't the best decorated – it probably hadn't seen an upgrade since the nineties. The seats were splitting, the booths cracking, the photos of naked cowboys faded beyond recognition, and the bar scuffed to fuck; but it was their place and where their friends were. Kirsty loved it here. There was comfort in the familiar. You always knew what you were going to get in Bar Orama.

Kirsty clinked her beer to Trip's. 'No doubt.'

'Did you know?' Dani asked Trip. Sarah, or Trip to her pals, worked as an English teacher in the same school where Ashley worked as an admin assistant.

'She did mention it, yeah. Just to get my opinion.'

Dani scowled. 'And you said it was a good idea?' she scoffed.

'No,' Trip replied, the word lasting a few syllables longer than usual. 'Obviously, given the conversation we had during the school holidays, I tried to talk her out of it.'

'What conversation?' Kirsty asked, surprised to be learning new information in the case of Dani and Ashley.

Trip waved her away. 'Irrelevant now. And what are you going to do?'

'About what?' Kirsty asked.

'Your hot photographer?'

Kirsty rolled her eyes. She'd get info out of Dani later. This thread of conversation needed shut down now. 'There's nothing *to* do.'

'I just can't get used to this new Kirsty. This time last year you would have had her in bed already,' Trip said with a chuckle.

Kirsty straightened herself, surprised to feel heat flush her cheeks. 'I'm older, wiser— '

'Boring-er,' Dani said, cutting her off.

'Would do you good to think like me,' she chided.

'As if. You going to text her?'

Kirsty pursed her lips. 'Not sure.'

'What's to lose?' Trip asked, taking another draw of her beer.

'It's more "do I want to open that Pandora's box?"'

'You really wouldn't just sleep with her?' Dani asked, picking at the label on her bottle.

'Nope. Over that. And I'm not being just a notch on her bedpost.'

'You've changed your tune. You were really into her yesterday,' Trip jibed.

'I'm just not—' Kirsty turned the words over, finding the

right ones. '—feeling her vibe.'

Dani snorted. 'Very hip of you. Four words,' she said, holding her digits up. 'Emotional numbing. Destructive behaviour.' She turned a finger down for each one.

'The fuck?' Kirsty said with an uneasy laugh.

'Two therapy sessions and you're suddenly a psychologist,' Trip said. There was an audible thud and Trip grabbed her shin, shooting daggers at Dani, who mirrored her glare. 'Ow.'

'Therapy?' Kirsty asked, the word sounding totally foreign.

Dani looked sheepish. 'I only told Trip because I needed to tell someone and you have enough problems on your plate.'

'You're not a problem.' Fuck, how had she not noticed her sister was needing help?

'I didn't mean it like that. It's just, it goes back to Dad, doesn't it? You don't need me dredging stuff up.'

'Still, you should have told me.'

'Well, I've told you now.' She grinned. Dani could never do serious. It was impossible to imagine her talking to a therapist.

'And is it helping?' An ache still panged in Kirsty's chest; the heavy weight of guilt.

'Too early to say, but it's good to have names for things.'

'Like?'

'Why I couldn't tell Ashley how I felt. Why I keep pushing her away.'

They were short sentences but they marked a massive milestone. Guilt was replaced by pride. 'You going to tell her you're seeing a therapist?'

Dani's eyes grew wide. 'No, no, no.' She downed the rest of her beer. 'Not yet, it's too soon.'

'And what about Hazel?' Trip asked, placing her empty bottle by Dani's, at the corner of the table.

'Won't last.'

'Got a crystal ball now?' Kirsty joked. 'So, emotional numbing, what's that? I don't do that.'

Dani pulled a face that could sink ships. 'You're doing with Rhona exactly what you did with—' She dropped her voice to a whisper. 'Travis.'

Kirsty snuck a quick look at the handsome bartender before returning her attention to Dani, her eyes narrowed. 'I didn't *do* anything with him.'

'You really liked him, but as soon as he declared feelings you self-sabotaged and ran a mile.'

'I wasn't ready for a relationship. I was different six years ago.' The way things ended with Travis was messy, no denying it, but they'd gone into things with an agreement to keep it casual. It wasn't her fault he caught feelings and wanted more. She wasn't numbing or sabotaging, or whatever Dani called it. It was circumstantial.

'Now Rhona comes along and you're already poking holes in her personality.'

'Will I get more beers?' Trip asked, already half-risen from the table.

The sisters chorused approval. 'I'm not poking holes in anything. I'm allowed to not like someone,' Kirsty snapped.

'Yes, but, you said yourself there was chemistry. Why not explore things a little? See where it goes? Instead of putting your walls up and shitting yourself?'

Kirsty tilted her head. 'Such a way with words.'

'Text her.'

'No.'

'Text her,' Dani said in a playful growl.

She wouldn't drop it. Kirsty grabbed her phone from her

jacket pocket, surprised to see a text notification on the lock screen. 'She's messaged me.'

Dani put her hands up as she leaned back in her chair, as if to say *told you so*. 'What's she said?'

It was a photo from today's shoot. Kirsty looked grumpy as fuck. *Oops*. Rhona's message read: *Think I should send Annie this one? X*

Kirsty turned the phone to Dani. 'Aww, that's cute.' She leaned forward, head resting on her hands, the epitome of innocence and attention. 'What you going to say back?'

Kirsty put the phone on the table. 'Nothing yet.'

'Boo.'

'What we booing?' Trip asked, divvying out the beers.

'Kirsty's new squeeze has texted and she's ignoring her.'

'The photographer?'

'Right, listen. I'm not ignoring her,' Kirsty said, on the defence. 'I'm just not replying straight away.'

'What does she look like?' Trip asked, savouring a long draw of fresh beer.

Kirsty tapped away on her phone, bringing up Rhona's personal Facebook profile. She'd been easy to find once she'd told Kirsty her surname. She passed the phone to Trip, who pulled a face of approval.

'Not at all what I was expecting.'

'What do you mean?' Kirsty joked.

Trip blushed. 'Just not who the name Rhona conjures. I was expecting some pale wee lassie from the Outer Hebrides. Not an Indian goddess. She's hot. Like, really hot.'

Kirsty rolled her eyes while tapping a molar with the tip of tongue. 'Yes, she is. But—' She emphasised the word with a finger in the air. 'Looks aren't everything.'

'I dunno,' Trip said, transfixed as she scrolled through Rhona's photos. 'Maybe you could introduce us.'

Kirsty didn't rise to the bait. 'Speaking of which. How's your hunt for Mrs Right?'

'Still going. And Mrs Right Now is good enough for the time being.'

'Anyone to write home about?' Dani asked.

'Same old, same old. Although—' Trip's face dropped and her scrolling finger froze.

'What?' Kirsty said, as frozen as Trip.

Trip gulped, her jaw tensed so hard she might break a tooth. She sucked on her bottom lip before talking. Kirsty's heart hammered in her chest. 'I've clicked something.'

'Trip.' Kirsty said, her voice deadpan.

Dani stifled a laugh, failing to hide a grin behind clasped hands.

'I've liked a photo.'

'Trip, are you serious?' The words came out in a torrent, merging into one.

Trip turned the phone to face her. 'Honest to God, it was an accident.'

Mortified didn't cover it. Was her passport still valid? How quickly could you leave the country and start a new life? *Suffering fuck.*

Trip looked like she'd just spat on someone's Granny. 'Kirsty, I swear. I didn't mean to do that.'

Kirsty couldn't do anything but stare at the screen. As if looking might magically take it back. She blinked. *Nope.* Still there.

Then a fucking drop down appeared, notifying her of a text.

Stalking me now? X

Kirsty set her jaw. 'She's texted. Sarah Gordon, I'm going to kill you.'

Trip pouted. 'Let me buy you a shot to make up for it. Or,

or,' she said, forcing a cheese-tastic grin. 'Maybe I've just initiated the greatest love affair of all time.'

'Unlikely.' She had to reply now. There was nothing else for it.

My friend Trip had my phone. We were trying to figure out how much of a player you were. Care to put us out of our misery? X

May as well lean right into this one.

Three dots appeared. She was typing.

'What did you say?' Dani asked, leaning on her forearms, trying to see Kirsty's phone.

'You two have done enough.' She waved them away.

A player? x

You're a bigger flirt than me. X

What does that mean? X

You know exactly what I mean x

Three dots. Nothing. Three dots. Nothing.

Kirsty could imagine her furiously typing, deleting, going at it again. She couldn't help but smile.

'What's going on?' Dani whined.

'Shh.'

How was Rhona going to style this one out?

You think I talk to everyone like that?

No kiss. Had she riled her? Too late now.

Yes x

The dance of the dots started again.

'Kirsty,' Dani said, impatience like a blanket around her words.

Trip fanned the air, reading over Kirsty's shoulder. 'She'll fill you in soon. Don't mess with her train of thought.'

Very zen.

Finally, a reply.

You're one to talk . . . but if it makes you feel better . . . I've not slept with anyone since moving to Glasgow. Last proper relationship was two years ago. I thought we had a connection but if you're not feeling it, no worries. Sorry I got the wrong end of the stick.

Shit. She had riled her.

'I've made her mad.'

Kirsty looked at Trip. Who pulled a face. 'Yep. You've fucked her off. Big time.'

'Right, it was your fat fingers that did this in the first place.'

'Steady on,' she retorted, flipping her annoyingly long, slim middle finger up at Kirsty.

'Let me read it,' Dani said, holding an eager hand out.

Kirsty held her hand steady, not surrendering the phone just yet. 'Don't fucking touch anything though.'

'Scout's honour,' Dani assured, hand over heart as she took the phone. She skim read, then handed it to Kirsty. 'You need to backpedal, fast.'

'I know, I know.' Kirsty's heart was still hammering. She hadn't meant to touch a nerve. She'd expected Rhona to be more playful.

Dani's earlier assumptions rang in her ears. Was she self-sabotaging? Was that even a thing? She actively wanted to find someone; why would she unconsciously stop that happening? She inwardly scoffed. Dani had her things – it was nothing to do with Kirsty. She was in control, always had been.

She typed a reply, unsure of every word.

Sorry, very grumpy today. Things are coming out wrong. Just trying to be funny. Sorry . . . x

She quickly followed it up with a joke, intent on lightening the mood:

Would a picture of my boobs help? X

'She's either going to love or hate that,' Trip said, taking a swig as she reclined in her chair.

'What?' Dani asked, on tenterhooks. Trip read the text to her. 'You're brave.'

She wasn't. But this was make or break; might as well go big. The thrill was nice. A tickle of adrenaline through her veins. No harm in taking chances.

I would rather see them in person x

'Back in the game,' Trip said with a fist pump.

'Right, okay, okay. Private conversation,' Kirsty said, only half-joking as she held the phone to her chest.

'I'll say. Give it a week. She'll be in your bed,' Trip said, draining the rest of her bottle.

'Are your expectations of me really so low?' Kirsty asked, tilting the phone so Trip couldn't see her reply:

You'd better hope our drink together goes well then x

'It was meant as a compliment.'

Kirsty didn't have time to dissect Trip's sentiment, never mind retaliate, as a call made her phone vibrate in her hands.

'Kat,' she said, staring at the phone like it had grown arms and legs.

Dani and Kirsty exchanged looks.

Kat rarely called Kirsty. Fair enough, she had been in touch more with the wedding stuff, but it was nearly ten o'clock on a school night. This felt odd.

'You'd better answer – might be Mum,' Dani said, her voice flat, her face just as serious.

Kirsty's heart stuttered as she answered the call. 'Hey, what's up?'

'Serious wedding issue.'

Not Mum, thank fuck. 'What's happened?'

'Know anyone that's good with a camera?'

10

More serious photographers might declare shoots like today's beneath them, but Rhona loved it. It was a job that was different every day, keeping her on her feet: you never knew what was going to come your way. She really was living the dream.

Plus, this gig was paying well, and the more money in her travel account the better.

Tibs the cat – Rhona had had to read the email a few times to check that was correct and not a trick of the imagination – was fast growing in popularity over on Instagram, so today's shoot was a massive celebration of her gotcha day, or the day her owners adopted her, in layman's terms.

She was a lovely, dainty calico and Rhona doubted she'd ever met a more appeasable animal. She was harnessed up but was quite happy to keep close to her owners, Jade and Stuart, and trot about, sniffing the grass and investigating other foliage. If it wasn't for the nearby dogs she probably would have been quite happy to be free range and do her own thing, with no threat of running off.

'We're going to take her in the camper van up to Applecross,' Stuart said, watching Tibs scrabble up a tree.

Rhona squatted level with the cat and shot continually, hoping for an action photo of Tibs dismounting. 'I've never been up there,' she said, moving position. 'But I've always wanted to go. I hear it can get pretty congested, though.'

'Yeah, it's kind of been taken over by tourists, but we'll go in low season.'

'If Applecross ever gets a low season,' Jade joked.

'You like travelling, then?' Stuart asked.

Tibs jumped and Rhona focused on capturing the moment before speaking. 'Yeah, I love it. Would be somewhere different every day of the week if I could.'

Rhona wanted to ask the couple what their jobs were but the moment hadn't arisen yet; no natural segue in conversation. Having the freedom to roam wasn't afforded to everyone. She was lucky her career would allow for some time off and would still be there when she came back. Well, in some capacity. She hadn't quite figured out how she was going to play it. Her time with Amber was very much temporary and owning her own business had been tough, even with June's partnership. Photography jobs weren't the easiest to come by, though, and you couldn't count on a steady stream of celebrity cats to pay the bills.

First and foremost, she had to figure out where to sink her pin on the map. The longer she stayed in the Shawlands the more she liked it, but maybe somewhere would grab her attention when she went on her big trip.

'Where are you from?' Jade asked, adjusting Tibs's pink harness so it was just right.

'North Queensferry,' Rhona answered, eyes still fixed on the cat. A particularly boisterous looking spaniel loomed on the edge of her vision. 'Do you want to do some shots of you holding her?'

'North Queensferry,' Stuart repeated, deep in thought. 'By the bridge, yeah?'

'That's the one.' Dad loved to joke that their house was the real focus on the Scottish twenty-pound note and, she hated to admit it, squint hard enough past the iconic landmark and you could kind of see their family home on the horizon. The notion brought up pangs of guilt for thinking of living in another country. Since her brother's accident she'd felt the need to be closer to home even more.

Jade lifted the cat into her arms and Tibs nuzzled into her neck. Without prompting, Stuart slipped into position, his head tilted to the cat, looking at her lovingly. These guys were well versed in photo composition. If only every shoot was like this.

'You into sewing?' Rhona asked, spying the tattoos of dressmaker's scissors and a Singer sewing machine that made up part of Jade's inked sleeve.

'A love passed down from my granny to my mum and then to me. I'm very lucky. I make cat accessories for a living – have my own Etsy shop.'

Self-employed crafter, nice. 'And I take it Tibs does some occasional modelling for you?'

'Just a little,' Jade said, kissing the cat on the cheek. She wriggled free of her mum's grip and scrambled onto her shoulder, using her as a bridge to paw at her dad. This cat was freaking adorable.

'And what about you, Stuart?' Bets were it was something else that could be done remotely. Maybe that was the answer. Could she take on photography jobs as she travelled the globe? Make money off TikTok, or something? With just a backpack she wouldn't need a massive budget.

The thought of her family tugged at her heart again. But that's what Facetime was for, surely?

'Website SEO master.'

'Sounds serious,' Rhona replied with a grin. She knew how to edit photos in her sleep; anything else to do with computers and websites, though? Whoosh, right over her head.

'I guess it is, but I'm a complete geek. I love it.'

'That's what counts, eh?' Rhona said, sidestepping to get a better angle. 'What is it they say? Do a job you love and never work a day in your life?'

Jade laughed. 'True. But also, work forty hours a week for someone else or do eighty on your own. Never feels like real work though.'

Rhona liked her attitude. Maybe she *could* own her own business again. June had tarnished her memories of self-employed-dom. Things might be different on her own. Especially if it meant travelling.

What would Kirsty make of it?

Rhona smiled to herself. She barely knew the woman, and yet here she was, wondering what she'd think of major milestone choices.

It had been a relief to see Kirsty wasn't as flirty with Ross, but her text had thrown Rhona. Did she really come across like that? It wasn't her intention. She'd thought they were on an equal playing field with the flirting. Maybe it was Kirsty's way of getting the lay of the land, figuring out Rhona's intentions. She'd asked her for a drink – was that not enough?

She had noted a shift in dynamics after their brief yoga sesh but Rhona had put it down to Ross's presence. Had she done something wrong? It wasn't worth dwelling on: they'd got over the blip and spent the rest of the evening texting.

Kirsty had only called time when she'd declared herself too drunk to be trusted. Rhona wished she'd had a little less willpower.

Apparently there was some long-winded story with Kirsty's sister and Ashley. She couldn't wait for Kirsty to fill her in next week. Where would they go on their date? This Bar Orama place Ashley mentioned seemed okay. She'd ask Kirsty later.

Tibs scooted into Stuart's arms with the arrival of another dog. They'd chosen the venue and Rhona couldn't help but wonder if somewhere a little less canine-filled would have been better. The customer was always right, though.

'Any other shots you'd love?' Rhona asked, camera on her hip.

'Just the one with her party hat,' Jade said, her smile a mile wide.

~

DRESS-UP BAG EXHAUSTED, Tibs the cat was now safely on her way home and Rhona was quite content taking her time in packing up her camera equipment, when her phone vibrated in her back pocket.

A text from an unknown number.

Hey Rho. Can I call you that? Too late now. It's Dani, Kirsty's sister. I stole your number from her phone. Hope you don't mind. You free for a chat? In Shawlands? Or want to call me? Got an urgent problem.

Well, this was intriguing.

In Queen's Park. You free now? Rhona replied.

The reply was instant.

Yeah, just in the flat. Where you at?

Rhona fired off her location.

Was this a good or bad thing? What kind of urgent problem could Dani be experiencing that Rhona had a solution to? And why wasn't Kirsty the one getting in touch? This felt fishy.

True to her word, Dani was in the park before Rhona knew it.

She couldn't be further from her sister. They shared the same wavy brown hair, dark eyes, and bright smile, but apart from that they were complete opposites. Dani had on a backwards baseball cap, just like when Rhona had met her in Café Odyssey the other day, along with an oversized hoodie and joggers. Even the way she carried herself oozed masc lesbian energy: the slight swagger in her walk, the way she held her head – she knew girls would look twice given the chance.

Dani was the type of woman that could either be a cocky little shit or sweet as an angel.

Time to find out which part she was playing today.

'Hey, Dani,' Rhona said, her voice betraying her uncertainty at Dani's visit. She hoisted her work bag onto her shoulder and walked off, Dani keeping pace. She'd stayed here long enough. Her bag was heavy but a stroll round the park would be nice.

'Rhona, you got a few mins?' Her expression gave nothing away.

'Yeah, sure. What's up?'

Dani took a deep breath as she stuffed her hands in her hoodie pocket. 'What's your plans for tomorrow?'

'Tomorrow?'

'Yeah, like the full day?'

'Huh?'

Dani shook her head, a smile splitting her face. 'Sorry,

let me explain. My little sister's getting married tomorrow, but her photographer fell down the stairs and broke their arm yesterday.'

'Shit.'

'Indeed. Don't suppose you're available?'

Rhona whistled through her teeth. She had the week's final Lovefest dates today; it was going to be a late one. Then tomorrow was earmarked for editing. Wedding season was in full swing, but Amber had booked her clients well before Rhona came on board and tomorrow was one of her days to ease back into business. 'I have plans. No one else that can do it?'

'Nope. Kirsty's having a full-on panic.'

'Should it not be your little sister that's panicking?' Rhona joked.

'You'll soon learn that Kirsty's the Queen of Spreadsheets. If she could plan her whole life she would. Kat's lucky she's had Kirsty to sort her wedding – she's a sucker for detail.'

'Is there really no one else she can call?' They were climbing a steep hill near the edge of the park now and Rhona's bag felt about ten times heavier.

'Kirsty's tried everyone. No one's free.'

'So I'm the last choice?' She raised an eyebrow, hoping to soften the accusation.

Dani looked sheepish. 'I don't think Kirsty wanted to bother you. She doesn't know I'm here.'

That explained a lot. 'She could have asked.'

'I know, but . . .' Dani trailed off. 'I know it's a long shot, but if you're not already booked for a wedding, would you consider it?'

'What's your budget?'

'Whatever Kirsty's written down,' Dani said with a

chuckle. 'I know this is cheeky as fuck, by the way. We don't even know you. I just want to take the pressure off Kirsty; she feels responsible for stuff a lot.'

'Let me talk to Annie. If she can wait until Sunday for the Lovefest stuff, I'll do my best to help.'

It was a surprise to find Dani's arms around her. She squeezed tight and Rhona brought a hesitant arm up to return the hug. 'You have no idea!'

Released from Dani's grip, Rhona smoothed her T-shirt out, relishing the breather from the hill. 'Annie-dependant, remember. Don't be getting Kirsty's hopes up yet.'

∽

'Alright, Amber,' Rhona said, sprawled out on her bed as she took a quick break from editing Lovefest pics.

'Hey, Rhona, what's up?' There was a thud and what sounded like a child screaming. 'Whoa, sorry, you still there?'

Rhona chucked. 'You okay? Should I phone you back? Bad timing?'

'Nah, it's cool. It's just *someone* doesn't like getting his clothes changed.'

'Ted?' Rhona joked. That was the name of Amber's husband: the old jokes were the best.

'I wish. It's been an age since I got anywhere near taking his clothes off. Hold on, will you?' Amber put her hand over the mic on her phone but Rhona could still hear her scream loud and clear. 'Yo, Ted!' Muffled voices hinted a conversation was taking place. Maybe she should just phone Amber back. It was no good trying to chat with so much going on. 'Hey, you there?'

'Yes,' Rhona replied, only just managing to stifle a sigh.

'Ted's taken him, so we're free to chat for a bit. What's up?'

'You ever done a gig at Carshine Castle?'

Amber whistled through her teeth. 'Carshine. Carshine. Now. Remind me where it is?'

'Near Edinburgh, I think. Off towards Peebles? I can get a postcode if you want to look it up?'

'Nah, it's ringing a bell. Wee castle, isn't it? Big tree-lined driveway? Grey bricks? Conservatory?'

'Sounds about right, but then that could be half the venues we go to.'

'It has a maze.'

'Yeah, that's deffo it. So, you've been?'

'Yeah. How come?' A piercing cry cut the air and Rhona could almost feel Amber wince.

'You need to go?'

'Nah, Ted's got things under control. I think. So, how come you want to know about Carshine?'

'I've been asked to do a last-minute wedding.'

'Oh wow, when? Don't forget you have Inverurie in two weeks.'

'Tomorrow.'

'Tomorrow?' Somewhere in the West End a dog was barking its head off, likely scared by Amber's sudden outburst.

'I know, I know. Kirsty asked me to. It's her sister's wedding and the photographer had to cancel last minute.'

'Kirsty? Oh, the hottie from Lovefest.'

'That's the one.' There was no point arguing despite the terrible nickname.

'Fair dos. Thought you had Lovefest stuff tomorrow?'

'It's going to be a juggle, that's for sure.' Rhona's front door slammed open and in poured a gaggle of blokes, by the sound of the monotone chat filling the hall. It was quickly followed by the sound of a Led Zeppelin album full blast in the living room.

'What's that?' Amber asked, her tone equal confusion and disgust.

'My flatmate's back.'

'Oh, that toad. Pal, you need to move. How do you sleep?'

'Thankfully I have enough to keep me up these days or I'd be murdering him.'

'Still, that's not on.'

'Anyway,' Rhona said, not wanting to focus on how horrendous Niall was. 'Any tips for Carshine? I don't have time for my usual recce. Any good spots? Manager okay to deal with? What's the goss?'

'Carshine. Lemme think.'

What sounded like breaking glass erupted in the living room. A chorus of cheers joined the ruckus.

She didn't have time for this shit. But what other option was there?

'Just bare minimum would be good, so I look like I know what I'm doing,' Rhona joked.

'I'll have notes in my journal. Can I help with Angus, then send you some pics?'

'That would be perfect – thank you.'

They said their goodbyes and Rhona rolled onto her back, staring at the ceiling. The steady thump of music continued. Maybe she could rent a hotel for the night. Nah, far too late for that.

At least it was only Kirsty and her family tomorrow; they would be more forgiving if she was a tired wreck than a normal paying gig. But the fact it was Kirsty was also terrifying. Rhona would meet her *whole* family tomorrow. Close and extended. Talk about pressure.

She wasn't usually one for pre-gig nerves. But then, this wasn't any old gig, wasn't it?

Rhona groaned before throwing a pillow at the wall. *I'm exactly where I'm meant to be.*

11

'On a scale of one to ten, how close to jumping her bones are you?' Dani asked her sister without losing the smile plastered on her face.

Kirsty dug her elbow into Dani's ribs as subtly as she could.

She was right though. In fact, it was worse. She was edging closer to a twelve the longer the day went on.

Wedding Rhona was very different to Lovefest Rhona. Gone were the T-shirts and skinny jeans.

Wedding Rhona had on sharp dress trousers, a matching waistcoat, and a collarless shirt, unbuttoned just enough to make Kirsty's pulse race.

There were no sly remarks either; no bravado. She had a job to do. This Rhona was professional personified.

Kirsty liked the way she took control without being forceful, directing people where they needed to be, how they needed to stand, and what they needed to do. If she could find a way to get Rhona alone for five minutes maybe she could take control of her, too.

She'd softened to the idea of Rhona again. Dani was

right: she was creating issues where there were none. The fact they'd been texting pretty much non-stop also helped matters. Not to mention that now they were Facebook pals, Kirsty had a wealth of photos to pore over.

'Yo, Kirst,' Dani said, waving a hand in front of her sister's face. 'Rhona wants us to do photos with Kat.'

Kirsty shook her thoughts free. 'Now?'

'She's asked enough times.'

'Really?' She couldn't stop the heat that flashed across her cheeks.

Dani pulled at her shirt, making sure it was sitting right. 'Girls in suits have always been your weakness.'

Kirsty silenced her with a look.

It was true, but she didn't need her face to burn any brighter. These photos would likely be on her mother's mantel forever more.

'Kat, you go in the middle,' Rhona said, turning to the side, avoiding the sun's glare as she adjusted her camera settings.

Damn, her bum looked good.

'If you say you're not attracted to her after this you're a liar. And a shit one at that,' Dani chuckled.

'You'd be cute together,' Kat said, getting into position between them on the castle's steps.

So far, everything else had gone to plan. The weather was perfect. The traffic had been bearable, despite Kirsty's pre-wedding worries, and the guests' transport between the city centre and venue was smooth. Just the speeches, meal, and first dance to negotiate, then Kirsty would feel like she could breathe.

Jesus. This felt as much her wedding as Kat's.

It had been great getting stuck into planning; being so involved. Mum and Dad never hid the fact that Katherine was their *little surprise*, but the twelve-year gap between her and Kirsty had been a wedge in their relationship, no matter how hard either tried. What happened with Dad definitely didn't help. Suddenly the wedge was a ravine; then, before Kirsty knew it, a cavernous canyon.

Kirsty didn't know the young woman her little sister had become – she'd blinked and suddenly her twenties were gone and the baby of the family was herself twenty-three, with wit as sharp as a knife and looks that could stop traffic. The past year had been like meeting her for the first time.

She'd taken Kirsty by surprise on her hen night, letting slip that she was often jealous of her and Dani's relationship. But the truth was, Kirsty was happy she wasn't on the inside of their little circle. Their bond was tied by time in the trenches; Kat was better to be on the outside, too young to remember how bad things had really been. Plenty of time to build bridges and forge new relationships.

She gave Kat's side a squeeze, unable to hide the grin on her face. Nothing like a wedding to make you a sap for family.

'Smile,' Rhona said, camera aimed at the sisters.

Kirsty focused on the rolling gardens behind her, scared that if she looked where she really wanted – the plunging neckline of Rhona's shirt – that the photos would give her game away.

It was a beautiful venue. Carshine Castle was just outside of Edinburgh and, in terms of weddings, pretty damn perfect. Small, grey, and with more turrets than you could shake a stick at, it was the ideal backdrop to Kat and Andy's day. The wedding was always going to be on the east coast of Scotland; Andy was from Burntisland, after all, but they'd had no clue what venue they wanted. Kirsty and Kat had scouted barns, hotels, converted mills: you name, it they'd seen it. Then Carshine Castle appeared, and wow. There was no getting past it.

And the rooms were amazing. Each one was deliciously modern but you still felt like you were a part of something old, like royalty. It was a castle, after all.

The idea of inviting Rhona up to her suite later had crossed Kirsty's mind, but she had a new problem.

Ross had messaged her yesterday and now it was painfully clear he thought they were actually dating.

Against her better judgement, she'd added him on Facebook when he'd sent a friend request. There was no sense in making the next three weeks awkward. But he'd soon messaged gushing about the fun he'd had (was he on the same date?!) and how he couldn't wait to see her again, blah-blah-blah. She was too busy with photographer drama to right him. She needed to let him down gently so he didn't run a mile and ruin her little publicity stunt.

It meant things with Rhona were going to be on the down low for the time being – if anyone saw them being coupley and it got back to the wrong people, it would cause chaos.

But damn. If Rhona's bum caught her eye again she was going to have serious issues.

Kirsty's face ached from smiling. It was a welcome relief when Rhona spoke.

'Let's take this to the drive – I want some photos with the trees on the approach,' she said, already leading the way. 'And Andy, you come too. We might as well start your photos there, limit the walking Kat's dress is having to endure.'

'I could get used to this,' Kat said as Kirsty and Dani automatically dipped to rescue the train of her dress, walking behind her like loyal dogs.

'Don't worry, I'm sure we'll find a way to get our own back,' Dani smirked.

'Planning on finally popping the question?' Kirsty said with a sly look.

Dani didn't retaliate, which was odd. She'd noticed a definite shift between her and Ashley. Even the way they'd sat at dinner last night: it was although Ashley had a rod in her, her muscles stiff and on high alert. Kirsty often joked with Dani that she was in a relationship without the sex, but now it felt like something might finally be about to give. And not in a good way.

There was no time to dwell, as Rhona fell in time with Kirsty's stride.

'Think you can handle dress duty for a second, Dani? I just need to chat with Kirsty about something. Might be easier if she's not got her hands full.'

'Yeah, sure, no probs.'

Rhona was quiet until they were safely out of earshot. 'I don't see any photos with your dad on the shoot sheet.'

Words lodged in Kirsty's throat; she couldn't even force a cough to dislodge them.

Rhona filled the silence. 'Don't worry, I saw his photo on the table by the bar. I've twigged the situation. It's just—' She took a deep breath. The flustered Rhona from their meeting in the café was back. It was cute. 'Usually, I'd have gone over important stuff like this way before the wedding. It's just I didn't want to upset Kat today if it was a difficult subject, and you seem to be the one that's got everything under control.'

'Our last photographer hadn't mentioned it,' Kirsty finally managed. The words felt like rocks in her mouth.

'Well, some brides like a photo with the memorial,

usually a family shot too. It's up to you. No shame in skipping it if you think it's inappropriate or weird.'

'I'll speak to Kat – thank you.'

Rhona smiled. 'No problem.'

It was nice Rhona had thought about him, but she didn't want to dwell on Dad. Today had already brought a whole host of emotions dangerously close to the surface. She couldn't take well-intentioned questions too. Best to change the subject. 'I was expecting something lewd.'

'Huh?' Rhona said, her face screwed in confusion.

'You've not uttered a single flirty thing to me all day.'

Rhona's face twisted into a rueful smile. 'I pride myself on having never slept with a bridesmaid while working. You're going to have to wait until I'm off the clock.'

'To sleep with you?' Kirsty barked with laughter.

'I've seen the way you've been looking at my bum.'

A wink and Rhona was off. Kirsty's cheeks burned.

∽

THE LEAD SINGER of the wedding band was AWOL. Of course he was.

'He's going through a break-up,' the drummer said, as if it made things better. He could have an arm hanging off for all Kirsty cared; he'd been hired to do a job and he was going to bloody well do it. The first dance was due in twenty minutes.

Kirsty blew her cheeks out slowly. There was no easy solution to this.

'I need to check on something. I'll be back in five minutes,' Kirsty said, walking away before anyone could protest.

She didn't have anywhere else to be, but she was about

two sentences away from blowing her top and it wouldn't be fair to shoot the messenger.

She slunk through the side door, grabbed a flute of champagne off a passing waiter, and found a seat away from other guests.

Kirsty emptied her lungs with a huge sigh, but it did nothing to relieve the weight on her chest.

She downed the champagne and tucked the glass under the bench's leg.

It helped a little, but the cinder block on her ribs didn't budge.

Today had gone well. Kat was happy. Andy was happy.

The speeches were amazing. Andy's best man, Dave, had nailed it, and Mum was an absolute blast as anticipated.

The first dance was Kirsty's last hurdle and it looked like she was going to finally fall.

Sometimes you do everything right and the world still finds a way to fuck you over.

She watched the guests mingling on the lawn. Thankfully, no one had seen her. She needed peace and quiet for a moment.

If Kirsty ever got married it wouldn't be such a grand affair. Her family and close friends; that was all she needed. Not that she thought today could be better – she just didn't like the thought of all that pressure, making sure a hundred or so people had a good time.

It was hard to imagine herself in Kat's shoes. She'd never been one for daydreaming about weddings.

The notion appealed: she just hadn't thought about it.

Dani, yeah. She'd figured she would marry Ashley.

But herself? It was a new concept, one she was still trying on for size.

'You okay?'

Rhona's voice broke Kirsty from her thoughts.

'The band's lead singer's disappeared.'

Rhona took a seat, nodding straight ahead, her eyes fixed on two very drunk guests as they playfully tussled with each other. Two of Andy's mates. 'Not ideal.'

'Nope. I bet you see shit like this all the time.'

Rhona laughed under her breath. 'I've seen way worse.'

'Does it not put you off?'

'Being a photographer?'

'Getting married.'

Rhona was quiet for a second. 'Not yet, anyway.'

A comfortable silence fell between them, like an old friend.

'Just get them to do an instrumental,' Rhona said, still facing the manicured lawn.

'Huh?'

'The band. If it's just the singer you're missing. Just get them to do the first dance without the words.'

It would work. The song was well known enough.

'Thank you. That's a brilliant idea.'

Rhona smiled. 'You'd be surprised how many fires I have to put out. Weddings rarely go to plan.'

'And yet you keep going to them.'

'I love my job. Life would be boring if they were all the same.' She scooted closer to Kirsty. 'Do you want a sneak peek at some of my shots? They'll need editing, of course.'

'Yeah, go on then.'

Rhona flicked through and Kirsty was in awe. Even without an ounce of editing they were great photos.

She'd instructed the sisters to 'act drunk' when getting some shots earlier and those in particular were phenomenal. She'd had them staggering down a slope together, arms linked, movements exaggerated and floaty.

They'd barely kept it together for laughing. There was an easiness about the shots, a candidness that would usually be impossible to capture, and yet Rhona had done just that. It was like you could reach inside the photo and feel the love.

'Thanks for today,' Kirsty said, still flicking through the photos.

'It's been nice seeing you away from Lovefest.'

'I don't really know what to make of that,' Kirsty said, her mind auto-driving conversation as her focus was still fixed on the pictures.

'Just that it's different without Ross.'

'Ah. Yeah, he is a bit of a third wheel, bless him.'

The sound of a guitar tuning up cut through the air. 'Sounds like your band is nearly ready.'

Kirsty twisted to face the castle. 'Once this is done I can relax.'

'You're a good sister.'

'I don't know about that.'

'Take it from an outside source. I've been to hundreds of these things. You're a good sister.'

Heat pricked Kirsty's cheeks. 'It was the least I could do.'

'I'd better boost too. Can't miss the big moment,' Rhona said, standing up.

Kirsty didn't budge. 'I know you don't sleep with bridesmaids, but do you dance?'

Rhona smirked. 'Not usually.'

'Willing to make an exception?'

12

'I'm going to head off,' Rhona shouted into Kirsty's ear. They were so close to the speaker that she could hardly hear herself over the music.

'Already?'

Rhona chuckled to herself. The day had passed in a flash and she was utterly knackered. Staying up until nearly midnight to work on Lovefest stuff hadn't been ideal, but volume of work trumped hours in bed. Not that she'd got much sleep with Niall and his mates carrying on. She could catch up on sleep once Annie had her files tomorrow.

Despite her dwindling energy, she'd had a blast today. Kirsty's family was lovely. Andy's too. Kirsty's mum was an absolute hoot though and completely stole the show. Her after-dinner speech had Rhona crying tears of laughter.

'I need to drive to North Queensferry,' Rhona shouted.

'What?' Kirsty shook her head before taking Rhona by the elbow and leading her off the dance floor and out to the hallway. Her cheeks were flushed with alcohol but she was nowhere near drunk. If anything, this was the first time

Rhona had seen her with a glass long enough to actually finish it. 'What did you say, sorry?'

'I'm heading to North Queensferry now. Just wanted to say bye.'

Kirsty's jaw tensed with disappointment. 'I've barely seen you today.'

'The mark of a good photographer.'

'You know what I mean.' She pouted. This gorgeous woman actually pouted. Rhona's insides flipped. God, that was cute. 'We've still not had our dance.'

'Another time.' After the spectacle of the first dance and with everything else Rhona needed to do, the night had slipped away.

Kirsty frowned. 'Take a quick walk with me?'

Nothing on earth could make her say no. 'Sure, why not?'

'Have you had a good day?' Kirsty asked, heading towards the doors to the terrace and garden.

'Yeah, it's been good fun.'

'Thanks again. I can't think of many people who would agree to do this at such short notice.'

'It was my pleasure, really.' It was a significant pay cut to what she was used to, but being with the Hamiltons had more than made up for it. There was a warmth to them, a gravitational pull that made you feel good.

'Kirsty!' A stout man with a bushy ginger beard boomed. He enveloped her in a hug and Kirsty fought to keep her remaining wine safe.

'Kenny, how are you? Long time no see.'

'I'm good, still up in Dingwall. You?'

'Same old, same old. Rhona, this is Mum's cousin Kenny. Kenny, this is my friend, Rhona.'

Kenny's eyes traced the length of Rhona and she

couldn't tell if it was disapproval or creepiness that glinted in his gaze. Guys could be hit or miss when she wore her suits.

He turned his attention back to Kirsty. 'You've still never visited. Soon?'

'We'll see how work goes. Listen, I need to help Rhona with something, but I'll be back soon.'

He winked. 'I'll be waiting on my dance.'

Creep. He was definitely a creep.

Safely through the double doors, Kirsty let out an audible groan. 'Cousin once removed, I must add,' she said with a shudder.

'He seems, erm, interesting.' There was always at least one weird relative: she'd seen a lot worse.

'He's forever trying to get us to see his hot tub. Yuck.'

Rhona pulled a face. 'A hot tub in Scotland. He's brave.'

'I dunno, I've had some good times in one out near Dunkeld.' Rhona desperately wanted to know more but Kirsty was already onto a new topic. 'Why are you going to North Queensferry?'

'Thought I'd better see my mum and dad while I'm in the area.'

'Ah, so y—' Kirsty rolled her eyes as she cut herself off, once again taking Rhona by the arm. 'Quick, down here.'

Rhona laughed. 'Another creepy relative?'

Kirsty took them down a path, towards the decorative maze at the end of the garden. The further away from the main castle they ventured, the darker it got. In other circumstances, this might be eerie, but Rhona was enjoying the thrill of sneaking about. 'Worse than that,' Kirsty replied with a huff as she dropped her arm from Rhona's. 'Andy's pal. He's been trying to fire into me for ages. I don't have the energy for him right now. I'd rather chat to you.'

'Do you just have a trail of would-be suitors everywhere you go?' Rhona joked.

Kirsty shook her head, hiding an embarrassed smile. 'Honestly, no. I've just been in some weird situations recently.'

'Speaking of which, how are things going with Ross?'

'He thinks we're dating.'

'Oh wow.'

'I know, right? Little did he know that my eyes were on the photographer instead.'

Rhona's gaze dropped to her shoes, self-consciousness washing over her like an icy shower. It was one thing to ask for a dance and share flirty jokes, but now she was off the clock it was a different matter. Things could actually go somewhere.

Kirsty stopped in her tracks, at the entrance to the maze. 'What? No comeback?'

'It's just—' Rhona shrugged as she stuffed her hands in her pockets.

'Shit. This is because of that text, isn't it?' Kirtsy wandered to the nearest marble bench, plonking herself down.

Rhona joined her, the cold stone bringing out instant goosebumps.

Usually shit like Kirsty's text wouldn't bother her. She had thick skin. But hearing it from Kirsty touched a nerve. There was nothing wrong with being a player, or whatever you wanted to call it, but she didn't want Kirsty thinking that's who she was. That's what was bothering her most. Why was she so bugged about Kirsty's opinion? 'Stuff like this doesn't usually get to me,' she said, deciding honesty was the policy.

'And yet, here we are.'

Once again, Rhona's shoes were the most interesting thing in the world. Kirsty downed her wine before placing the empty glass on the grass beside the bench.

'Getting sensitive in my old age, I guess.' She forced a half smile, making herself lock eyes with Kirsty. 'And I'm tired. Hard to be witty when my mind's half asleep.'

'Then don't be witty. Just be honest.'

Rhona chuckled under her breath, straightening herself. Now, there was an invitation. Where to start? She considered her options, finally settling on a thought that had been at the forefront of her mind for most of the day. 'Okay.' Kirsty bit back a smile and Rhona couldn't help but return it. 'I've seen my fair share of bridesmaid dresses, but this one,' she said, waggling a finger up and down Kirsty's torso. 'This one is a new favourite. The neckline is particularly inspired.' Lilac was a nice colour on Kirsty, but it was the way the loose neckline draped over her cleavage that sealed the deal.

'This old thing,' Kirsty feigned pawing at the neckline to reveal even more of her breasts.

Their attention shifted to the castle. Someone must have propped a door open and music spilled into the night air, carrying it down to their private haven like it was a whisper meant only for them.

A slow song came on, something by Ed Sheeran – they all sounded the same to Rhona – and she took the chance to get to her feet, extending a hand to Kirsty. 'I believe I owe you a dance.'

Kirsty smiled, taking Rhona's hand and closing the gap between them. She placed her free hand on Rhona's upper arm, bringing them closer still.

The air was electric.

They swayed in time with the music, moving as one, Rhona's hand around Kirsty's waist, locking them together.

'Much better without any eyes on us, eh?' Kirsty said, resting their clasped hands against Rhona's chest.

'Much,' Rhona said, and lightly kissed Kirsty's knuckles.

Her whole body tingled with anticipation, and maybe it was her imagination, but it seemed the stars were shining a little brighter just for them.

They slotted together perfectly, Kirsty's body now pressed against Rhona's as they shuffled to the song.

If she closed her eyes they could be anywhere, just the two of them. It was perfect.

Before they knew it, the song was over and another tune took its place. Rhona extended her left hand into the air, keeping hold of Kirsty's, inviting her to spin. She twirled, the light from the castle highlighting her face and curves. Rhona wished she had her camera, but she wouldn't want to take herself out of the moment, anyway. Instead she focused on committing the image to memory.

Kirsty returned to their original position, nuzzling into Rhona's neck.

Nothing had ever felt so natural. It was like they'd known each other for years.

The spell was broken when some weird 80s pop song came on.

Kirsty lifted her head and Rhona felt the thrum of her heartbeat as she snagged her gaze. You didn't need to be psychic to know what she was thinking. Rhona closed the gap and was surprised when Kirsty spoke, her lips so close she could feel them graze hers with every word.

'You're so—'

'Kirsty,' a woman's voice called. 'Oh, shit, Jesus, sorry.'

Rhona couldn't help but laugh at the way Ashley spun

with her hands covering her eyes. You'd think she'd just walked in on them naked.

Kirsty cleared her throat, her body relaxing as she stepped back, creating an inch of space between them. 'Ash, what's up?'

Even in the dim light, it was obvious Ashley was the colour of a tomato. She dropped her hands, crossing them over her chest, still embarrassed. 'It's just I saw you come down here and I thought it would be a good chance to have a private chat about something. I didn't know you were already doing that.' She looked back to the castle like making eye contact was the hardest thing in the world.

'Honestly, it's fine. I'm going home anyway,' Rhona said, letting go of Kirsty. The moment was gone. They could rekindle it when they went for a drink next week. She dipped so her lips were level with Kirsty's ear, a hand on her waist to keep steady. 'Until next week.' She kissed her on the cheek before straightening her waistcoat. 'See you, Ashley. Say hi to Hazel for me.'

Rhona wandered back up the path with a final look to Kirsty. She was beautiful. Probably a good thing they'd been interrupted or she never would have made it to her parent's house.

∼

'Rho, Rho.'

The distant voice cut through her dream, bringing her back to reality. Her childhood bedroom came into focus. The bed, windows, and door remained in the same place, but everything else was different. Her white walls were replaced with floral wallpaper, her tasteful bedding now patterned and garish. It was the guest bedroom now. Still, it had more personality than her room back in Glasgow.

'Rhona!' her brother's voice barked from downstairs. She ignored him. Not like he could do anything about it, anyway.

She rolled onto her side, grabbing her phone for the bedside table. Just after half eight.

She smiled at a text from Kirsty – *You still up? xx* – sad she'd missed it, but as soon as she'd got in last night and exchanged pleasantries with her parents there was no holding her back from sleep.

She fired off a quick reply, joking about Kirsty's likely hangover, and made her way to the toilet.

Finally awake, she wandered downstairs and into the kitchen to find her parents and brother gathered around the kitchen table.

Michael's face broke into a grin as he swivelled his wheelchair to face her, running his back wheel right over her foot.

Instead of hugging him, Rhona punched his upper arm. 'Mum,' she whined. 'He just ran over my foot. On *purpose*.'

Michael pulled a face out of his mother's sight, confirming it hadn't been an accident. He yanked his sister into a hug as Mum spoke. 'Rhona, don't tell tales on your brother.' She didn't even lift her eyes from the newspaper. At least her input was more than Dad offered. The room could be on fire and he'd still just sit, poring over the paper.

Rhona squeezed her brother tighter. 'What are you doing here?' she asked, pulling back and walking towards the kettle. 'Why aren't you in Edinburgh? Charlene finally sick of you?'

'As if. Can't a guy surprise his big sister if he wants? Does he need a reason?'

Rhona pulled a face as she picked up the boiling kettle

and poured water into her mug. 'He does if it's only just gone nine on a Sunday.'

'Mum said you were stopping by unexpectedly and I thought it was the perfect chance to see you. There's something I need to tell you.'

Rhona stilled the spoon stirring her teabag and studied his face. Michael looked okay. The same goofy smile, dark eyes and thick black hair that he never did a damn thing with but it still looked styled. He'd always be her baby brother, even with a big bushy beard. He'd been through enough operations; surely he didn't need to endure another?

'Everything okay?' she asked.

His face changed, his features shifting from goofy to concerned. 'Nothing bad,' he said, his eyes lighting up. 'God, sorry. This is exciting. Promise.'

She fished the teabag out and dumped it in the bin, her features still laced with scepticism. Maybe she was still half asleep, but something wasn't adding up.

Rhona took a seat and tried to gauge the room. Her parents didn't bat an eyelid.

'They already know,' Michael said. He was fidgety, playing with his wheels, making himself move back and forth.

Mum put the paper down and raised her eyebrows at Michael, a smile pulling at the corners of her mouth.

Okay, this was getting weird.

'Spit it out, then!' Rhona joked, taking a sip of tea.

Michael couldn't talk for smiling. Suddenly, his face dropped, and Rhona felt her stomach flip. 'Mum, can you get the box? I left it in the living room.'

Nervous energy flooded Rhona's veins. 'What's going on?'

Love Detour

'You'll see.' Michael looked close to euphoria as his smile returned. 'Charlene's sorry she can't be here, by the way. She wasn't feeling good this morning.'

The way his eyes sparkled hinted this might be part of a joke, but it was lost on Rhona.

Dad lowered his paper when Mum came back. Not quite away – it was still open across the table – but it was the most attention Rhona had ever seen him give before ten o'clock.

She felt like the odd one out. Her heart tapped against her ribs, not sure if it should be racing or not.

Michael handed her a parcel. A neat little box covered in a swirly pink-and-green paisley pattern, finished with a ribbon.

Rhona looked at it like she'd never seen a gift before in her life.

'Open it,' Mum urged, standing behind Michael, her hands on his shoulders.

Rhona was almost shaking as she undid the ribbon. She placed the box on the table and shimmied the lid off, her eyes going between the box and her brother.

Finally, it was open. She placed the lid on the table and parted the yellow tissue paper inside, to reveal clothing. A top?

Carefully, she pulled it out.

A white babygro.

Mum squealed; Michael was quiet, but his attention never left Rhona. She wasn't even sure she'd seen him blink since she got up. She could almost feel the ache in his cheeks as he fought the smile pulling at his lips.

She turned the babygro around. 'Auntie Rhona will teach me the fun stuff,' she said, confusion clear as she read aloud the grey script decorating the tiny clothing. The penny dropped. 'Are you having a baby?' She leapt to her feet, her voice louder as she repeated the question. 'Are you having a baby?'

Michael leaned forward, grabbing her for another hug. 'You're going to be an auntie!'

She didn't even feel the tears start, but the next thing Rhona knew, her cheeks were soaked. 'This is the best news ever!'

Mum joined in the hug. Dad watched from a safe distance.

She slumped back in her chair, wiping the tears from her face and unable to stop smiling. 'My wee brother, a daddy,' she said, still in shock. 'When are they due?'

'February twenty-third. So we're not quite at three months yet, but when I heard you were here I couldn't wait. And it saved me driving to Glasgow,' he added with a chuckle.

Mum took a seat and gave Dad's hand a squeeze. 'Our first grandchild.'

Dad smiled. He was a man of very few words, but Rhona could tell he was over the moon.

'February twenty-third,' Rhona repeated, her voice dreamy. That would cut travelling short. Or at least add a pit stop. There was no way she would miss her niece or nephew being born.

'You going to be around?' Michael asked.

'Of course.' The tug in her bones pulled once more. Scotland was calling her to stay.

13

'Self-sabotage,' Dani sung as she walked past Kirsty's bedroom door.

'Fuck off,' Kirsty sung back, mimicking her tune.

Two minutes later she appeared in Kirsty's doorway, two open beers in hand. 'Drink?'

'Why not?' Kirsty said, not taking her attention from her reflection in the mirror as she put on bronzer.

Dani took a seat on the edge of her sister's bed after placing the beer bottle on the floor by her.

'Excited?' she asked, swigging the booze.

Kirsty took a ragged breath, finally pausing the brush's motion across her cheeks. 'Yes and no.'

'No?'

'Also shitting myself.'

'First ever date; bound to have nerves. You might be shit at this.'

Kirsty glared at her sister's reflection. 'You're *meant* to be helpful.'

Dani chuckled. 'Just trying to make you laugh. So, what's

the crack with the coffee machine? Do I need to do anything tomorrow?'

Kirsty huffed, stuffing the brush in her make-up bag before searching for her mascara. 'No. That's why I stayed back.'

The coffee machine wasn't holding pressure this morning, which had made their day a nightmare, but thankfully the engineer guy had managed to swing by and fix it that evening. It had put Kirsty's plans into disarray, but it was fine. She had it under control. She'd topped up her fake tan last night. So she didn't get the nap she wanted this afternoon? No biggie. A quick shower and now she was putting on her make-up. Everything would be fine. If only someone would tell her stomach: the butterflies were twirling at supersonic speed.

Yes, she could have asked Mum to wait for the engineer, but she didn't know the machine like Kirsty did. All that would do was tempt fate and have Dani calling her at God-knows-what o'clock tomorrow morning, saying the problem wasn't properly fixed. It was one thing to push her plans back; it was another to deal with problems hungover. Plus, if everything worked out as planned, Rhona would still be here in the morning. She'd have no time for coffee machines.

The buzzer went, making every muscle in Kirsty's body tense.

'I'll get it,' Dani said, jumping to her feet.

Kirsty took a deep breath. *It's just Rhona.* It had been a fantasy-filled forty-eight hours since their interrupted near-kiss and Kirsty felt like a tightly wound spring.

Before she knew it the door to the flat was opening and Dani and Rhona's polite chit-chat filled the hall. 'She's still getting ready, but that's her room,' Dani said.

Kirsty watched as Rhona's head popped round her door. Suddenly she felt silly sitting on her floor, putting on make-up in her wardrobe's mirror. Surely real adults had vanity mirrors, or something? Too late now.

'Hey.' Rhona bit her bottom lip, a cheesy grin taking over. 'Can I come in?'

Kirsty swivelled to face her. 'Yeah, sure. Take a seat.'

Wow. Kirsty pretended to be searching for something in her make-up box for fear of her mouth hanging agape. Rhona looked amazing.

She had on black skinny jeans, black boots, and a loose printed tee. Her hair was up, showing off the undercut that drove Kirsty wild. Rhona hovered her hands over her black denim jacket. 'Should I take this off, or are you nearly ready?'

'Pretty much done,' Kirsty said, picking up the beer and taking a gulp. 'Beer? Dani just opened it.'

Rhona accepted the bottle and sat, taking a long draw as she watched Kirsty in the mirror. God, she looked so cute perched on the end of her bed. Kirsty gave her own reflection a once-over: everything looked in order. She got to her feet and stretched, sore from sitting on the floor. She was getting too old for this malarkey. Maybe she did need a vanity. No room in here, though.

'You look good,' Rhona said, her eyes still trailing Kirsty's body. She felt good; confident. You couldn't go wrong with skinny jeans and a floral top. Especially not one with a plunging neckline.

'As do you.' Kirsty sat by Rhona on the bed, taking the bottle from her. She could feel the heat from Rhona's leg through her jeans. She took a swig before speaking. 'So, I have a confession.'

'Uh-huh?'

'I've never been on a date before.'

'Never?' Rhona didn't look convinced.

Kirsty tilted her body, facing Rhona as best she could. 'Scout's honour. So, you'll need to keep me right tonight.'

Rhona relieved Kirsty of the beer bottle and took a drink. 'Keep you right?'

'Yep. Dates have etiquette, yeah? Like, something that's always confused me is—' She took the beer back and took a long slow draw, her eyes locked with Rhona's. 'Are you meant to kiss at the start or the end of the date?'

Rhona chuckled, shaking her head as she quickly got the gist of Kirsty's intentions. She hid a smile behind her hand, feigning, or at least Kirsty thought she was hamming it up, embarrassment and shock. 'Start, always at the start.'

'Oh, really?' Kirsty said, edging closer. 'Well, I'd hate to go wrong so early in the evening.'

She shut her eyes and closed the gap, the feeling of Rhona's breath hot against her lips, the smell of beer fresh in the air.

Rhona's hand gripped her waist, pulling her closer, until finally their lips met.

Kirsty hadn't quite decided if this was going to be a quick peck or more, but Rhona was already aiming for the latter. A flush of desire erupted low in Kirsty's stomach as her lips moved in time with Rhona's. Their mouths parted and she couldn't help but groan as Rhona's tongue found hers.

Fuck, Rhona was a good kisser. Her core tingled, coming more alive with every pass of Rhona's lips.

Her free hand cupped Rhona's jaw, wanting to keep the connection for as long as possible.

Kirsty fought the urge to move her thigh over Rhona's, well aware she was still holding a bottle of beer.

Much more and they wouldn't make it out tonight. But this was too good to stop.

Rhona's hand snaked under her top and Kirsty's muscles stiffened at the contact. She felt drunk, delirious with desire.

It took all her willpower to pull back, and she was surprised to find herself breathless.

Had she ever experienced a first kiss like that? Usually her kisses were more carnal, shared in pubs or clubs, the promise of something more or just drunken fun. Maybe first date kisses were different.

Rhona smiled, their faces still centimetres apart. 'Worth the wait.'

'I'm glad you think so.'

'Still want to go out?'

She was joking but the heat between Kirsty's legs wasn't. She had to convince herself more than her date. 'Erm, yes! I just spent an hour getting ready,' she playfully scolded.

Rhona stole a quick kiss. 'Well, we'd better go before I change your mind.'

~

'Have you really never been on a date?' Rhona asked as they walked by Queen's Park.

'Nope.'

'How old are you?'

'Er, you can never ask a lady that,' Kirsty joked. 'But off the record, I'm thirty-five. Not that it should make any difference. I just haven't been interested in dating before now.'

'So what's changed?'

Kirsty shrugged. She didn't want to get deep so early on

with Rhona. She didn't need to know about her baggage yet. 'Just getting older, I guess. Done with playing around.'

'And you thought I wasn't?' Rhona asked with a wicked glint in her eye.

'Never going to live that down, am I? I guess . . .' She took a deep breath, preparing to be blatantly honest. 'I just wanted to be sure of your intentions. I don't want a fling.'

Rhona nodded, her eyes saying she was thinking. *Shit. Was that too much? Too serious?*

Rhona still hadn't spoken when they reached the Battlefield Monument. They had a decision to make about their destination for the evening, but Kirsty needed her own answers first. 'Does that scare you?'

'No. Not at all. I'm just thinking.'

'Good thinking or bad thinking?'

'Not sure yet.'

Well, fuck a duck. That can't be good. Now wasn't the time to over-analyse. 'So, we can go here,' Kirsty said, pointing to the converted church across the road. 'Or we can keep walking for ten minutes, go to the unofficial gay bar of the Southside.'

'Bar Orama?'

'You know it?' Kirsty asked, unable to hide the shock in her voice.

'Ashley mentioned it. Let's go there. I want to see what the fuss is about.'

'Bar Orama it is, then.'

They walked in comfortable silence as they negotiated crossing the roundabout, although Kirsty's mind was in overdrive. Had she overstepped a mark by saying she wanted a relationship?

She didn't want to sound desperate, but she also couldn't relax if this wasn't cleared up soon. 'So,' she began, not really knowing where the sentence was going. 'You enjoying living in Glasgow?'

What was that? That wasn't clearing things up. This was a totally new tangent.

'Yeah, I am. I love it. Although, I wish I'd got a place in the Southside instead of the West End. I much prefer it here. I don't know the place, though. I just went on Amber's advice.'

'That's easily done. Glasgow varies from street to street, never mind suburb to suburb. You never know until you move somewhere.'

'True: that's what I love about getting to know somewhere new.'

'So, when's your lease up? Moving south soon?'

They were well into the suburb of Battlefield now. It was less lively than Shawlands, but still oozed Southside charm, with its long stretch of indie shops. They crossed the road and walked towards the hospital, taking the quickest route to Mount Florida.

Rhona waggled her head, thinking. 'The rent's cheap. I think I'll just stick it out until Christmas. Then I'll head home before I go travelling.'

'Eh?' The word caught in Kirsty's throat, like it was too big to pass. Travelling? What?

'I'm only covering maternity leave for Amber. I want to spend next year travelling. Well, maybe not a year. I'll have enough saved for a few months, maybe six if I really shoestring it.'

Kirsty's brain froze, every connection fizzling out. She opened her mouth to speak before realising she didn't know how to form sentences any more.

This was a disaster.

A force gripped her stomach, pulling it down and

making her feel sick. Christmas. Six months of travelling. Why hadn't Rhona mentioned this before?

Why was this news having such an effect on her? It was like her brain was wading through tar; tears pricked at her eyes.

Rhona was searching her face for an answer. Kirsty had been quiet for an uncomfortably long time, so she couldn't blame her. It was just . . . what the actual fuck?! Christmas wasn't far off.

This was over before it had even begun. She fought the urge to turn on her heel and go straight home. She'd need to see Rhona at Lovefest events; there was no point in acting like a petulant child and making things awkward.

'Where are you going to visit?' Kirsty finally managed, her voice not sounding like her own.

Rhona's face lit up with excitement. Kirsty's stomach swooped again. What was the point? Three months with the girl then she was off, Kirsty forgotten forever. She could scream. So much for a first date.

'I've not decided where I want to start yet,' Rhona gushed. 'But I know I want to visit India. I've got relatives in Punjab, so I guess it would make sense to start there.' She was in full flow now, her eyes sparkling with excitement. 'But I also want to see Sri Lanka, Indonesia. I know I can't do them all. Waaaay too much distance between. And India could take a lifetime in itself, but that's what's exciting. There's so much to explore.'

Kirsty's stomach had sorted itself out but now her heart refused to act normally. Each beat vibrated with a dull ache. 'Sounds good.' It did. She just didn't like the timeline. They crossed the road again, still navigating through hospital car parks and outbuildings. Bar Orama was only five minutes away. Thank God. She really needed a drink. 'You've never been to India before?'

'Once, when I was younger. I don't really remember it. Is there anywhere you're dying to go?'

Kirsty had never really thought about it. America and Australia had always intrigued her, but she had no burning desire to travel. 'Not really. We used to go on holiday to Spain, but Mum and Dad were always so busy with the café that it didn't happen often. My friend Kim – you'll probably meet her in a minute – her parents have a villa in Ibiza. Me and Dani and our pals try to go there every year. That's about the extent of it.'

Rhona nodded. 'Always nice to get away from the same four walls. Doesn't matter where you go.'

Kirsty stifled a sigh. *Does if you're going for a half a fucking year.*

Finally, they were at the lights, and Bar Orama was within sight. It didn't look like much from the outside; in fact most people probably walked past, lumping it with the other bars in the area. Its flaky black facade didn't give much away. And its Western-style lettering even less so. Kev liked his cowboys, that was for sure.

The green man appeared, along with a shrill beep, and they crossed the road. She was here and still wanted to enjoy the evening, but her temper was triggered, annoyance gripping her like an ever-tightening screw. She wanted to travel back, go down a different route of conversation, and not find out about Rhona's plans until it was too late. Ignorance would be bliss.

'I hope it lives up to the hype,' Kirsty said, standing aside so Rhona could enter the bar first.

Music filtered onto the street, some acoustic indie tune

Kirsty didn't recognise, and in they went. Rhona looked pleasantly impressed.

This was Kirsty's domain, her little safe haven, and she was fiercely protective of it.

She and Dani had this thing; it was silly, but it perfectly explained how she felt right now. Dani had aptly christened it *dick-coloured glasses*: when someone has pissed you off so much that they can literally do no right. Everything is annoying. You're seeing them through a different lens to everyone else.

Kirsty was annoyed at herself for feeling that way about Rhona. She'd pissed her off and now the edges of her personality were fraying: the woman she'd kissed not even an hour ago was unravelling, someone else taking her place.

But this was a Kirsty problem. It wasn't fair to take it out on Rhona.

'Kirsty!' Kim shouted from the bar, her smile on full beam.

Tuesday evening and the bar was quiet. Only two other tables were filled and it was no one she knew. Pity. She could have done with a distraction.

Rhona let Kirsty lead them to the bar.

'Rhona, this is my friend Kim I was telling you about.'

Kim bobbed her head. 'Oh, really? Good stuff?'

'Just about your villa.'

'Ah, using my parents' credentials to score points with your date?'

She never should have mentioned Rhona in the group chat. Now she was going to have to explain how they'd crashed and burned before they'd even got out the gate.

'You know me, always out to woo,' Kirsty said, forcing a smile. 'What do you want to drink?'

Rhona put her hand on the small of Kirsty's back as she

leaned forward to study the bottles lined up at the back of the bar. It was annoying how nice the contact felt. Kirsty edged herself free in what she hoped was a subtle move. 'I'll have a Chardonnay please, Kim.'

'Sailor Jerry and Coke for me. I'll get this round,' Rhona said, producing her card.

'You sure?'

'Yeah. My treat. Start as we mean to go on, and all that.'

Kirsty felt like someone had put her emotions in a washing machine and started a spin cycle. Her heart wanted her to kiss Rhona and her head wanted her to bawl her eyes out.

'Thank you. You grab a seat and I'll bring the drinks over,' Kirsty said.

Travis scuttled to her end of the bar, never one to be shrewd. 'So you *are* on a date.'

'Meaning?' He was being jokey, but Kirsty's mood didn't match. Grumpiness was seeping out in every direction: it was like trying to hold water in a sieve.

He narrowed his eyes, sizing up the tone. 'Excited for you, I guess.'

Fuck. Kirsty grappled her anger and stuffed it down like she was tamping coffee grounds. 'Thank you. Sorry, not having the best day.'

'How so?' Kim asked, setting Rhona's drink down on the mat.

'Coffee machine broke and some customers were dicks about it,' she lied. Well, it was true; it just wasn't why she was grumpy.

Travis nodded. 'I'm sure your date will cheer you up.'

'She's doing her best.'

'It's not an easy job, so cut her some slack.'

Kim whacked him with a bar cloth. 'Go grab me another Chardonnay, will you? I just finished the last bottle.'

Travis pulled a face, crossing his eyes in the process. 'Yes, boss.'

Kirsty picked up the drinks and said a quick thank you to Kim. She could do this: time to relax and enjoy the evening. Say it enough and she might believe it herself.

14

'So, you've never been on a date,' Rhona said, sipping her rum and Coke. 'Does that mean just one-night stands, or long-term partners you just had fun with?'

She'd bagged a booth near the back of the pub. She could see the appeal: it had a laid-back vibe and felt pleasantly familiar, even though Rhona had never visited before. Some of the furniture was a little aged, but it just showed love.

Kirsty shifted in her seat. 'I guess a bit of both.'

'My longest relationship was eight years,' Rhona said, battling to carry on the conversation. Kirsty had been weird since they got here. The sudden shift in dynamics was throwing Rhona. Had kissing her been the wrong thing to do? Kirsty had initiated it, though. No, the issue came after that. Maybe Kirsty just ran hot and cold. This was the yoga day all over again.

'That's a long time. Why did you break up?'

Rhona scrunched her face up. No point in sugar-coating things. 'We had a business together. June saw the business bank account as a better asset than me. She drained it and ran off.'

'Jesus.'

'I know, but it's water under the bridge. Sometimes you put your chips on the wrong person. I wouldn't be in Glasgow if that hadn't happened.' She took another sip of Coke. 'I like to think when really shitty stuff happens it's just the universe giving you a boot up the bum, steering you in the right direction. Sometimes you need a slap in the face to pay attention.'

'That's a very optimistic way to look at things.'

'I like to stay positive. Keeps me centred. Like yeah, it hurt, but I wouldn't be here otherwise. So I'd say it worked out.'

Kirsty didn't look convinced. 'It's a nice concept, but I think sometimes life is just shit. It's not always about direction.'

Now wasn't the time for debating Rhona's beliefs. She'd already rubbed Kirsty up the wrong way about something. 'That too. And I've definitely had moments when I thought the same. But hindsight is a wonderful thing.'

'What do you mean?'

Rhona finished the last of her drink, the alcohol warming her throat and chest. 'My little brother was in a car accident when he was nineteen. A drunk driver ploughed into him. Left him paralysed from the waist down.'

'I'm so sorry,' Kirsty said, consolingly, her features softening.

'Completely changed his life goals: his life is nothing like he ever imagined. It's been tough. Some really, really shitty times, I won't deny that. But he's happy. I found out on Sunday I'm going to be an auntie.' Rhona's face broke into a smile at the thought.

'Congratulations,' Kirsty said, returning her smile.

'Due in February. I can't wait.'

'But you'll miss it all if you're travelling.'

There was a lilt to Kirsty's voice, the hint of venom touching the surface of her words.

'Has something about my plans annoyed you?'

Kirsty pulled her bottom lip between her teeth, her eyes fixed on her wine. Rhona let the moment simmer: she wasn't going to give Kirsty a way out of the conversation.

Finally, she spoke. 'I don't see the point in pursuing a relationship if you're just going to leave in three-and-a-bit months.'

Ah. There it was. So she had pissed Kirsty off. 'So, what? That's it? You won't even give us a chance?'

'What's the point if it won't exist after Christmas?'

'Surely every relationship has the potential not to work at the start. Why bother exploring any of them?'

Kirsty's muscles stiffened as she thought. 'Fair. But this one already comes with an expiry date.'

'I'm not going forever. And chances are I'll come back to Glasgow. I like it here.'

Kirsty snorted with frustration. 'It gets better and better. So, Glasgow might not even be on the cards. Do you not think you should have told me?'

'It just hadn't come up until now. I didn't think it was important. I might stay here. I might not. Maybe you'll be the reason I come back.'

'Whoop-de-do. Lucky me.' Kirsty grabbed her bag and scooted out of the booth. 'I'm going home. You can do what you like.'

Rhona was too shocked to answer. Instead, she watched Kirsty leave and did her best to avoid the glares of Kim and the barman standing beside her.

Fuck.

There really was no choice but to go after her.

Rhona hoofed it out the door and was relieved to see Kirsty at the traffic lights. She'd made it a fair distance, but she could see her; that's what mattered.

She jogged along the pavement, her calf muscles already protesting. She wasn't used to doing cardio. Especially not in boots.

Kirsty was already crossing the street when Rhona came level with her.

Not a word.

'Kirsty, don't leave like this,' Rhona said, falling into step with her.

Kirsty crossed her arms, tucking her hands away, and kept her gaze on the pavement ahead.

'This feels bigger than me not telling you I was leaving,' Rhona said, still keeping pace.

It suddenly dawned on her that she didn't know this woman at all. Yes, they'd shared a few flirty moments and Rhona had *felt* she'd got to know Kirsty and her family at the wedding, but not really. Maybe this was standard for her.

But instinct told Rhona it wasn't. And maybe that's what was annoying Kirsty more than anything.

'Can we at least be friends?'

'I don't need any more friends,' Kirsty grumbled.

'So, that's it? You're just going to write this connection off?'

Kirsty's stare could kill: Rhona had never felt anything so weighted in her life. 'Rhona, we kissed once. We had nice conversation. It's barely the romance of the century. I think we'll both cope.'

Wow. Harsh. Rhona was sure she saw the glint of tears rimming Kirsty's eyes, though.

They were back at the spaghetti scramble of lights between the hospital buildings now, forcing Kirsty to stay rooted. She couldn't go anywhere until the traffic presented a gap. It was now or never to build a bridge.

'I know you don't need any friends,' Rhona began, her voice unsteady as she picked her words. 'But I've enjoyed hanging out with you. And I think you've enjoyed talking to me?' It wasn't meant to be a question but she lost her nerve near the end of the sentence. 'I think we'd be silly to let this go to waste. At least, you know, as a future option? You can't expect me to just walk away and forget about you. You're amazing, Kirsty. I can't just pretend we never met.'

The last part was cheese central, but if ever there was a time to ham things up it was now.

Kirsty stared at the coffee shop across the street.

'Plus, you're going to have to see me on Thursday anyway. You can't escape me while Lovefest is on. And, heads up, I can be pretty insufferable when I don't get what I want.' Fingers crossed the joke landed as intended.

'I can already see that.' *Bingo.*

'So?'

'So?'

The green man finally appeared, letting them cross.

'Give me a chance? As a friend.'

Kirsty marched ahead: thankfully Rhona's long legs made catching up a doddle.

She stopped when they reached the other side and Rhona nearly crashed into her. 'We'll play it by ear. But I need to be alone tonight. Okay?'

Rhona nodded. 'Okay.'

15

Thursday came around quicker than Kirsty would have liked.

She'd decided on Sunday to keep Ross at arm's length and simply not date him by skilful omission. A few texts here and there were harming no one, and if she managed to keep their 'dating' to Lovefest events it shouldn't be too painful. The only issue with that plan was the extra-curricular activities the other couples were involved in; dates between their dates. *Urgh.* Annie was taking great delight in posting photos online and the public were loving it. She was going to have to up her game or Ross might become suspicious. And suspicious meant complications she didn't need.

Her head was dealing with enough without adding Ross into the mix. She was still swimming in indecision from Tuesday. No. Drowning was more apt.

Kirsty was a little embarrassed by how she'd acted, but her agitation had wound itself so tightly by the time Rhona brought up travelling again it was a case of losing her temper or crying, and she didn't want to do either in public.

It was leave or make a fool of herself. Could she have executed it better? Absolutely. Did she have a time machine? Sadly not.

She wasn't keen on pursuing a friendship, but it would keep things civil for the remainder of Lovefest.

It wasn't Rhona's fault her plans didn't align with Kirsty's, but it was a kick in the teeth nonetheless. The first time she'd met someone and felt there could be something worth chasing, and that person only wanted a temporary fling. Past Kirsty would be taking her by the shoulders and giving her a good shake. This would have been her perfect set-up back then.

Especially given how damn attractive Rhona was.

She could go back to old habits and see where it went, but doing so would feel like failure. She'd all but made a promise to herself to change her ways. Getting into a relationship with Rhona, no matter how casual, was setting herself up for heartbreak. Her priorities were different now. She owed it to herself to take her new motives seriously.

Someone equally as alluring would come along.

Maybe.

Kirsty focused on the drink she was currently turning between finger and thumb. Oh, to be anywhere but here.

This week's date was all about getting to know the other couples. They'd been summoned back to Cal's and had taken over the seated area in the pub section of the venue. Couples' pub quiz. Fantastic.

It wasn't busy. but a few other patrons were scattered over the pub area. They looked slightly perplexed as to what they'd wandered into. Kirsty knew how they felt.

Ross had his arm draped over the back of her chair and she'd caught Rhona looking more than once. It made her feel like she was doing something wrong. Being honest with Ross wasn't an option, though.

Another date next week, then the Lovefest closing event. Two weeks. It was better this way. No one got hurt and Mum would be happy.

Business was certainly booming at Café Odyssey. There was no denying that Kirsty's involvement was having a positive effect. Mum had even made Lovefest scones – strawberry, white chocolate, and vanilla – and they were selling out every day. If she could just keep Ross's attention, the public would continue to flock.

She hadn't told Mum about Rhona, and Dani had been sworn to secrecy. There was no point complicating stuff. If everyone thought she was dating Ross, so what?

'Hello, everyone,' Annie chirped into her microphone. There were only ten of them over two tables; the mic might have been a little overkill, but whatever.

Rhona hovered near Kirsty and Ross's table and she couldn't help the pang in her chest, wishing the two would swap places. Despite their fight, Rhona would still be better company than Ross. Everything was stiff and wrong this evening.

Ashley sent her a half-assed smile, but it did little to make Kirsty feel better.

'Welcome to the first ever Lovefest Couples' Pub Quiz!' Annie said, almost giddy with excitement. 'One of the things our couples wished for last year was the chance to get to know the other couples, so I hope you'll stay for some complimentary drinks after our quiz.'

Ross's hand found her shoulder, and even through her hoodie his touch made her tense. It wasn't him, per se. She didn't want anyone near her.

She caught Rhona's eye again and knew that wasn't true.

'You all have your pens and paper, yes?' Annie checked, giving the two tables a quick glance. 'Then we'll begin. Question one...'

'I'll write,' Ross said, snapping the pen up from between him and Kirsty. He was trying to be helpful but it just made Kirsty's mood worse. But at least if he took control she could sit back and do the bare minimum.

'What do you think?' Ross asked, leaning in close so the other couples wouldn't hear them. They were on a table with Ashley and Hazel and Greg and Yash. Kirsty wondered if Annie had meant to create an LGBTQ+ table. What would Ross think of that? His weirdness about pronouns hadn't been forgotten.

'Huh?' Kirsty asked, having not listened to Annie in the slightest.

Ross's brow furrowed. 'What Disney film was hyped as "The Greatest Love Story Ever Told?"'

'*Beauty and the Beast*,' Kirsty said with a shake of her head. Easy stuff.

'You sure?' he whispered. She could smell his cologne; it was annoyingly nice. He leaned closer. 'What about *Aladdin*?'

Kirsty snorted with laughter. 'That's not a love film.'

'It is.' He scrunched his face, intent on being indignant.

'Sorry to interrupt, guys,' Rhona said, squatting so her head was level with the two of them. 'I'm just going to take a few photos. You carry on.'

Professional Rhona was back, but Kirsty could tell there was more behind her eyes tonight.

Ross scribbled down Kirsty's answer as Rhona snapped away.

Her hair was down tonight but she'd paired a tight T-shirt with perfectly fitting cigarette trousers. It was almost unfair how good she looked. If Rhona was playing a game to make her look twice, Kirsty had gone the opposite. She really couldn't be arsed. A hoodie and skinny jeans was all she could muster today.

'Who wrote the following: "If music be the food of love, play on"?' Annie asked.

Ashley pulled a face. 'Come on, you must know that?' Kirsty asked before sipping on her wine.

Another face and a shrug before erupting into giggles with Hazel. 'How do you know this?' Ashley asked between laughter.

'School,' Kirsty jested. Ashley had sat beside Dani in English: there was no way anything would have stuck with that clown by her side.

Surprisingly, Ross looked just as clueless. Kirsty couldn't help but sneak a look at Rhona, who looked smug as fuck behind the camera. She knew. Of course she knew.

'Go on then, write the answer,' Kirsty whispered to Ross, accidentally so close she almost brushed his earlobe with her lips.

That confused the poor man further. Kirsty plucked the pen from his grasp and jotted down *Shakespeare*.

Maybe it was her imagination, but Rhona seemed to be lingering on Kirsty, taking more photos of her than anyone else. It felt like all eyes were on her.

'How many roses are sent each year on Valentine's Day?' Annie asked.

Kirsty and Ross exchanged looks. 'Millions, surely?' she whispered.

She studied the two other couples at their table: both were deep in discussion, no obvious numbers being said.

'I think billions,' Ross ventured.

Rhona moved on, or at least by way of her subjects. She

positioned herself behind Kirsty, getting a shot of Ashley and Hazel.

Kirsty was doing her best to block them out, so she side-eyed a view of Rhona's chest as Ross stared into the corner of the room, presumably doing some hardcore mental maths.

Her chat with Ashley had put Kirsty in an odd position. She'd actually wanted to hash it out with Rhona on their date, get an outsider's opinion; but well, that never happened.

She liked Hazel, no denying it. But Ashley had wanted Kirsty's opinion on the whole Dani thing: it was like she was pushing for her blessing. She couldn't do that to Dani. Especially not now she knew about her sister's therapy sessions.

Kirsty had brushed it off, wiggling her way out of the conversation, and dropped some serious hints to Dani when back in the castle. They'd obviously fallen on deaf ears, though, given how touchy-feely the two women were together now.

They looked ridiculously cute.

It was how Kirsty had imagined herself with Rhona on Tuesday.

Before she knew it, a massive sigh had escaped her.

'You okay?' Ross asked.

'Yeah, sorry. Tough question.' Kirsty lied, forcing a smile. 'So, what do you want to go for?'

'I say seventy billion.'

That was ridiculously high. 'How about seventy million?'

Ross shook his head. 'Nope. I'm telling you, it's billions.'

'Sure, go for it.'

Not like anything mattered anyway.

~

'It's all a bit surreal isn't it? Tom said, between gulps of beer. The quiz was over, with Helen and Philip declared the winners, and now they were expected to mingle. The other couples were nice enough. Kirsty was surprised how geographically spread they were: she'd expected most people to be Southsiders. Ross, Tom, and Yash were all from the West End, though, and Helen had travelled over from Paisley. It would seem the success of Lovefest was drawing a crowd from beyond the Shawlands border. No wonder the café was busy.

'Probably much better when the camera isn't in your face,' Ross said and Kirsty wondered if it was as much about Rhona as it was the absurdity of being photographed.

'Oh God, yeah.' Tom agreed. 'Did you guys do anything extra last week? We went to the park.'

'We didn't,' Kirsty said, shutting things down as quickly as possible. 'My sister got married so I didn't have a spare moment.'

'This week, though,' Ross said, looping an arm around her and squeezing her side. Her stomach lurched.

'Yeah, hopefully,' she lied with a smile.

'Who do you think will win?' Sophie asked, possibly picking up on Kirsty's hesitation and throwing her a lifeline: girl power for the win.

'Us, obviously.' It was disguised as a joke, but Ross was being serious. Kirsty wouldn't mind five grand, though – she wasn't going to argue with him.

Tom retaliated with a joke about them being the rightful winners, backed up by Sophie, then all eyes were on Kirsty. Truthfully, she was backing Ashley and Hazel, but this didn't feel like the right moment to declare treason on her own chances.

'Guess it's all to play for,' she said, after a swig of wine. 'What are you spending your money on, Ross?'

That got a rueful look from Tom: good. She was pulling this off.

Ross pondered the question. His hand was still gripping Kirsty's waist and the sensation made her want to scream. 'Okay, so, not the full two grand, but a few hundred quid. I'd like to get a hot composter.'

Kirsty wasn't the only one who looked confused.

Ross continued. 'It's a type of compost bin.' His eyes lit up, excited to share his facts. 'It can give you compost in sixty to ninety days. A regular garden bin can take up to two years, although I've got compost in as little as six months.' He looked very pleased at this.

Kirsty exchanged a look with Sophie. She opened her mouth to talk but snapped it shut, wanting to make sure she'd fully understood. 'A compost bin?' Kirsty asked, her head tilted to the side.

'Not just any old compost bin. A hot bin.'

'A dream's a dream,' Kirsty said, happy for Ross. Somewhere out there, his own little Charlie Dimmock was waiting.

'What about you, Kirsty?' Sophie asked, somehow keeping a straight face.

'A holiday somewhere. Don't really care where, as long as it's hot.'

'I can't go anywhere too sunny,' Ross said, assuming he was invited. 'I burn even in the Scottish sun.'

Could she have landed anyone less compatible?

'And a sun hat for Ross, by the looks of it. Don't worry,

I'll splash out and get you a good one,' Kirsty joked. She stepped free of his grasp. 'Just going to see Ashley.'

Rhona lingered on the periphery and it was excruciating not to detour in her direction. Whatever tension hung between them had to provide better conversation than fucking compost.

That was unfair. He was allowed an interest. Kirsty just wished it was one that aligned with hers.

'Hey, guys,' she said, perching on the sofa arm by Ashley. 'How's it going?'

A tumble of *okay*s and *not bad*s rippled through the group. Greg and Yash looked very cute together. They were good fun, too. Yash had got excited and blurted an answer earlier, only to have Greg playfully tell him off. You could feel the chemistry between them: things were obviously going well.

Same went for Ashley and Hazel. The hand on Hazel's knee was duly noted.

'What about you?' Ashley asked.

Kirsty shrugged. 'I've learnt that Ross likes compost.'

'Compost?' Ashley repeated.

'Yeah.' She didn't quite know how to follow that up. 'You guys staying out after this?'

Helen shook her head. 'I need to get back to Paisley.' She and Philip were older than the other couples – late forties, if Kirsty was going to hazard a guess – but they seemed like they could keep up with the best of them. It was a shame she couldn't stay.

Philip held up his glass of what Kirsty presumed was straight Coke. 'But I'm driving, so it won't take too long.'

God, was everyone actually a couple but her and Ross?

The lads shook their heads. Kirsty turned her attention to Ashley. 'Nope. School's back in.'

A night out with Hazel might be awkward and the feeling was mutual: both kept quiet.

'Probably for the best. I'm cream crackered,' Kirsty said, exaggerating a stretch.

'Not heading out with Ross, then?' Ashley asked, a wicked smile playing on her lips.

'He's not asked. Besides, I'm on an early tomorrow. I need an early night.'

'Strange, when you do the rotas.'

Kirsty fought the urge to throttle Ash; it was obvious what she was insinuating. 'Dani needed to start later. She's meeting someone.'

That got her attention. 'Anyone interesting?'

'Some woman,' Kirsty replied with a shrug. Her therapist, but Ashley didn't need to know that.

'Like a date?'

'I decided not to ask. So, does anyone know what they're doing next week? Annie's not told me yet. Although rock climbing was mentioned in passing.'

There was a mumble of frustration through the group. 'No idea,' Helen said. 'And I need to know what day we're scheduled so I can juggle work.'

'I'm sure it won't be long,' Kirsty said reassuringly, wishing she hadn't brought up a touchy subject. She was quite used to Annie's laid-back approach. You always had to factor in a little waiting time.

'Can you not ask Rhona? I'm sure she knows,' Ashley offered.

'Rhona?' Helen echoed.

'The photographer,' Hazel clarified.

'Ah, you know her?' Helen asked, perking up at the notion she might be able to circumvent Annie for information.

Kirsty shot Ashley a look that was thankfully received. Dani had probably told her that they'd kissed. Anything Dani knew, Ashley knew too. Some habits die hard. 'Only as much as you guys do. But if I get the chance, I'll ask her.'

Helen's shoulders slumped. 'Thank you.'

'Right, I'd better get back to my date,' Kirsty said, getting to her feet. Time to talk compost.

16

How close Ross was to Kirsty was driving Rhona insane.

Okay, so they'd agreed to be friends and exchanged a few texts yesterday, but the memo obviously hadn't reached Rhona's head. Because by God, Kirsty looked cute tonight.

Attraction wasn't a tap. She couldn't just turn it off. Two days ago they'd been on a date and shared an off-the-charts kiss. How could she not look at this gorgeous woman and feel jealous?

It wasn't a new emotion for Rhona, but she'd never felt it like this before. Probably because, unlike every other scenario, this one could play out exactly like it did in her head.

Ross and Kirsty would kiss. He thought they were dating. It was inevitable. There was absolutely nothing Rhona could do to stop it.

Friends don't give into the urge to pull two people apart and keep it that way, she reminded herself.

But then friends don't usually kiss so passionately that you see stars.

Rhona tensed her jaw, hiding her frown behind the camera as she took photos of Tom and Sophie. They had good chemistry, especially in the photos of their unofficial Lovefest dates. Tom had surprised Sophie with a picnic in the park over the weekend. Very romantic.

Rhona swallowed a sigh. That's what worried her. What Kirsty and Ross would be up to when no one else was around.

Kirsty had been honest about her lack of attraction to Ross, but she'd also not set the record straight with him about their dating. That spoke volumes.

She moved closer to the bar, getting a few wide shots of the evening. It was going well: lots of chatting and smiling, even more so now the quiz was over.

Rhona jumped when she lowered her camera and saw Kirsty was standing beside her, ordering drinks.

'Did I scare you?' Kirsty asked, only just suppressing a laugh.

'Just in the zone. You having fun?'

Kirsty turned to lean her back on the bar as the barman sorted her order. She surveyed the room before answering. 'Yeah, I am actually. You?'

'Me? I guess. I'm working.'

Silence hung between them, only interrupted by the barman placing Kirsty's drink order down.

She kept her back to the room as she spoke. 'Sorry again for Tuesday. I just—'

'It's fine,' Rhona said, cutting her off. It wasn't, but it felt like the right thing to say.

'Can we go for a drink after this? I need your opinion on something.'

∾

Love Detour

Rhona could listen to Kirsty talk all day. Thankfully, getting up to speed on Ashley and Dani took a lot of backstory, so she almost got her wish.

She'd hung back and let the couples' evening play out. It wasn't long before things naturally wound up and everyone parted ways. But she wished she'd had the foresight to go ahead instead of enjoying a lone drink in Cal's. Then she wouldn't have had to endure seeing Ross kiss Kirsty on the cheek as they said goodbye. It was little, and nothing compared to what they'd shared, but it stung like a slap in the face.

Then Kirsty had doubled back and joined Rhona, like *that* wasn't super suspicious. Now wasn't the time to bring it up, though: she already felt like she was on a fine line. She had Kirsty all to herself now – that was the main thing.

They'd moved on from Cal's and were now in a pub a few doors up. The Griffin. It was almost dead. One other couple and a lone man. It suited Rhona fine; much easier to listen without noisy punters.

Wine had added a rosy tint to Kirsty's cheeks and the way she pulled faces and gestured with her hands, getting more animated as the story went on, was tugging at Rhona's heartstrings. She looked adorable.

'So, that about sums it up,' Kirsty said, finally taking a breather. 'What would you do?'

It was a tough one. Rhona took a sip of her Pepsi. She'd never been more disappointed to have her car; who knows where the night could have gone otherwise.

'I think it's unfair of Ashley to put you in the middle. If she's looking for validation it's only because she feels guilty. She knows that she's hurting Dani.'

Kirsty nodded. 'Thank you. Yes. See, I knew you would get it. But what about me? What do I say?'

'Just keep out of it. Let things run their course.'

'But I don't want Dani to get hurt.'

'You're not responsible for either of their actions. They're grown women. You've got no control over what they do.'

'Life would be so much easier if I did.'

Rhona shook her head. 'Nope, because then you'd be responsible for everyone. That's a lot of weight on your shoulders.'

Kirsty pursed her lips. 'I think I carry that anyway.' Her eyes wandered to the huge flat-screen TV in the middle of the far wall. She watched for a bit, as if she'd suddenly developed a keen interest in football.

'I know it's tough,' Rhona said, despite Kirsty's still watching the screen. 'But you need to let them make their own mistakes. If they get hurt, it's not your fault.'

Her attention came back to Rhona. 'Kind of is, if I don't do anything to stop it.'

'You spoke to Dani at the wedding. What more can you do?'

'I dunno. I feel I want to give her a shake. She could be happy if she would just give Ashley a chance. I don't know if it's because she doesn't want to get hurt, or if she's worried about ruining their friendship. Who knows? She never wants to talk specifics,' she said with a frustrated waggle of her head. 'But why be miserable when the opportunity is there to take a chance?'

'Humans are programmed for comfort. It's a defence mechanism. Much easier to protect yourself from potential upset if you avoid change.'

'Makes no sense,' Kirsty said with a huff before taking a draw of her wine. 'Thanks again for letting me rant. You're a good listener.'

Rhona smiled. 'I have my moments.'

Kirsty's eyes darted to the screen again. Rhona watched as her jaw muscles clenched and unclenched a few times. She let Kirsty own the silence, giving her peace to think. Finally, she spoke: 'I think, this friendship thing, I'd like to give it a bash.'

Rhona cocked her head. 'I thought we agreed to that on Tuesday.'

'Yeah, well, I wasn't exactly all in.'

'Sneaky.'

'I guess I have my moments too.'

17

The week passed without much excitement. Kirsty tried to fob Ross off as much as humanly possible, but when she ran out of excuses she had to give in and go for a coffee. The daytime setting and lack of intimacy worked a treat, and she escaped with only another peck on the cheek.

The thought of doing anything more with him made her skin itchy.

One date to go, then seven days stood between her and freedom.

This week's activity was rock climbing at a business called Southside Bouldering. She'd always wanted to have a bash at climbing and had been abuzz with excitement all day.

'Is Ross okay?' Annie asked, bouncing on the balls of her feet as they waited.

'I dunno; he's taking ages,' Kirsty replied. She was ready fifteen minutes ago. What the hell was taking him so long? This was eating into her climbing time.

It was an impressive set-up and Kirsty was eager to get

going. The wooden walls jutted out at all angles with a jumble of technicolour grips starring the walls, like blobs of misshapen chewing gum.

This was going to be fun.

Rhona wandered over from chatting to the instructor. She tilted her head in his direction, her eyes on her camera as she adjusted the settings. 'He's going to nip to the changing room, see if he's okay.'

Her hair was styled in two plaits today and Kirsty was weak at the knees. Until this evening she'd had no idea that was even a thing for her. Now her heart refused to go at a normal pace.

'I can still do it if he's ill or whatever, yeah?' Kirsty asked Annie.

Rhona bit hard on her lower lip, battling a smile.

'What's that face for?' Kirsty asked with a quiet laugh.

'Just noting your concern for the poor man,' Rhona said, only just holding back the giggles.

'Of course. It's just, this looks fun.'

'You'll be fine to do it,' Annie said, looking at the top of the wall. Lord knows how high it actually was. Kirsty chose not to dwell on that. 'It's the couple photo I'm concerned about. Got to keep you in the running for that cash prize.' She punctuated the sentence with a wink.

'I think that ship's long sailed.' Kirsty had gotten over the cash a while ago. Publicity for the café was more than enough of a reward.

'Not feeling the spark with Ross?' Annie asked, not sounding the least bit surprised.

Kirsty shrugged. 'He's nice, I just, dunno...'

'Mhhm,' Annie said with a knowing smile.

'What?' Kirsty asked as she laughed nervously.

'Attention has perhaps wandered elsewhere?' Annie replied, a singsongy lilt to her voice.

'Huh?'

'I have eyes, ladies.' She looked at her watch. 'I need to be home soon. Jack will kill me if I miss bedtime.'

Kirsty exchanged a look with Rhona, who returned a shrug.

Finally, Ross appeared out of the changing room, followed by the instructor.

He looked white as a sheet.

'You okay?' Kirsty asked as he came to a stop at her side.

He let out a fractured breath. 'Really not good with heights.' He looked like he wanted the ground to swallow him up.

Shit. Poor guy. Kirsty gave the thick matting that covered the floors a good kick with the toe of her trainer. 'This place seems pretty padded – nothing bad can happen.'

Ross wasn't convinced. He shook his head, his tongue lodged in the side of his cheek.

'Right, you guys ready to get going?' the instructor asked.

'Why don't we take some photos first, ease into this?' Rhona suggested, already heading for the nearest climbing wall.

Ross was as pale as fresh snow but he nodded, walking over like he had on lead boots.

Kirsty felt sorry for him. Still, if it came to the worst he could sit this out and watch her.

Rhona snapped away, not going for her usual dynamic shots: this was an exercise in speed. Kirsty could feel Ross's hand tremble as he held her waist for the final photo.

The instructor clapped his hands together. 'Right, I'm Scott, one of the owners of Southside Bouldering. Have either of you climbed before?'

No surprise when Ross shook his head.

Kirsty watched Annie and Rhona chat on the edge of the mats, the occasional glance coming her way. Rhona showed Annie an image on her camera's screen then pointed to the wall; Annie nodded. There was a quick goodbye, then Annie was off.

'Come over to the wall – let me talk you through what the different coloured holds mean,' Scott said, beckoning them over.

Ross looked close to vomiting. 'You don't need to do this if you don't want to. I won't judge you,' Kirsty said, putting a hand on Ross's back. His T-shirt was clammy.

'No, no, I'll try.'

'So, the purple holds are the easiest, but you'll find you get into a natural rhythm when you start,' Scott said, ignoring Ross's fears for the time being. 'But I would always aim for purples or yellows. Keep things simple for now.'

Kirsty nodded. 'Purple and yellow. Got it.'

Scott grabbed a canvas drawstring bag off the ground. 'Chalk. Stick your hands in and let's start with some basic moves.'

You'd think Scott was asking them to put their paws in a bag of snakes with how hesitant Ross was.

He gulped.

Looked at Kirsty.

At the wall.

Finally at Scott.

Then back to Kirsty.

'I need to go.' He didn't wait for a reply: he was off, trotting to the changing rooms, a hand to his mouth.

'Okay,' Rhona said with a whistle.

'Should we check on him?' Kirsty asked, not sure what to do.

'He'll be fine. Just a bit peaky,' Rhona said, eyes on the now-closed door.

'You okay to continue?' Scott asked.

Kirsty nodded. 'One hundred per cent. I can't wait,' she added with a grin.

'If he's not doing it, can I?' Rhona asked, her eyes wide with excitement. 'I have my gym bag in the car. I can get changed while you take Kirsty over the basics.'

Scott shrugged. 'Don't see why not. That okay with you, Kirsty?'

'Sure,' Kirsty replied with a smile.

KIRSTY HAD to pretend to focus on identifying holds when Rhona reappeared – it was either that or have her jaw hang open. Her cheeks had already betrayed her, though; the heat flushing over her was undeniable.

Rhona in shorts and a sports bra with plaited hair.

Wow. Wow. Wow.

Her heart thrummed against her ribs, a swell of desire erupting in her belly.

If Kirsty ever felt sad in the future, this was going to be the image that brought back happiness. As if the look wasn't enough, Rhona's full-beam smile was like sunshine. Kirsty couldn't help but be warmed by her glow, her own face breaking out into a grin.

Rhona slammed a fist into her palm, ready for action. 'Where do you want me?'

Right here, right now, on the mat.

Kirsty swallowed her X-rated thoughts away. This was about climbing. Rhona was her friend. Her very fit, gorgeous friend.

Scott held the chalk bag out to Rhona. 'Get chalked up,

then I'll quickly run over the basics. You done bouldering before?'

Rhona shook her head. 'No, but I do a lot of yoga. I've heard it can kind of translate over. Is that true?'

Scott looked intrigued. 'It certainly can. Flexibility is definitely good.' He walked them over to the training wall and the furthest set of holds. He patted the long purple hold nearest his chest. 'So, these guys are basically a ladder – super easy, you can just climb up. Who wants to give it a go?'

Rhona looked at Kirsty. 'Ladies first.'

Kirsty gave her a little nod on the way past. 'Thank you.'

Scott was right; it was easy. The holds were rougher than she'd imagined and it took a second to get used to climbing on the balls of her feet, unlike a normal ladder where you'd put your foot straight through, but it was fun. She jumped to the ground, landing on the soft mat.

Couldn't have been more than a few feet. Ross was really missing out.

'Good,' Scott said. 'Now, Rhona, something a little harder for you.' He got into position, climbing up four yellows to the right of the ladder. He pulled in tight, his muscles stiffening. 'This is called pausing. It's really good for training your muscles. You'll need to do this when you climb and scan for your next hold.' He pushed out then back in, taking the same position. 'Rhona, want to give it a bash?'

She shot Kirsty a smile before getting into position.

It was hard not to take Rhona in.

You could tell she worked out. Her arms curved in all the right ways, the shadow of her bicep muscle making Kirsty short of breath. Then there was her stomach. *My oh my.*

This wasn't going to make sticking to her guns easy. At this moment in time, Rhona could be going travelling tomorrow and Kirsty would still beg to touch those toned abs the first chance she got.

The hairs stood up on Kirsty's neck, a fresh bloom of sweat forming over her chest.

This woman was intoxicating.

'Great,' Scott said. 'While you're there, do you want to try reaching for that far yellow? Yep, that's the one.'

It was a little too far and Rhona almost slipped trying to reach it.

Scott chuckled. 'How about jumping to it? It's not far.'

Rhona looked over her shoulder, as if seeking encouragement.

'You can do that, easy,' Kirsty said. Anything to see her stretch again.

Rhona flexed back and forth, psyching herself up. Finally, she was ready and launched into the air. She hung for a second, the hold firmly gripped in her hands.

The air all but left Kirsty's lungs. Her eyes traced the line of Rhona's arms. Just over a week ago she was close to experiencing them all to herself. It felt like the universe was taunting her.

Rhona dropped to the ground with a thud, slightly out of breath. She smiled at Kirsty. 'That was fun; you should give it a go.'

People like Rhona had a gravitational force. She was a magnet. You couldn't help but be pulled in and feel the happiness beaming off her. There was no option but to give it back. A new feeling rippled over Kirsty; a fresh emotion running over her skin. It was hard to put a finger on what it was, but it felt good. *Rhona* made her feel good.

Lover or friend, Kirsty wanted to be around her.

Dani was right: she'd put up defences the day they did yoga. She'd poked holes in Rhona that didn't deserve to be there. Now was the time for leaning into a friendship that brought out the best in her, not for building walls and over-analysing.

'I don't think I have the same upper body strength you do,' Kirsty said, hoping it wasn't obvious she'd been looking at Rhona's arms.

'Nonsense,' she replied, hands on hips, still slightly out of breath and riding her high.

Kirsty stepped into position, looking to Rhona for guidance. 'You're taller than me as well.'

'Now you're just making excuses.'

The confidence Rhona was emitting was almost palpable. *Okay.* She could do this. And if she couldn't? So what? There was a soft mat to land on.

Scott shuffled into position behind her. 'So, just do what Rhona did. Weight on your right foot, leap when you're ready. You're looking to grip right there,' he said, pointing to the yellow hold.

Getting into the first position was easy. Her muscles were fatigued but a fire roared in Kirsty's belly. Maybe bouldering could be her new thing. Could she and Rhona get a pass to come every week? She'd need to check it out online.

She leaned back once, twice, three times, very aware that all eyes were on her. Finally, on the fourth go, she felt ready and launched herself. Kirsty's hands gripped the yellow holding, safe as houses. Her face split with a smile. 'Whey! I did it!' she yelped.

Rhona shouted encouragement, glee lacing every word. 'I knew you could.'

Now there was the matter of getting down. It seemed higher now she was here. Her muscles burned: it was now or never.

Kirsty dropped to the ground, but her footing didn't

quite compute and she stumbled, only to be caught by Rhona's steady arms.

'Almost,' Rhona said, their faces millimetres apart.

Under any other circumstances there would have been a moment here, Kirsty was sure of it. Instead, Scott cut in. 'Want to try something horizontal?'

∽

'THAT WAS AMAZING,' Rhona said, opening her locker.

'It was, wasn't it?'

Rhona pulled a towel out of her bag and ran it over her face. The gesture tied Kirsty's stomach in knots. Her cheeks burned as she realised she'd stopped mid-walk to her own locker. Hopefully she was too red from exercise for Rhona to notice.

She continued to her space on the other side of the tiny changing room, with only the dividing bench and its coat rail standing between them both. She stole another look at Rhona as she unpacked clothes. God, her back was a sight – just as toned as her lovely stomach.

Kirsty gulped and returned her attention to her belongings.

Why was she torturing herself? She'd debated their relationship a thousand times since their drink in The Griffin. Today was only making the decision harder. Could she really expect them to only be friends? The way Rhona made her head swim was going to make that difficult. Still, it was only until Christmas. There was nothing to say they couldn't be more after Rhona was done travelling.

'Are you—' Rhona said and stopped mid-sentence, her eyes searching the room.

'Yes?' Kirsty asked with a laugh.

'I might just get changed in the loo.' She was off before Kirsty could say another word.

They shouldn't have kissed. This whole debacle would be easier if she didn't know how perfect Rhona's lips felt, the sensation of her tongue against hers, the way even thinking about it made Kirsty's stomach swoop, desire pinging in her core like a beacon calling Rhona back.

Kirsty tilted her head to the ceiling and let out a long, sad sigh.

Her melancholy moment was interrupted by the changing room door opening, the lady aiming straight for the centre bench.

Back to reality: their little bubble was burst once more. It was going to be a long winter, Kirsty had no doubt.

18

It felt like there was no air in the tent.

Niall had been particularly obnoxious last night. The noise until the wee small hours was bad enough, but Rhona had woken up to the stench of weed and a cracked kitchen sink.

It was his problem, but one that directly impacted her. How soon, if ever, would he get that fixed? She didn't want to do her dishes in the bathroom until Christmas.

Rhona stepped out the back of the marquee and into the dregs of the crowd. Lovefest's closing event was wildly busy. Annie was over the moon, and rightly so. The air was thick with excitement and revelry, everyone in high spirits, enjoying themselves. There was a buzz to the atmosphere and it was nice to see so many smiling faces. Thankfully, the good mood was rubbing off on her too, bringing her energy levels up to where they should be.

She positioned herself between crates of mixers, grateful for the metal barriers blocking the back door that meant the crowd couldn't spill any closer, giving her room to breathe.

The August heat showed no sign of waning and Rhona

wiped her brow for the thousandth time. No matter what she did, sweat bloomed.

Rhona revelled in the relief the tent's shadow brought, lingering by the back door. She wasn't needed for a good thirty minutes and Annie was off working the crowd, hobnobbing where needed. She could chance staying outside until she was called.

She looked at her camera's viewfinder, busying herself by reviewing her shots so far. Being places on her own was never an issue, but without a beer in her hand and free rein to mingle her options were limited. The crowd outside the tent was too thick to negotiate and take photos; it was better to stick to controlled areas. Less risk of being jostled about.

'Rhona, hey,' a familiar voice called.

She snapped her head in the direction of her name to see Annie weaving through the throng, a man following her.

'Hey,' Rhona said as Annie joined her in her little backstage bubble.

'This is Isaac – I thought you guys might like to meet.'

He wasn't what Rhona was expecting. She wasn't sure what she *had* been expecting, to be honest, but it wasn't the guy standing in front of her. He was shorter than her by a few inches and had a mound of curly dark hair on the top of his head. It was his bright red glasses and crazy floral shirt that were throwing her slightly.

'Hey,' he said with a little wave. 'So good to finally meet you. Annie's been singing your praises. I've had serious FOMO, if I'm honest.'

His words were as lovely as his smile and Rhona felt heat flush her cheeks. Always good to know she'd done a job well. 'Don't worry – the reins are all yours after this.'

Annie and Isaac exchanged looks. 'Actually, I'm not a fully trained photographer. It's more of a hobby, really. The board has had a chat and we have the budget for more events, if you're keen?' Isaac said, his smile widening.

Words escaped Rhona. She wasn't expecting that.

'Nothing permanent, unfortunately. All freelance. But we'd love to have you back if possible,' Annie added.

'I'd love that,' Rhona replied, mustering her best smile. It was an amazing offer, but if she wanted to pay her bills and properly settle down she'd need a lot more than the occasional freelance job. Plus, did she really want to be tied down to one suburb? After photographing Tibs the cat, the idea of working while travelling had danced around her brain, the concept growing arms and legs as time went on.

Still, Glasgow wouldn't be a bad base, and a job was a job. It was definitely one to keep in the back pocket.

'Next month is dedicated to shopping local and we've got loads of events planned, if you're free?' Annie asked, looking hopeful.

'I'll need to check with my other job, but I think that should be possible.' Now, that was a lifeline. She'd considered upping sticks and moving back home in order to save more dosh, as Amber's need for her was winding down, but another month in Glasgow would be good, especially if she was getting paid to stay.

'Amazing,' Isaac said. 'I can't wait to work with you.'

'Likewise.'

'Café Odyssey will definitely need some promotional shots done,' Annie said with a wink, before shifting her gaze to the metal railing at the far side of their little pen. There leaned Kirsty, wearing a floral tea dress and looking as radiant as ever. She gave Rhona a wave and a smile.

'There's nothing going on with me and Kirsty,' Rhona said, hoping not to sound too disappointed. She needed to stop the way her heart skipped a beat and her mouth broke into a smile every time she laid eyes on the woman. It was impossible, though. Kirsty's mere presence was enough to put Rhona on cloud nine.

'I might have only been hosting Lovefest for two years, but I know a spark when I see one. Besides, I really am serious about promotional shots. There's a hundred and twenty retail businesses in Shawlands and I'm sure most of them will want to take advantage of you if we're paying.'

Pound signs *kerching*ed in Rhona's eyes. That could be another month of travelling paid for. 'You tell me where you need me, and I'll be there.'

'You might regret that,' Isaac said with a chuckle.

'Right,' Annie said with a little clap of her hands. 'Meet us here in forty minutes?'

'Sounds good.'

Goodbyes said, Rhona ventured over to Kirsty, who was still propped on her forearms, leaning on the metal barrier. 'I could have you done for loitering,' she joked.

'Charming,' Kirsty said with a chuckle. 'I'd not seen you around; I was worried you'd bailed.'

'On my final hurrah as Lovefest's official photographer? Never.'

'You allowed out your pen?'

'Just avoiding the crowds. It's bloody boiling.' It was probably a good job there was a physical barrier between them. It was noisier down this end and the urge to use the excuse to get close to Kirsty was strong.

Ever since their time bouldering, Rhona had struggled to shake the idea that there might still be a spark between them, despite Kirsty's desire to stay just friends.

'Think you could brave them for a moment? I'll be on stage soon, then God knows when I'll see you again.'

The sentiment sent butterflies through Rhona, swooping

from her chest to her belly. It was innocent, but Kirsty admitting she wanted to hang out meant a lot. Their blatant flirting had all but gone. To Rhona, it felt like teasing herself. Plus, they'd agreed to just be friends; no point in embarrassing herself.

Still, *something* had lingered as they climbed those walls.

'I think I can spare you five minutes.'

Kirsty's smile was euphoric. If Rhona could bottle that and sell it, she'd be a millionaire.

'Out you come, then. My friends are over by the food trucks.'

Free of her confines, the air was suddenly stiff between them. There should be a greeting but nothing was natural. A kiss on the cheek was way too much. A hug was just wrong. She was one step away from shaking hands and making this a formal affair. Might as well be, given how foreign Rhona's body felt. What to do with her hands?

Kirsty's eyes lingered with hers for a second, like she might be feeling the same. The moment was broken as she set off in search of her friends.

'If you see Ross, let me know,' she said with a nervous laugh.

'Why do I feel like you're serious?' Rhona said, returning the same energy.

They weaved through the crowd, keeping close to each other. 'Because I *am* serious. I've managed to avoid him so far. We went out for drinks on Wednesday,' she said with a shake of her head. 'He really is lovely, but just so dull. And don't, by the way.'

'What?' Rhona said, truly confused.

'Look at me like that. I feel really bad about it. Okay? Let's not talk about it.'

That hadn't been the plan, but okay. Rhona ran her

finger and thumb over her lips, mimicking a zip. 'My lips are sealed.'

'There's everyone,' Kirsty said, leading Rhona to a small huddle of women.

She recognised Dani, and Kim from their disaster date. Ashley and Hazel stood opposite. Rhona gave them a little wave as the group made space. A glamorous blonde woman hid a mischievous smile behind a plastic tumbler of wine. The glare Kirsty shot her didn't go unnoticed.

'So, you know these guys,' Kirsty said, looking a little sheepish. 'And this is Izzy.' She pointed to the blonde. 'And Trip.' A tall brunette gave a nod.

'Trip? Like, to fall?'

'Not exactly, but same spelling. Long story,' Kirsty said. 'So, Trip works with Ashley, and Izzy is my best friend. There, that's the family tree.'

'You guys having a good time?' Rhona asked. This felt oddly like a test. For what, she wasn't sure, but she sure as hell hadn't studied for it.

Dani's face said she was having a crap evening, but everyone else seemed chipper. Rhona had never had a group of queer friends. Singular, yes. But a whole gang? Never. They seemed tight, and going by the way she was getting the once-over Rhona got the impression they looked out for each other. Kirsty had put her in front of the firing squad. She stood a little straighter.

A chorus of *yes*es rippled through the group. 'Oh, I've got news,' Rhona said to Kirsty, but was well aware everyone was still listening in.

'Yeah?'

'Annie wants me to hang about, do some promotional stuff next month. Then she says they'll need me ad hoc.'

'So you're staying in Glasgow for a bit?' Izzy asked. For a

fleeting moment Rhona thought she recognised her from somewhere. Impossible. Blonde with blue eyes? She could be anyone.

'For now,' Rhona replied, her gaze snagging Kirsty's. 'I need to be somewhere, so why not Shawlands?'

'Will you stay in the West End?' Kirsty asked.

Rhona pulled a face.

'South is where it's at,' Trip proclaimed as she raised her nearly empty glass to the sky.

'I don't know if I can be arsed moving, to be honest. But my flatmate's a dick.' Niall was becoming more nocturnal by the day. The longer she stayed, the more he relaxed, and the more Rhona understood why the rent was so cheap. He knew he was hard to live with. There always had to be a snag. At least it wasn't forever.

'We've all been there,' Izzy said with a roll of her eyes. 'Just do what Kim did and pop the tyres on their bike.'

Kim's eyes flew wide. 'Hoi! That makes me sound mad. It's a long story, right, but just believe me: he deserved it.'

Kim couldn't be more different to the super feminine Izzy. She was barely over five foot, with faded purple hair and she had on grungy flannel over a printed tee. The sides of her hair were buzzed short and tattoos snaked out from the sleeves of her shirt. Rhona liked her style.

'Don't mess with Kim. Noted,' Rhona said, pulling a face. 'Plus, I don't think he has a bike.'

'Good you're staying, though,' Kirsty said, her eyes wistful.

'Incoming,' Izzy mumbled into her drink.

It was too late. Ross's hands found Kirsty's waist and she jumped a mile. Rhona's insides were scrambled, jealousy searing through her like acid.

He kissed Kirsty's cheek and Rhona felt the heat through her veins.

'Guys, this is Ross,' Kirsty said, looking like she wanted to wriggle free. Rhona couldn't help but feel sorry for the guy, but at the same time she wanted nothing more than to tell him to fuck off.

'I need to steal Kirsty for a bit,' Ross said, already trying to lead her off.

She locked eyes with Rhona as if wanting her to formulate an excuse. She had nothing.

'Right, I won't be long,' Kirsty said, defeat clear.

And just like that, Rhona was alone with Kirsty's pals.

'She'd better dump him tonight,' Izzy declared when Ross was safely out of earshot.

Rhona's attention was stolen by the dynamics of Ashley and Hazel. They'd been strangely quiet. It probably didn't help that Dani's mood was like a black cloud drowning those beside her. She leaned in, lowering her voice so only Dani could hear her. 'You good?'

'Nope.'

'I'm going to the bar – want to chum me?' Rhona asked Dani, now loud enough that everyone could hear.

She agreed with a shrug.

'I'll come too,' Trip said. 'I could do with another beer.'

A safe distance away, Rhona spoke to Dani. 'I'm not really going to the bar, but I thought you might want a breather.'

'I definitely need the bar,' Dani said, her shoulders still slumped.

'Want to do shots?' Trip asked.

'You on a mission as well?' Rhona asked with a rueful smile.

'Too right. I'm off school tomorrow. Would be rude not to.'

'That, and I've seen you eyeing up half the women,' Dani joked, her mood lightening a little.

Trip gave Dani a playful shove. 'Aye, well. It would be rude to ignore that, too.'

Dani mustered the kind of melancholy smile that sits pleasantly on the surface, perfectly masking the pain buried deep beneath, keeping present company satisfied you aren't about to walk into the River Clyde and never return. Sometimes all you could do was put on a brave face and schedule a cry for later on.

'Let's make them doubles,' Dani said, falling into line for the outdoor bar. 'Will you do one, Rhona?'

She shook her head. 'I need to work. Later though, if you're still compos mentis.'

'Hopefully not. Although if Kirsty wins, I might be persuaded to stay out,' Dani replied.

'If Kirsty's buying the drinks you'd better come out. Once in a blue moon, and all that,' Trip joked.

Dani's social tank was empty again and Trip only got a weak smile in return.

Rhona gave her a squeeze on the shoulder. 'See you in a bit.'

She made her way backstage and slipped into position behind one of the bigger speakers, giving her a bird's-eye view of the dance floor in the tent. Packed didn't cover it. There was barely an inch of free space. No wonder it was stifling. Between all the bodies and the muggy August air, there was no chance.

She snapped away, getting a few great shots of the busy tent.

On the edge, by the open door, stood Chloe and Holly,

two of the contestants from last year. Could be good to get some candid pics of them before Chloe did her formal bit on stage.

Rhona hopped off the stage and made her way over, expertly avoiding the mass of sweaty bodies and precariously held drinks.

'Hey; Chloe, isn't it?' Rhona asked.

'Yeah, what's up?' The redhead replied with a smile.

'Rhona. I'm the Lovefest photographer,' she said, holding her camera up. 'Mind if I get a few photos? You too, Holly, if you're keen?'

'Sounds good to me,' Chloe replied, changing her stance to face Rhona face on.

'Where's your other half?' Rhona asked, her eye to the viewfinder.

Chloe looked like a deer in headlights. Shit: hopefully they'd not had a fight right before their time on stage. She looked at Holly and pulled an exaggerated face somewhere between a smile and a grimace. 'He's busy.'

Okay. 'And Jen?'

'She's at the bar.'

'Just you two, then. That's cool. We'll do proper shots later.'

Rhona snapped away, but picked up strong vibes that these two had something else they'd rather be doing. She let them go: there'd be plenty of time to get better photos later.

Alone again, she scanned the crowd, looking for more of last year's participants. Instead she spotted Kirsty, Ross's arm wrapped firmly around her.

It wasn't his fault. He was proud of her and wanted to show Kirsty off to his mates, but Rhona couldn't help the envy that gripped her chest. It was like there was a cork in her throat, plugging the bitterness that welled so it lodged in her ribcage, growing heavy and tight.

This wasn't a side of herself that she wanted to discover.

Yet here she was. Kirsty wasn't a fleeting attraction. Somewhere along the line she'd made a home in Rhona's heart.

19

There was no polite way to get out of this, so the only option was to endure it. They'd be called to the stage soon. Ross's arm around her waist made her want to gag, though.

She zoned out as the guys made idle chit-chat. There were no girls in this friend group. It wasn't usually a problem, but they were discussing work and someone to make polite side conversation with would be nice.

Kirsty smiled and nodded in what she hoped were the right places. It was so noisy, so muggy, that her brain had no more room for deciphering what was being said.

She could have jumped for joy when Izzy appeared.

'Kirsty, can we have a chat?' She turned to Ross. 'Girl problems.'

Ross's arm didn't move. He looked at his watch. 'Can it wait? We'll be on stage soon.'

'Not really,' Izzy said. Her face was stoic, but Kirsty knew her well enough to catch the flicker of annoyance in her eyes.

She wriggled free. 'I won't be long. I'll get you by the stage in five.'

He furrowed his brow. 'Don't be late.'

Wow. She'd leave it to the last minute, just to wind him up. Who did he think he was?

Izzy took her hand and led them through the crowd. Kirsty took a deep breath when they finally exited the tent.

'Thank you,' she said to Izzy as they found a spot by the railings.

'Figured you wouldn't want to be left alone too long.'

'Where's Rhona?'

Izzy bit her lip, cutting short a smile. 'She went off with Dani and Trip.'

'And what's that look for?' Kirsty asked, masking her uneasiness with a laugh.

'You really like her.'

'No I don't.' Internally, she scolded herself. It was a knee-jerk reaction and one she gave into far too quickly.

'You do. It's cute. I've never seen you like this.'

She chose to ignore her. 'How is Dani? She's been in a mood all day.'

'Same. Worse. Dunno. I think Trip is keeping a close eye on her.'

Kirsty nodded. Ashley might be Dani's best friend, but Trip was a close second. She could be on stage and not worry about her little sister. Otherwise, there was a good chance she'd be glued to the bar. 'I'd better go soon – can't be arsed with Ross getting nippy with me.'

'He seems charming, by the way.'

'Tell me about it.'

∽

'You coming out for drinks?' Ross asked as they stepped off the stage.

Kirsty's heart was still battering her ribs, on a high from being in front of the raucous crowd.

She shook her head. 'Honestly, I've got a really sore head. Too hot and not enough water.'

Ross's face creased into a frown. 'You sure? We're all going to Cal's. It'll be fun.'

'Nah. I need my bed. There's my mum – I'm going to say bye to her then head off.'

He followed her eyes to see her mum and stepdad lingering behind the metal railing. Her mum waved. 'Not going to introduce me to your mum and dad?' He raised his eyebrows, making it look like he was joking, but Kirsty could feel the weight in his tone.

'Another time.'

The other couples passed around them, filing out of the event space. In the corner of her eye, she saw Rhona pause before heading off.

Kirsty and Ross were static, the loaded atmosphere that hung between them rooting the couple to the spot.

'You didn't introduce me to your friends, either.'

There it was. She'd been a dick to him and she knew it, but it wasn't all on her.

'You didn't really give me a chance.'

'What do you mean?'

'You saw them for all of two seconds before you whisked me away.'

'The photographer was there.'

'Well observed.'

'You fucking her?'

Kirsty felt like she'd been punched in the gut. *Okay.* She didn't feel so bad now. 'Excuse me?'

'You heard.'

She stood, mouth agape, a breath of frustration escaping.

'That's a yes, then.'

'This isn't the time nor the place for this conversation.' She crossed her arms. Her legs felt like jelly, her heart racing from the unexpected accusation. 'You really think you can talk to me like that?'

He tensed his jaw and searched for the right words. His muscles relaxed. 'You're right. I'm sorry.'

'This isn't working for me. I'm out.' She turned on her heel, only for him to grab her wrist.

The malice in his eyes didn't fade when Rhona spoke.

'You good, Ross?' she asked, stepping closer. At full height, she wasn't far off him.

They stood for a second, Rhona and Ross with locked eyes, her shoulders squared and his grip on Kirsty still tight.

Rhona didn't even blink. Kirsty's stomach flipped. She didn't want a fight.

After what felt like an eternity, he let her go.

Ross looked at both women, shaking his head as he laughed under his breath. 'Fucksake.'

Rhona didn't budge. The only movement was her pinky finger, which hooked Kirsty's and gave a quick squeeze.

She turned and was still watching him over Kirsty's shoulder when she finally spoke, both hands now holding Kirsty's. 'You okay?'

Kirsty nodded. 'Yeah. Bit shaken, but yeah. Thank you.'

'Why did he do that?'

'Doesn't matter. Silly fight.'

She wanted to hug Rhona. Anyone else and she would. But with Rhona, the gesture felt laden.

Fuck. She felt like the biggest arsehole on the planet.

Yes, Ross shouldn't have done that, but she'd goaded him into a bad mood.

'You're really pale. Let me get you some water.' Rhona said, giving her hands another squeeze. She hadn't even noticed their fingers were still laced together.

'I'm fine. Honestly.'

'Everything okay?' Mum asked, appearing at her side.

Rhona dropped her hands.

'Yeah, good, Rhona sorted it.'

Mum gave Kirsty a hug. 'We're heading off now. Want us to walk you home?'

Kirsty shook her head against her mother's chest. 'Nah. We're going to the pub. Celebrate Ashley's win.'

'Well, look after Dani, will you? She's already three sheets to the wind. Are you going out with them, Rhona?'

'I've got my car. I'll probably just head home, if I'm honest. Been a long day.'

Kirsty released herself from Mum's embrace. 'No, please come out. You can stay at mine.'

~

BAR ORAMA WAS A BLAST, even with Dani's sour mood. Which was probably fair given how touchy-feely Ashley and Hazel had been all night. They had just won five grand, though. Kirsty was buzzing for them.

More than once she'd caught herself watching Rhona. She was so easy-going; it was like she'd always been part of the gang and Kirsty couldn't help herself, zoning out as she took in her smile and the way she listened to her friends. She'd gravitated towards Dani and Trip and it wasn't long before the newly formed trio had broken off to their own little bubble. It didn't take a rocket scientist to see that Dani appreciated the distraction. To give Rhona her due, she'd kept up with her sister too. Keeping Dani's spirits high with, well, spirits.

Which now made for a very drunk, beautiful, photographer in Kirsty's bedroom.

Her thoughts felt like a blender, and it didn't help that the booze was making her head spin. It would be so easy to kiss her, cross the line, and cope with the consequences tomorrow. But Kirsty didn't want to do that, not with Rhona. As drunk as she was, Kirsty knew that regret wasn't an option. Tomorrow was for hangovers only.

Rhona reached under her T-shirt, flicking her bra open before fishing one strap out of her sleeve, then the other. She threw it to the ground.

Kirsty gulped.

'Close your eyes – I don't want you getting too excited,' Rhona said, her fingers fumbling with the top button of her black skinny jeans.

'I need to pee anyway. You do what you need to while I'm gone.' She yanked her boot off and placed it by the other, shoving them under the bed.

The room tilted on its axis when she stood. Not good.

They'd got chips on the way home, so the chances of being sick were low. Still, a feeling sat low in her belly. Shame? Guilt? Embarrassment? Hard to tell.

Toilet done, Kirsty gripped the sink and studied herself in the bathroom mirror. Maybe Dani was right. Her life was one big self-sabotage.

After a sigh so loud that Rhona surely heard it next door, Kirsty wandered back to her bedroom. It was only then she realised she probably should have taken the opportunity to get changed herself.

She couldn't be fucked now. Sleep was calling.

'You took ages,' Rhona said, a pillow propped behind her head as she scrolled on her phone.

Kirsty narrowed her eyes in mock anger. 'Didn't.' She yanked her PJs out from under her pillow. 'Forgot to get changed.'

Rhona slammed her phone against the bed with a gentle thud as she cocked her head, a devilish grin spreading across her face. 'That's a shame.'

'Enough.' Kirsty shimmied into her pyjama trousers, pulling them up under her dress. She turned her back to the bed. 'Can you undo this?'

It might have been the booze, but it was like Kirsty was watching herself. One version of herself leaned into the moment, initiating a kiss; the other held strong and kept Rhona at arm's length. For a heartbeat, it could have gone either way.

Sensible Kirsty kicked in when Rhona's fingers ghosted over the bare skin on her back as she took hold of the zip.

'Still just friends, remember.' There was no room for error. If Rhona gave her an inch there was no way she could stop herself taking a mile.

Rhona's sigh rivalled Kirsty's earlier one in the bathroom. 'Friends. Yep. Got it.' Kirsty would have understood if she was mad, but she wasn't. Only disappointment swamped Rhona's words.

Zipper down, Kirsty stepped out her dress, dropping it to the floor. She was careful to keep her back to the bed as she pulled on her Tt-shirt but she'd forgotten her wardrobe was one massive mirror. She snagged Rhona's gaze and held it for a second before Rhona closed her eyes, shaking her head along with a quiet smile as she slumped back into her pillows. Neither said a word.

She hadn't worn a bra today. But then, she hadn't expected company in bed.

Desire flushed over her, making her hairs stand on end and her nipples stiffen. She pulled the covers close, tucking them under her arms.

Kirsty stared at the ceiling, happy to find it wasn't spinning.

'You putting the light out?' Rhona asked, sitting up on one forearm.

'Do you think I'm an arsehole?' She'd been so lost in her own thoughts that Kirsty hadn't even clocked what Rhona had said.

'Huh?'

'Do you think I'm an arsehole?' she repeated.

'Why would I think that?'

'The way I've treated you and Ross is hardly fair.'

'Circumstances,' Rhona said, scooting closer.

Kirsty kept her eyes on the ceiling. 'Not really. I made the choices. I could have done things completely differently, if I'd wanted.'

Rhona was quiet. Kirsty checked she wasn't sleeping, only to be met with thoughtful brown eyes studying her face. 'You want me to be honest?' Rhona asked.

'Always.'

'You could have treated Ross with a little more respect.'

Kirsty was surprised to find her muscles relaxing, like a weight had been lifted. She'd expected the truth to sting but instead it was a relief, confirmation she wasn't being too hard on herself. 'I thought I'd grown up, that I'd changed. But I guess I've just found new ways to hurt people. I should apologise.' She grabbed her phone off the bedside table and was surprised to find herself typing Travis's name into Messenger, not Ross's. Now there was a gaping wound she'd happily slapped a band-aid on and shoved to the back of her mind.

Rhona reached over and replaced her phone on the table. 'Not when you're drunk.'

Kirsty looked up, unable to take her eyes away from Rhona's. 'You should be thankful you've dodged this bullet.'

Her hand slotted by Kirsty's waist, holding Rhona steady over her. Time slowed; not even the air moved between them as they unknowingly held their breath. Kirsty could feel the heat of Rhona's skin through her T-shirt where their bodies touched.

'You think I wouldn't have already run a mile if I wanted to?' She lowered onto her forearm, so close Kirsty could feel Rhona's nipples pressed against her chest, despite their clothing.

'I have no idea why you haven't.'

Rhona pecked the end of her nose with a quick kiss and Kirsty had to close her eyes to stop herself from groaning. Since when had her nose been a major erogenous spot?

She could feel Rhona's gaze on her, so wasn't surprised when she opened her eyes to find the same searching look from before.

The kiss was a question, a toe in the water, seeking permission before diving in. Kirsty gave her answer by snaking a hand under Rhona's T-shirt, resting it on the small of her back at the hem of her pants.

Rhona dipped her head to Kirsty's neck, her lips grazing the skin under her ear as she spoke. 'You're not as bad as you think. Everyone makes mistakes.' She kissed Kirsty, lightly biting at her skin before pulling back. This time the groan couldn't be contained. 'Good intentions. Terrible execution.'

Kirsty inhaled a long, jagged breath. There was no

denying how wet she was, but somewhere at the back of her mind, sober sensible Kirsty was using a megaphone to voice her concerns.

She was softening to the idea of Rhona; but not like this, not drunk.

Rhona's lips connected with her neck again and for a moment the world went foggy and sensible Kirsty was lost to the ether.

She allowed herself a moment of delicious defiance and moved the hand on Rhona's back lower, cupping her toned bum cheek and squeezing lightly. Not that she needed encouraging, but Rhona took the gesture to heart and deepened her kiss on her neck. Kirsty's hips moved of their own accord, arching to meet Rhona's.

'Fuck,' Kirsty groaned. It was a mix of pleasure and frustration. The voice in her head was back with a vengeance. 'Stop,' she said, her breath catching. She brought her free hand to Rhona's stomach, leveraging a little distance.

Rhona stilled. 'Stop?'

'We can't. Not like this.'

'Okay.'

Rhona slid her hand out from Kirsty's T-shirt. The grazing of her fingertips down Kirsty's stomach made her shiver. She'd been so caught in the moment that she'd not even noticed Rhona sneak her hand up there.

'Like, I want to,' Kirsty said, a twisting feeling in her gut worrying she'd upset Rhona. 'At least I think I want to. And I don't want our first time to be while we're drunk.'

Rhona relaxed into the pillows, still facing Kirsty. 'It's okay,' she said, brushing a stray strand of Kirsty's hair behind her ear. 'You're right.'

The air prickled between them.

Kirsty turned around, clicking the bedside lamp off before getting comfy. Tears threatened, the lump in her throat making her mouth wet. This was her comeuppance. Of course she'd find someone wonderful, only for them to be temporary.

'We'll chat in the morning,' Rhona said, scooting closer and spooning her.

There had to be a way to make her stay.

20

'Fuck, I'm so rough,' Rhona said, slumping into Kirsty and Dani's armchair.

'Where did you get that?' Kirsty asked from her equally slouched position on the couch where she'd been watching TV.

'Get what?'

'The hoodie.'

'It's yours.'

Kirsty laughed. 'Well, obviously. I forgot I even had that.'

Rhona looked at the baggy purple hoodie. She was experiencing the kind of hangover that made her skin feel sensitive and sunburned. The skinny jeans were bad enough, but nothing Kirsty owned would have fitted. With her clingy T-shirt, the combination would have been a step too far, so she'd gone in search of something looser. 'Do you mind?'

'Not at all. But full disclosure: the reason it's bigger than my other stuff is because I stole it off someone who was taller than me.'

'Ah.'

'Yep.'

'So, is it weird I have it on?'

'Honestly, I don't care. Do you want a cup of tea?'

Rhona sat up, but had second thoughts as her stomach churned and quickly collapsed back down. 'I would love one. I think I need to chill here for a bit before I'm legal to drive. Is that okay?'

Kirsty's pace to the kitchen slowed. Even through bleary eyes Rhona could see Kirsty's muscles stiffen for a moment. 'Yeah, of course,' she said, her voice less confident. 'We should probably have a chat anyway.'

'Not yet,' Rhona said, rubbing at her temples. Her brain was suffering from lag. Everything was on the go-slow and fuzzy at the edges.

Kirsty took the hint and remained quiet while she made the tea. When the click of the kettle signalled it was nearly ready, Rhona mustered all her strength and ventured to the sofa. May as well have been a marathon. Talk about the sweats. *Jesus.* It had been a long time since she'd had a hangover like this.

'You're not that bad, surely?' Kirsty asked with a chuckle as she passed Rhona the steaming hot mug of tea. 'Shit, do you want sugar? I don't even know if we have any.'

'This is fine. Thank you.' The first sip touched her very soul and she groaned with pleasure. Her mouth was still like sandpaper, though, and the taste of tequila coated her tongue. She gulped. Even the thought was enough to turn her stomach.

'I didn't think you were that drunk last night.'

'I was drunk, but—' Rhona cut herself off as she did a double take at Kirsty's neck. 'Have you, erm, have you looked in a mirror today?'

Kirsty pulled a face, running her tongue along the inside of her upper teeth before she spoke. 'I have, yes.'

'Sorry.' A huge, dark love bite bloomed under Kirsty's ear lobe, spreading right down her neck.

'I thought about killing you but I guess it's only fair I accept half the responsibility. After all, I didn't stop you.' She took a sip of her tea. 'I'll fix it later.'

Rhona leaned the back of her head against the sofa. 'Have you got any food?'

'There's bacon in the fridge. We can have that when Dani gets up.'

'Vegetarian,' Rhona said, sounding more pitiful than she'd ever done in her life.

'Oh, poor wee lamb,' Kirsty soothed, cupping Rhona's cheek with her palm and guiding her head to her shoulder. She gave a few gentle taps before retracting her hand. 'No food for you then.'

Rhona kept her head on Kirsty's shoulder and got comfy as she let out a long sigh. 'I'm never drinking again.'

~

THEY STAYED on the sofa until nearly lunchtime, naturally slotting into a position where Rhona rested her back against Kirsty's chest, safely held in place by her arm. Once Rhona had brought her hand up to skirt over Kirsty's, only to feel her muscles react, and not in a good way.

This was a bubble of inbetweens. If lines weren't crossed and discussions remained unhad, they could sit like this forever. It was like existing on a knife's edge, though, and Rhona knew it couldn't last.

When the sound of Dani's shuffling footsteps echoed down the hall, Kirsty wriggled free and the bubble burst.

Rhona instantly missed the contact.

'Please tell me you feel rough too,' Rhona said, twisting to face Dani as she entered the living room.

She certainly looked rough. Her hair was a mess and the way she had one eye scrunched up to look at them didn't shout tippity-top.

'I've spewed twice. Hopefully not aiming for a hat-trick, but—' She fell into the armchair, her legs dangling over the side. 'You never know.'

'Well, just make sure you make it to the bathroom. I'm done cleaning up after you,' Kirsty said, making herself comfy in her new position at the opposite end of the sofa to Rhona.

They watched TV in silence for a while before Dani spoke again, her voice low and whiny. 'Kiiiirsty.'

'No.'

'Just a little cup of tea, please.'

Kirsty gave in, presumably knowing that it was a losing battle and it was better to keep the peace. She stood up and collected her and Rhona's mugs. 'You want a fresh brew?'

'Yes, please,' she replied, forcing a grin. What a sorry pair she and Dani were. Booze was no good in your thirties.

Rhona got her tea first, then Dani. She took the mug from Kirsty, her head cocked to the side. 'What's on your neck?'

'Nothing.'

'It's definitely something.' She leaned to the side, getting a better view as Kirsty sat down. 'Are you two . . .?'

'Nope,' Kirsty replied, quick as a flash. Rhona's stomach flipped and this time booze wasn't to blame. 'Now shut up and drink your tea.'

Dani didn't need to be told twice.

Rhona's stomach grumbled. She really needed food in

her. She downed half her tea and psyched herself up. She was definitely legal to drive, but could her stomach hack the twenty minutes of motion?

She put her hands on her knees: it was now or never. ' I need to go. I'm starving.'

'There's stuff in the fridge,' Dani offered.

'Vegetarian,' Kirsty said, like it was an affliction.

'Ah. Okay, well let's order Uber Eats.'

'I bought bacon,' Kirsty scolded.

'We can eat that tomorrow. Live a little, deviate from the plan.'

All eyes fell on Rhona, who was still sitting, hands on knees, ready to stand up. She relaxed. 'I mean, I would totally eat a McDonalds if you got one.'

Kirsty groaned, but the smile on her face was undeniable. 'Right, but Dani's paying.'

∽

FED AND WATERED, Rhona felt a little more human and it was finally time to go. She sat on the end of Kirsty's bed, putting her trainers on.

She was braced for a chat but still, when Kirsty appeared in the doorway, she winced. A part of her had hoped it could be avoided. Kirsty's intentions were perfectly clear.

'So,' Kirsty said, taking a seat beside Rhona.

Kirsty held her hands in her lap, playing with her fingers, giving them all her attention.

'So,' Rhona repeated, her trainers now tied.

'Last night.'

It was Rhona's turn to focus her attention anywhere but Kirsty. She fixed her eyes on her trainers, giving her feet a wee wiggle. 'You said you wanted to take things further but today I'm guessing you've changed your mind.'

'What makes you think that?'

Hope ricocheted through Rhona, giving her strength to meet Kirsty's gaze. 'Just your body language this morning. The way you shut Dani down.'

'I—,' Kirsty paused, her head tilted towards the ceiling as she thought. She took another run at the right words. 'It's not that I don't want to. It's just, I need to take a rain check. I don't think I really know what I want right now.'

Hope turned sour, like curdling milk, and sat heavy in the pit of Rhona's stomach. 'I understand. Take as long as you need.'

They sat for a moment, silence draping over them.

'When do you leave?' Kirsty asked before chewing on her bottom lip.

'I was going to go now.'

She laughed under her breath. 'No, when do you leave Glasgow?'

'My flight's booked for the twenty-seventh of December.'

Kirsty's brows rocketed skyward. 'Shit, you've booked it already.'

Rhona nodded gently. 'Yeah, did it this week. Figured now or never.'

'Wow.' Silence was fast becoming a third wheel. Rhona wondered if the conversation was over. Finally, Kirsty spoke again. 'December. Okay. Well then, I'd better hope Santa gets my letter this year.'

21

September was uneventful, but as promised, Annie had found plenty to keep Rhona in Shawlands with the Shop Local campaign. Mum was so impressed with Rhona's photos that she'd hired her to take proper promotional shots for the café.

Which was how Kirsty found herself posing for photos in front of the coffee machine one Thursday evening.

With Lovefest done and dusted, reasons to hang out were depleted, and Rhona seemed busier than ever. That or she was avoiding Kirsty, which wouldn't be a surprise given she'd failed to make up her mind about what the hell she actually wanted from her.

Whenever she felt like she had it figured out, a new voice would pipe up and throw her thoughts back into a tailspin.

Why Rhona couldn't commit to Glasgow was beyond Kirsty. Talking about it felt too close to begging, though, and she definitely wasn't at that stage. Yet. The way butterflies had erupted in her stomach when Rhona walked through the door this evening told Kirsty everything her heart needed to know.

'Now, try and look happy to be here,' Rhona gibed.

'Do I not?' Kirsty asked with a laugh.

'Wee bit pensive there. Start thinking happy thoughts.'

'Think about the glass of wine we're having when we're done,' Mum called from over Rhona's shoulder.

'Better be more than a glass,' Kirsty replied through gritted teeth as she tried to hold her smile in place.

'Dani, you jump in now.' Rhona guided her. 'Stand in front of Kirsty and we're just going to have a chat, okay? I'll snap away; pretend the camera isn't here.'

Easier said than done. Modelling was hard. Kirsty's face ached.

'Susan, got any funny stories about these two?' Rhona asked Mum.

Kirsty shot her a *don't-you-dare* look but there was no holding her back. Mum whistled through her teeth. 'How long have you got? Kirsty, do you remember the time you locked Dani in the shed and told me she'd run away?'

'She was being particularly annoying that day,' Kirsty retorted, pulling Dani into a playful headlock.

Dani wriggled free. 'I still hate confined spaces.'

'Dani got her back, though,' Mum gleefully informed them. 'There was the time Dani tricked Kirsty into eating a raw onion.'

Rhona's eyebrows arched behind the camera. 'How the heck did you manage that?'

'Coated it in chocolate,' Dani said, matter-of-factly.

'I've never forgiven you for that.'

'But they love each other really,' Mum added.

The sisters pulled exaggerated grossed-out faces at each other.

'Sometimes,' Kirsty said, giving Dani a wink.

'Remember when Dani broke her arm on the rope swing? You were distraught, Kirsty.'

'Yeah, because I was six and her bone was poking out.'

Dani motioned like she was dry-heaving, a hand to her mouth. 'Don't.'

Rhona straightened herself. 'Right, I think I've got what I need here. You still wanting a team shot on the stairs, Susan?'

'Yes please. I'll get everyone lined up.'

Kirsty hung back, watching Rhona switch out the lenses on her camera.

'You still enjoying Glasgow?' she asked.

Rhona smiled weakly. 'It has its moments.'

'I expected you to be more chipper than that. You okay?'

'Yeah, just tired, and this campaign finishes soon. I'd be more relaxed if I had a few extra jobs lined up.'

'They'll come.'

Rhona looked distracted. 'I'd like both my lights for this, to cover the height difference. Got an extension I could borrow?'

'Yeah, sure. It'll be in the store cupboard upstairs.'

Rhona was off before Kirsty could offer to get it for her. That cupboard was a guddle; it would be a heck of a lot quicker if she nipped in for it.

By the time Kirsty went through the kitchen and crossed the ground floor, Rhona was up the stairs and nowhere to be seen. She cut through her lingering relatives and bounded upstairs, certain she'd hear the crashing of boxes at any moment as Rhona moved something she shouldn't.

She was slightly out of breath when she reached the store door. Rhona looked tiny in the packed space. An old light bulb flickered over her head.

'Let me help,' Kirsty said, stepping into the room. Suddenly it felt smaller than ever.

Rhona's eyes skimmed the boxes, bags, and display stands precariously stacked on the shelves and floor.

'How do you find anything in here?' she asked with an amused chuckle.

'Organised chaos. Here, let me scoot past and I can grab it.' She placed a hand on Rhona's hips and meant to use her for leverage as she sidled past, but instead she was frozen, painfully aware how close Rhona's neck was, the desire to kiss her building in her muscles. Had the room been bigger it would have been hard not to give into the urge to spin her, find her lips and do what Kirsty had spent weeks fantasising about. Thankfully, there wasn't enough room to swing a cat, never mind a beautiful woman.

Kirsty swallowed and, still keeping one hand on Rhona for stability, dipped to pull the lead out from between boxes.

'Here,' she said, passing it to Rhona. 'Need anything else while we're here?'

Rhona tried to turn but her foot caught on the corner of a box and she nearly toppled over. Thankfully, Kirsty's hands were ready to steady her.

'Not really big enough in here for two, is it?' Rhona said with a smile.

Kirsty opened her mouth to speak but was interrupted by Mum. 'Rhona, love! Do you want us in height order?'

'Duty calls,' Rhona said and shuffled out.

Kirsty sighed.

Before she knew it, the time had come for Rhona to leave. Kirsty hovered by the table Rhona's kitbag was on as she carefully put her equipment away.

'Sure you can't stay?'

Rhona shook her head. 'Sadly not. Got a shoot early in the morning tomorrow and I want to stay fresh.'

'Anything exciting?'

'An engagement announcement, in Kelvingrove. Amber passed it on to me. She couldn't get childcare.'

Kirsty slowly nodded her head. 'The jobs are still there, then?'

'Yeah, I mean weddings are definitely slowing down,' she replied, putting a lens in its bag. 'But I have a few more jobs lined up for October.'

'Then what?'

Rhona lifted her gaze to snag Kirsty's and the weight was almost crushing. Rhona shrugged. 'Things are petering out so I guess I'll move back home, save more money, travel for jobs if I have to.'

'I thought you were staying until December?' It was one thing not having a good excuse to see Rhona, but knowing she was at least in the same city was a comfort. North Queensferry felt like the other side of the world.

'Staying in Scotland, yeah. Doesn't make sense to stay if the jobs aren't here. My outgoings would only just balance my income.'

That made sense, so why did it feel like Kirsty's stomach was in knots?

'That was fantastic, Rhona,' Mum said, appearing from the next room. 'When will we get the photos back?'

'Might be the end of next week, if I'm honest. I'm juggling a lot and my flatmate, Niall, isn't the easiest to work around during the day.'

'Then come here,' Kirsty blurted. 'Free coffee,' she added to sweeten the offer.

'If time allows, I'll give it a bash.'

~

Rhona obviously wasn't as busy as she'd made out because she'd been here every other day since. And just like that, September trickled into October.

'He's called Chet,' Kirsty said, showing Rhona the photo of the grey tabby on her phone. It had quickly become their daily routine for Kirsty to take her lunch break at Rhona's table, and today was no different.

'And Dani really thinks this will help?'

Kirsty bobbed her head from side to side as she put her phone away. 'Ish. She's got it in her head he'll do something. I guess anything is worth a try.'

She hadn't been sure about a cat at first. Vet bills. Food. Not to mention stinky litter. But one look at that rescue cat's face and Kirsty had been smitten.

'I'll need to come and meet him.'

'You should. He's so sweet. Dani carries him around like a baby.'

'Now that I need to see with my own eyes.'

'What are you working on today?' Kirsty asked, leaning over to look at Rhona's screen. Memories of their first meeting in the café floated to the surface. It felt like a lifetime ago.

'Another engagement shoot for Amber. This one was out at Loch Lomond. It's beautiful there. Have you been?'

'When I was younger.' Kirsty studied the couple on the screen. She knew it was partly down to Rhona's skill with the camera, but they looked euphoric. Did love really make you feel that way? 'They look happy.'

Rhona beamed. 'They were. Childhood sweethearts. Been together since they were seventeen. Sometimes when you know, you know.'

'Must be nice.' The words were distant, Kirsty lost in her own thoughts.

It was bad to keep Rhona hanging and a part of Kirsty worried she'd soon get bored and move on, but every day she turned up at the café was another win.

Their new routine was making Kirsty complacent. She needed to decide soon, assuming that Rhona still wanted her. Now there was a thought. Kirsty's stomach tightened. Had her window to act passed?

'Listen,' Rhona said, and Kirsty's heart stuttered. No good sentence started with *listen*. 'I really appreciate you letting me work here. Niall is unbearable.'

'Why do I feel a *but* looming?'

Rhona smiled as she rubbed at her chin. 'Jobs are getting sporadic and Niall is doing my nut in. I need to move home.'

Kirsty swallowed, buying herself a moment. 'I get it. When?'

'This weekend, probably.'

'Always so quick to make your plans reality.'

'I've never seen the need to draw things out.'

Kirsty looked at the screen again, at the couple's grinning faces. For a heartbeat there was no one else she hated more in the world.

'Will you come visit?'

'If I'm near Shawlands again.'

'So chances are, I might never see you again.' Her eyes were back on the screen but she wasn't looking at the image this time. She wasn't looking at anything. Her brain was closing down, like a computer shutting off.

'Would you be that bothered?' There was no malice to Rhona's voice, it was a simple, honest question.

Kirsty's mind sprung back into action. 'Of course I'd be bothered.' She took Rhona's hand in her own and squeezed tight.

'Okay. Cool. It's just I wasn't sure.'

'I know I've avoided—' she paused, searching for the right word. '*Us* for longer than I should, but I'm still getting my head around a few things.'

She stroked the back of Rhona's hand with her thumb. Her heart fluttered with every caress.

Rhona's eyes shifted to the ceiling and narrowed as she thought. 'At the risk of sounding desperate, I just . . . I need a sign you want me to stick around, because right now I feel like you just want to be friends. Which is totally cool, but I'd rather you said now instead of keeping me waiting. I won't be offended – promise.'

'If I said I wanted more, would you stay in Glasgow?'

'Well, no. I've told Niall I'm moving out, but I could make more of an effort to visit. I've liked working here. But I'm not going to be some lovesick puppy that hangs out here every day, wasting time and petrol money when you don't want me.'

'Is any girl really worth wasting time and petrol money on?' Kirsty said with a smile.

'Don't joke. I'm being serious.'

'Well then, don't waste either. Come stay with me for a bit. That buys me time to get my head straight but it means you won't forget me in the interim.'

'I couldn't forget you if I wanted. And believe me, I've tried.'

'I don't know if you're being serious,' Kirsty said, smirking. She didn't want to know the answer. 'But I'm being serious. Will you stay at mine for a bit? If it doesn't work, you can move home.'

Rhona looked hesitant.

'Means you can meet Chet too,' Kirsty added.

'Let me think about it.'

22

'Is that all you've got?' Kirsty asked.

Rhona looked at the stack of boxes and her big black suitcase. 'I travel light. Most of my stuff went into Mum and Dad's storage right after Manchester.'

Kirsty's face screwed in confusion. 'It's hardly anything.' She shook her head free of thoughts. 'Right, well, I've cleared a drawer for you. And made some space in my wardrobe. Do you have any house-y stuff? What's in the boxes?'

'Nothing worth unpacking.'

'No priceless antiques, got it. I'll leave you to it, and I'll be in the living room if you need me.' She threw a thumb in its direction. Rhona's chest ached at how cute she was.

Standing here, actually putting her boxes in Kirsty's bedroom, this suddenly felt like a godawful idea.

If a friend was looking for advice in the same scenario she would label them insane. There were so many red flags it might as well be Bondi Beach. They'd kissed twice, and while Rhona agreed being drunk wasn't ideal, there had been plenty of opportunity to pick things up sober. Yet Kirsty was avoiding it like the plague.

Maybe Rhona was subconsciously a masochist. Why else would she put herself through so much pain?

It was bad enough that she'd soon found herself visiting Kirsty's work every other day. Now she was going to share a bed with her. Talk about torture.

With Kirsty, Rhona was like a moth to flame. It didn't matter how many times she was burned: she'd keep gravitating back.

She lifted her case onto the bed and spread it open. First out was her grey tartan waistcoat and trousers, pressed and ready for a wedding tomorrow. It was down in Ayr and the couple had requested their photographer stay over to get family shots in the surrounding woodland the day after the wedding. It was unusual, but Rhona liked accommodating odd requests. Humans were strange and delightful creatures, every one unique, and it was important people got what they wanted on their big day. Plus, it kept the job interesting, one of the biggest reasons why she loved what she did.

Next she decanted her underwear and tops into Kirsty's empty drawer. Everything else went in the wardrobe. It didn't take long. Rhona stood, hands on hips, and surveyed her new room. It was nice to be somewhere with personality. It wasn't her personality, but it was Kirsty's and that was more than bearable.

～

'Is that you done?' Kirsty stilled, her head poking over the back of the couch like a meerkat caught mid-action. 'You going out?'

Rhona unfurled her yoga mat in the space between the sofa and breakfast bar. 'No, I wanted to do some sit-ups. There's more room here. I won't distract you from the TV, promise.'

The glint in Kirsty's eye said it was too late for that. Rhona had chosen the same outfit she'd worn bouldering. Kirsty's appreciative glances hadn't gone unnoticed then and today was no different. She disappeared back behind the couch without another word.

Yes, it was resorting to underhand tactics, but she really did want to get a workout in. She'd been so busy organising the move she'd barely had a chance to sit, never mind keep her body active.

Rhona started easy: just a few normal sit-ups, followed by a set of crunches.

It wasn't long before she felt the weight of Kirsty's gaze. She glanced up at the sofa to find two brown eyes watching her.

'That explains so much.'

'Huh?' Rhona stopped, resting on her elbows.

'You could crack eggs on that stomach.'

Rhona snorted. 'I've never heard it put like that before.'

'Well, you know what I mean. I doubt I could even do one sit-up. Never mind all that.'

'I'm only getting warmed up just now.'

Kirsty scoffed. 'Alright, alright. Show me your best moves, then.'

'No pressure, eh?' Rhona started an oblique twist but had second thoughts mid-move. 'Let me show you how easy it is. More fun than just watching,' she said, gesturing with her hand for Kirsty to join her.

After a moment of hesitation Kirsty padded round,

adjusting her sweatshirt as she towered over Rhona. 'Where do you want me?'

Rhona rolled off the mat and gave it a firm pat. 'Just here.'

Kirsty dropped down and lay on her back, knees bent. 'Don't laugh.'

'You must be able to do a sit-up. You've got a great body.'

The tinge on Kirsty's cheeks was instant. 'Genetics. I think the last time I did a sit-up I was reaching for the remote.'

Rhona switched positions, moving to sit by Kirsty's feet, her thighs either side. She gripped a hand around each ankle, her fingers snaked in Kirsty's joggers.

It shouldn't have roused Rhona's core; there was nothing overly sexual in what they were doing, and yet it did. She swallowed, painfully aware of the heat between her legs.

'Okay,' she said, her voice a little croaky. 'Sit up – use your stomach, not your legs, and certainly not your neck.'

Kirsty put a hand to each temple and tried to raise herself. The movement was minimal.

Rhona bit back a laugh. 'You're winding me up.'

'I would never.' The smirk suggested otherwise.

She edged forward, Kirsty's trainer socks making contact with Rhona's bare legs.

With her feet securely lodged, Rhona's hands were free to wander to the sides of Kirsty's stomach. It was a little bit of a stretch so she leaned against Kirsty's knees to make it easier.

'Pull from here,' Rhona said, squeezing Kirsty's oblique muscles.

Kirsty nibbled at the corner of her bottom lip. 'I'll do my best. You staying there?'

'Nothing like an incentive.'

Rhona felt Kirsty's muscles tense and it wasn't from a sit-up. The air was charged between them. Maybe moving in wouldn't be so bad after all.

'Here goes,' Kirsty said, pulling herself up. She came to a stop inches from Rhona's face before collapsing onto the mat. She let out an exhausted huff.

'You done after one? I thought you had stamina.'

'Well, you thought wrong.'

Rhona bounced her next sentence around her head. To say or not to say? *Stuff it.* 'I never had you pegged as a pillow princess.'

Kirsty chuckled before turning sultry. 'Actually, I think you'll find I'm a top.'

Rhona pulled a face. 'Now that I don't believe.'

She knew what was coming and did nothing to stop it; in fact, she encouraged the swift change in dynamics. Kirsty opened her legs wider, letting Rhona sink between, freeing her feet. In one seamless motion her ankles were hooked around Rhona and before she knew it, Kirsty was on top, thighs straddling her stomach, her wrists held to the ground.

Kirsty's long hair brushed Rhona's face as she hovered over her. 'What do you prefer?' she asked, leaning close to Rhona's ear, her voice a rumbling purr.

Rhona's core pulsed. There was no beginning, no end, no sides to the world. Someone had put a hand to the universe and jumbled it all up, like a jigsaw puzzle in a bag. Her mind was blank. All that existed was Kirsty's weight bearing down on her centre; the way her wrists felt pinned to the ground, Kirsty's hands gentle but firm; and the sensation of warm breath against her skin.

After what felt like an age, Rhona remembered how to

talk. 'I'll take what I'm given, and this is certainly working for me.'

Kirsty's lips lingered under Rhona's ear. 'You know,' she said, pushing down harder on Rhona's wrists. 'I still need to get you back for that mark you left on my neck.'

Rhona snapped back to reality. 'I have a wedding tomorrow,' the words came out in a panic, merging into one.

It didn't faze Kirsty. She held steady and Rhona's heart rate rocketed. Her lips sweeped Rhona's skin as she spoke: 'Then I guess you're off the hook. This time.'

It was impossible to know if the TV was still on. All Rhona could hear was the sound of her own breathing, a low pant that screamed want. She gulped, fit to burst. If this went further she would come with one touch, she was sure of it.

Kirsty released her wrists and sat up straight. A scream lodged in Rhona's throat. She couldn't tease her like this.

She leaned back, shifting her weight to Rhona's thighs as she motioned for her to sit up too. Rhona had no idea where this was going but happily complied. She looped her arms around Kirsty's waist and held herself steady.

Kirsty locked eyes with her as she cupped a hand to Rhona's cheek. 'Why not just lie to me? Tell me you're coming back, that you're going to stay?' The words were nearly a whisper.

'Do you want me to do that?'

Kirsty shook her head.

'I'll only ever be honest with you, Kirsty. I can't be anything else,' Rhona said, leaning her forehead against Kirsty's.

They sat like that for a while. Rhona was vaguely aware of the cat padding by, but apart from Chet they could have been the last two beings on earth, frozen in a moment.

Rhona's racing heart slowed, but each beat still felt like a bomb going off in her chest.

Kirsty broke the connection and planted a chaste kiss on the tip of Rhona's nose. Her stare was piercing.

If this could never end, if she could find a way to keep Kirsty in her arms and hold onto her forever, that would be perfect.

She could say it. It would be so easy. Two little words. *I'll stay.* But the thought pulled her muscles taut and made her stomach twist.

Kirsty sighed. A colossal exhale that emptied her lungs and was so heavily loaded it could put your back out.

'Tell me what you're thinking,' Rhona said, her fingers tracing Kirsty's lower back.

Kirsty watched the cat jump onto the arm of the sofa, then fixed her attention on the corner of a cushion. 'I've already been through so much heartache, I don't know if I can do it again.'

'I'm not going to break your heart.'

'You will. One way or another.'

What can you say to that?

As Rhona thought, Kirsty filled the silence. Her eyes returned to search Rhona's. 'Now you tell me what you're thinking.' Her voice was piqued with trepidation.

'I'm not going to force you to take a chance you don't want to take. You either walk away now or you stay and see what can happen.'

Rhona's throat tightened. She knew moving in was a dangerous game, but hadn't expected things to progress so quickly. She's gone to the living room with the intention of being a little flirty, not having Kirsty break her heart.

Fuck.

'And what about you?'

'Me?' Rhona repeated, confused.

'Do you want to stay or walk away?'

'I don't really have a choice. You're sitting on top of me.'

Every muscle in Kirsty's body relaxed and Rhona felt the shift against her thighs. Kirsty closed the gap, their noses now nearly touching.

'You're something else.'

Rhona didn't get the chance for a smart reply as Kirsty's lips found hers. It was quick at first, then Kirsty drove it deeper, slower. It was the kind of kiss that didn't have a care in the world; it was a lazy Sunday morning with a paper, a day off with no plans but to get lost in yourself. Or get lost in Kirsty, which was exactly what happened to all of Rhona's senses when their lips parted. Kirsty's tongue found hers and a heady mix of happiness and desire exploded in Rhona's belly.

If she was stuck on a desert island Rhona would take one thing: Kirsty's kisses. There was nothing in life she needed more.

Kirsty's hand slid around to the back of her neck, her fingers dancing through Rhona's undercut.

She'd have more chance of picking the winning lottery numbers than containing the moan that escaped.

Rhona pulled Kirsty closer as she rocked against her hips.

Kirsty stilled as she giggled into Rhona's mouth. She opened an eye to find Chet's front paws resting on Kirsty's arm, his inquisitive face inspecting what the fuss was about.

'Hi Chet,' Kirsty said, her voice husky. She scratched the top of the cat's head. 'Don't tell Mummy; she'll only get jealous.'

'Before I put the light out, can I explain myself?'

Rhona couldn't help but chuckle. She'd be lying if she said she'd not been expecting sex tonight, but they had all the time in the world. If Kirsty needed to get something off her chest then priorities had to shift. She scooted closer in bed, looping a hand between Kirsty and the pillows and pulling her into a hug.

'Of course.'

'Okay. But just listen, yeah? Don't interrupt. This might meander a bit.'

Rhona refrained from laughing again. Instead she kissed the top of Kirsty's head as a signal to continue.

'I know we've just spent the last thirty minutes making out, which was fantastic,' Kirsty said, holding a finger aloft before lacing her hand with Rhona's. 'But this whole thing still makes me anxious.'

'Yeah? Sorry, no more interruptions,' Rhona joked, only to mask the dread that now balled in her stomach.

'I'm just . . . it's just, you see . . .'

Rhona bit her lip, burying her nose into Kirsty's hair. 'Hmm?'

Kirsty let out an exasperated sigh. 'Dani has all these grandiose ideas about self-sabotage but I don't think that's what I'm doing. I'm more, like, focused on self-preservation.'

Rhona skirted her free fingers over Kirsty's bare arm to show she was listening but still giving her space to talk.

'It's like, my heart's a watch,' Kirsty's voice pitched, excited to have landed on something she could run with. 'And for the first eighteen years it was an amazing watch: worked perfectly, looked good, top-notch. A Rolex or something, yeah?'

Rhona nodded silently. *A watch, got it.*

'Then my dad died and the watch stopped. And I

figured, why fix it? Even a broken watch is right twice a day, yeah?' Sadness pulled at her words and Kirsty burrowed deeper against Rhona's chest.

'So I left it. And it got battered, and tarnished, and I didn't treat it very well. But I didn't see the need for a watch. If I could do everything right, and control everything I could and my watch still got broken, why have one? You don't need a watch. You can just ask other people for the time.' She paused. 'I don't know if that's saying what I want it to, but anyway. So now, *now*,' she said, elongating the word. 'I'd quite like to know the time again, and all the pieces are there and I'm doing everything right, and I just don't know how to get it ticking. Well, no, maybe it is ticking, yeah? But it's an hour out, or something. Does that make sense?'

Not really. But Rhona kinda followed. 'Yeah, I think I know what you mean.'

Kirsty nodded. 'So now I'm looking at this watch and it's really fragile, and I'm thinking, *Thirty-five years I've kept this priceless watch going and you want me to just hand it over to someone else?* Cause you know, it might not tell the right time, but it's the only watch I've got. What if you drop it? Or lose it? Or you see another watch you like better? There's no way I could fix it again. It's already almost beyond repair.'

Rhona unravelled Kirsty's words.

'Is this analogy still working or do I just sound mad?'

'No. I think I get what you're saying. Can I speak now?'

'Please. Before I go off on a tangent about clocks or something.'

'I get why you'd be cautious, as the owner of such a rare and unique curiosity, but I promise not to wear it swimming. . .?' Rhona wasn't sure if that was the right conclusion.

The gentle whack to her chest confirmed it wasn't. 'Rhona, be serious. Please.'

Rhona steeled herself, growing sincere. 'I've never knowingly broken a watch. My little Casio's taken a beating or two, but other people's? I always treat with the highest respect. And I don't care if yours runs a little different to the rest. That's why I like it so much. I'm just sad it got broken in the first place.'

Kirsty was quiet.

'He would have liked you,' Kirsty said, her voice a broken whisper.

'You think?'

'Yeah.'

Rhona felt Kirsty shift. She sniffed quietly, but Rhona didn't say anything. This was Kirsty's moment.

Her voice cracked when she spoke, but soon levelled back out. 'I know it's super sad, but he was my best friend. These past few weeks I've been trying to imagine what advice he'd give me. I told him everything and he always knew the right thing to say.'

'What do you think he would have told you?' Tears welled in Rhona's eyes, she widened them, hoping they'd dry out.

'He would have told me off for a start. For keeping you hanging.' Kirsty laughed but Rhona could tell if she touched her cheek it would be wet. 'And then he would have said something corny about how great love is. He proper worshipped Mum. He'd want me to have that, I think. The longer I go without him, the further away he gets.' Kirsty pawed at her face, getting rid of the evidence of tears.

Rhona's heart ached. It was no wonder Kirsty was cautious.

'How did he . . .?' Rhona trailed off, not sure if it was appropriate to ask, never mind say the word.

'Sudden Arrhythmic Death Syndrome. He went to bed

and just never got up the next day. Nothing you can do. It just happens.'

'Fuck.'

She'd assumed cancer, or something, but that was . . . *fuck*.

'Sorry for making this such a downer,' Kirsty said, attempting to sound jokey. 'I just, well, you deserve to know what's going on in my head. Maybe it will help you understand why I need a little patience.'

'Thank you.'

Kirsty sighed. 'I never talk about my dad. It makes my skin feel weird. But this. . . it feels okay, I guess. Can we not talk about any of this again, though?'

'If that's what you want then consider it forgotten.'

'Not forgotten. Just silently sealed away.'

'In the watch vault.'

'What's a watch vault?'

'I dunno. Somewhere you keep expensive watches?'

'Doesn't sound right.'

'It was your analogy,' Rhona said, playfully tickling Kirsty's side.

'You're a fool,' Kirsty joked, pulling Rhona in for a kiss.

23

'So?' Izzy asked as their cocktails were placed on the table.

'So?'

'You said you wanted to chat.' True. Kirsty had invited Izzy to Cal's cocktail lounge, intent on getting her head in order. If an one could make sense of her muddled thoughts, it was her best friend.

A sigh tumbled out as Kirsty rolled her eyes. She was fed up with herself.

'Oh God, you still haven't slept together, have you? It's been nearly a week.'

'I know.' Kirsty took a sip of her margarita. God, it was good.

'Sex aside, how's it going? You've lived with Dani for as long as I've known you. Weird to have someone else's milk in the fridge?'

'It's actually been strangely easy to adjust.' A smile pulled at Kirsty's lips as she remembered something. 'You know what she asked me when she first moved in?'

'No, pray tell.' Izzy leaned closer, excited.

"'Do you have a cleaning rota? Just tell me what jobs you want me to take over.'"

'Fuck. How did you keep your pants on?' An older couple at the table opposite gave an disapproving look, but Izzy ignored them.

'It was close, let me tell you,' Kirsty said, signalling a minute distance between her finger and thumb as she scrunched her face up.

'That's pretty much porn to you. But let's be serious. What's going on in that head of yours?'

Another sigh. Kirsty looked out of the window, watching passing Southsiders battle against the wind and rain.

Izzy waited patiently for an answer, sipping on her martini as she studied Kirsty's face.

Nothing was falling into place. 'I dunno, Iz.'

'You do like her, yeah?'

Kirsty couldn't look Izzy in the eye. This was too big. 'That's the problem. I more than like her.'

'Oh.'

'Yep.'

'That's massive.'

'Yep.'

'Still no budging on the coming-back-to-Glasgow thing?'

Finally, Kirsty could look at her best friend again. 'She won't commit. That's what I don't get. Why not? It makes me think she has no intention of coming back.'

'I thought you said her brother was having a baby?'

'He is. So what?'

'Well,' she replied with a shrug. 'She'll surely be back in Scotland at least.'

'Okay, so one,' Kirsty said, holding up a finger. 'I'm not doing long distance. And two, if she doesn't want to move to Glasgow, why bother? I'm never leaving.'

'So what are you going to do? Keep snogging like randy teenagers? What's the point? You can't go on like this until she leaves. You need to make a decision now. It's been months, Kirsty.'

'I know,' she whined.

'Have you told her how you feel?'

'Of course not.'

Izzy shook her head, biting her bottom lip to hide the grin she was battling. 'Kirsty, tell the girl, for God's sake.'

'She won't say it back.'

'You don't know that. Plus, you need to give her a reason to stay. Maybe if she knows you love her, she'll commit.'

The word felt like a punch to Kirsty's stomach. She'd never felt like this before. Outside of family she'd never uttered 'I love you'. This was a huge step. Did she really want her first time to have the potential to crush her?

'It's too much.'

'Nonsense. Look, invite her over now. Let's have a drink together. Let me get to know my future best-friend-in-law better.'

'It's minging outside.'

Izzy leaned towards the window, craning her neck. 'I can see your flat from here. She'll be fine. And there's something called a brolly. Amazing the technology they have these days.'

'Nah.'

'Come on.'

'Nope.'

'Please.'

'You're insufferable.'

'One of the reasons why you love me.' Izzy's eyes turned wistful. 'You're not going to abandon me when you go all loved up and coupley, are you?'

'You mean like you did with Emmie?'

'Hardly.'

'And Carly.'

'Now you're just changing the subject.'

'Correct.'

'I'll behave. Promise.'

There was little point in arguing. Izzy wouldn't be averse to crossing the road and dragging Rhona over herself. 'Right, okay, I'll text her.'

Izzy clapped excitedly as Kirsty sent the message.

'See? That was easy.'

'Anything to shut you up.'

Was it Kirsty's imagination, or were the older couple now leaning a little closer and looking strangely invested now the topic of their conversation was potentially en route? *Nosey gits.*

'While we wait, what's the deal with you?'

'Me?'

'Still on Tinder?'

'Totally over it. One minute I'm in a serious relationship, the next I'm asking some random girl on Tindy what her favourite colour is.'

'No you do not.'

'I would hate for it to be beige. Minimises disappointment further down the line.'

'Shouldn't surprise me. That's such an Izzy question.'

'I hate dating. I just want someone to get me. Someone to sweep me off my feet. Someone to have easy conversation with, no hanging about, you know: an instant connection.'

'Not asking for much.'

'I've read enough romance books to know what I deserve.'

'Real life is a little different, Iz. Hate to break it to you.'

Izzy scoffed. 'Life's what you make of it. My princess is out there, waiting for me. I just have to be patient. Our paths will cross sooner or later.'

'You're disgustingly romantic when you're optimistic.'

'Keith gave me a pep talk. He said he was sick of me crying.'

'Good on him. He's got the patience of a saint to live with you.'

'I give good tummy scratches. He can never leave.'

The eavesdropping couple looked confused.

'Keith's a cat,' Kirsty said to thin air. Izzy looked confused. The couple looked satisfied to know the dynamic of Izzy and Keith.

'He is a cat. Well done. Now, any reply from your live-in lover?'

Kirsty resisted the urge to pull a face and checked her phone. 'She's on her way.'

Izzy danced in her seat.

'Please don't embarrass me,' Kirsty said, draining the rest of her cocktail. She needed a little courage. Her heart rate was threatening to rise beyond what was acceptable. Why was she getting nervous? This wasn't just about Izzy. Seeing Rhona made her heart leap. Even if she had just seen her thirty minutes ago. *Fuck*. Kirsty had it bad.

'There she is,' Izzy said.

Kirsty turned, spotting Rhona across the street. Her hoodie was pulled tight and she hugged her black denim jacket close. The other way round and Kirsty would have stuck to the cosy flat if invited out.

Rhona crossed the road, taking advantage of a gap in the traffic, and did a cute wee run. It was ingrained in everyone when crossing a busy road, but when Rhona did it Kirsty's breath stuttered.

In a flash, Rhona was pushing open the glass door to Cal's.

She flipped her hood down and searched the room. Kirsty bit down on her bottom lip, not wanting to be a grinning idiot when Rhona finally spotted them.

Izzy raised her hand. 'Rhona!'

Their eyes met, and seeing Rhona's perfect smile made Kirsty's heart boom.

'Hey,' Rhona said, putting her jacket on the back of the spare chair.

'Hey,' Kirsty said, her voice dreamlike.

'You want a drink?' Izzy asked, already knowing the answer as she caught the waiter's attention.

'Yeah, that would be good.' She turned her attention to Kirsty, placing a hand on her knee. 'You okay?'

'Yeah, why?'

'You said Izzy needed me for something. I was worried something was wrong.'

'Me? I need something?' Izzy repeated, cocking an eyebrow. Kirsty kicked her under the table. 'Oh, God. Yeah. Now I remember.'

Kirsty was grateful Rhona was now obscuring her view of the couple opposite. This pantomime didn't need awkward eye contact thrown into the mix.

'So, what's up?'

The waiter appeared and took their order, giving Izzy precious time to think.

'I need your professional opinion. Winter wedding. Okay to wear heels, or is that tempting fate with soggy grass?'

Rhona screwed her face up. It was a ridiculous question. Kirsty couldn't have done better though. Her mind was blank. All she could do was take Rhona in, the feeling of her hand resting on her thigh the only thought filling her mind.

'That's a tough one. Unlikely that there will be a lot of grass to contend with at this time of year. People tend to stay in.'

'True. But it's out at Brinkley House. You know how much they like to encourage a firework end to the evening. Do you remember the one during the summer? They had us waiting until eleven.'

'How do you know I was at Brinkley House this summer?' Rhona's eyes narrowed with intrigue.

The waiter sat their drinks down and Rhona's gaze never broke with Izzy's.

'I guess if you're sticking around,' she added a subtle but definite cough to her sentence. 'Then you deserve to know what I do for a living.'

Rhona looked at Kirsty then back to Izzy.

Izzy sipped her drink, building the suspense. 'After Lovefest, you said you felt like you knew me from somewhere. I said no. Well, sorry, it was a lie.'

'Really? So, how have we met? At a Brinkley House wedding? Why hide that?'

Kirsty sipped her fresh margarita. This was an interesting development. Izzy's job was a sacred secret. Most people, her parents included, thought she was an accountant.

'I go to a lot of weddings.'

'Okay.'

'And other things. Mainly weddings, though.'

Kirsty sat in silence, enjoying her drink and front-row entertainment.

'So?' Rhona's tone elevated. Kirsty had never seen someone look so confused.

As if sensing the attention of the third party at the neighbouring table, Izzy beckoned Rhona closer with a finger. As she whispered the truth in Rhona's ear, a smile formed.

'That's not a real thing,' Rhona said with a chuckle.

'I promise you it is.'

Rhona looked at Kirsty. 'Is she telling me the truth?'

'One hundred per cent,' Kirsty confirmed.

'Then you whisper to me what you think Izzy said.'

She leaned closer and the urge to kiss her was all encompassing. She smelled good, like she'd spritzed fresh perfume before leaving the house.

Kirsty lingered, enjoying the proximity. She put a hand on the back of Rhona's chair, closing the gap by a few more inches. Her lips grazed Rhona's ear. 'She's a date for hire.'

Kirsty leaned back. 'Only men, though.'

'Why?'

'Can't risk feelings getting involved,' Izzy said before sucking on her straw to drain a hefty amount of cocktail.

'Like, for real? You're not having me on?'

'Nope. And tell anyone, I'll kill you,' Izzy said, deadly serious.

Rhona's mouth refused to close. 'That's wild.' She stared at the ceiling, deep in thought. 'Brinkley House. You were with the brother, weren't you? I remember the family portraits now.'

'Yep, that sounds right. Was a busy summer. Once it's done I tend to forget. Frees up brain space for the next one.'

'Why do you remember me? You must meet loads of photographers.'

Izzy flashed one of her trademark glances, the one that could melt hearts. Or set them on fire. Depended how she felt. 'You might not be exactly my type but I can appreciate a hottie in a suit when I see one.'

A faint blush ghosted Rhona's cheeks. 'Ladies do love my waistcoats.' As if feeling Kirsty's glare, she switched gears. 'You like your job?'

'I love it. The pay certainly helps.'

Kirsty smiled. It took a lot for Izzy to trust someone; the fact she was being so open with Rhona counted for a lot.

Rhona rubbed at her chin, still shaking her head in disbelief. 'So, if I see you again should I pretend I don't know you?'

'Probably easiest. If we're at a wedding, of course, not like normal times. You're coming to Izzy-een, yeah?'

'I think so.' Rhona didn't sound so sure.

'Izzy-een, or Izzy's birthday party, for the less informed.'

'Ah, right, yeah. Of course.'

'Good. Now, ladies. I think Keith's hankering for a furball, so I need to scoot.' She downed her drink while locking eyes with Kirsty. 'I'll get these – you girls have a nice chat. Stay out for a few more.' She winked and was off before Kirsty could protest.

Not exactly subtle, but then Izzy never was.

'Got your outfit sorted yet?' Kirsty asked. Her phone's lock screen lit up.

Izzy: *Tell her.*

Kirsty stuffed the phone into her pocket.

'I think so. I'm seeing Amber tomorrow. I might call into town on the way.'

'Amber? So, a work meeting?'

'Yeah, kind of, I guess. I feel like we're ships in the night just now: she might employ me but I never see her. She was my friend before she was my boss. I'm looking forward to catching up with her.'

All the while Rhona was talking, the voice in Kirsty's head was getting louder. She couldn't tell her. Or could she? *Three words. That's all it takes.* And Izzy was right. Maybe it would be the incentive to make her stay.

'You okay?'

'Yeah, why?' Kirsty laughed.

'You totally zoned out there.'

'Nah. Well, maybe a little. Been a long day.'

'Busy?'

'Winter weather. People are starting to think about Christmas. Nights are drawing in. They want to be cosy and drink coffee and relax.'

'Cosy and relaxed sounds good. Do you want to finish these and go home? Dani and I were going to watch a film. We still could if we leave soon.'

They could, but she couldn't say what she needed to if Dani was within earshot. Never in a million years.

'Yeah, it's just I—'

Rhona tilted her head, listening.

The words were caught in her throat, far too big to come out of her mouth.

'I—'

'Yes?'

'I—'

'Are you sure you're okay?'

'I think we should get snacks on the way home.'

Fuck's sake.

Kirsty was certain she heard a groan from the table opposite. This wasn't the time or the place.

∾

'So, what was that about with Izzy?' Rhona asked now they were sheltered from the rain. They'd hoofed it from Cal's down to the arcade – a row of shops under a covered walkway. Kirsty's brolly had protected her hair and face but the driving rain had still managed to pelt her lower body and she was soaked to the bone.

'Ach, she's just being silly.' As she spoke, Rhona took her hand. Warmth swelled in Kirsty's belly. She'd never walked holding hands with a partner before.

'How so?'

'She thinks we need to have a chat about us.'

Rhona's pace faltered. 'Do you think we need to have a chat?'

Kirsty shrugged.

'We totally can if you want,' Rhona reassured her.

'Nah. This is our relationship. She just doesn't get it. Slow suits me fine.'

Rhona nodded but didn't look fully satisfied.

The sentence sat in her chest. She had to say it. There was no way she could live her life never telling Rhona how she felt. It was like having a beast sit on her ribcage, restricting her breath.

Before she knew it they were at the shop. No one says I love you for the first time in Sainsburys.

But, if she didn't do it now she would have to sit through a film with the words growing inside her.

By bedtime they would be a coiled spring, ready to explode.

'Something's definitely up,' Rhona said as the automatic doors slid open.

'It's nothing.'

'So, it's something?'

With a huff Kirsty picked up speed, dropping Rhona's

hand and overtaking, leaving her in the chiller aisle. Crisps. She needed to find the crisps.

'Kirsty. Speak to me.'

'Salt and vinegar or sweet chilli?' she asked, holding up two family bags.

'Let's get both. Dani will want some too. Now, tell me what's going on.' Rhona took the bags from her, their eyes locked.

She couldn't, not here. Life-altering moments didn't happen in supermarket aisles.

A guy resembling a drowned rat skirted round them, aiming for the snack bags of nuts.

Rhona's eyes didn't budge. Maybe if she kept the connection she would know what Kirsty was feeling. Wishful thinking.

She gulped, but it did nothing to dislodge her words.

'Are you still having second thoughts?' Rhona asked, breaking the spell that held them in place.

'Second thoughts? I don't think I ever said I was having them.' Kirsty was on the move again, whipping to the far side of the shop in search of booze.

'Well, anxiety, whatever. Is that what's wrong?'

'In part, I guess.' Anxiety about making an utter fool of herself, did that count?

Even with the gap between them, Kirsty heard Rhona sigh. She hated planting the seed of doubt. This conversation was having the opposite effect of what she intended.

'I don't know what I can say to put your mind at rest,' Rhona said, stopping by Kirsty's side as she perused the wine fridge.

'Honestly, it's fine. I was just talking to Izzy about stuff and she wouldn't drop the idea of us having a chat and I gave in and now it feels like a really stupid idea and you probably think I'm nuts.' The tinny music coming from the shop's speakers were all that filled the void between them as Rhona unpicked her jumble of a sentence.

'I don't think you're nuts. But if something's on your mind you should say.'

They stood, both facing the wine, and Kirsty wished she could be brave.

When she was fourteen, she was completely infatuated with a boy called Darrel. He was in her English class. Short brown hair, glasses, a smile that would light up every room.

The Christmas dance was coming up and Kirsty figured it was the perfect time to make a move. Only, courage wasn't her strong suit. Up until then guys had always made the first move; she'd never been the one to put her heart on the line.

When she'd confided in her dad, he said, 'Better to take a chance than live a life of what-ifs.'

So, she did. Darrel had shot her down in flames and she fought not to think about the heartache that followed, but the advice was still golden.

She had to say it.

Maybe Izzy was right and these were the magic words to make Rhona stay.

Kirsty gulped, her mouth as dry as sandpaper.

No what-ifs.

'I—'

'Sorry, girls, can I just. . .?' said a guy, not waiting for their response. His dripping wet arm snaked between them and over Kirsty's shoulder, retrieving a bottle of Riesling.

Kirsty stepped aside, biting down the anger that formed in the pit of her stomach. 'Yeah, sure. Sorry.'

Rhona pulled a face, as if to say *Impatient, much?*.

The moment was gone, courage diluted and all but washed away.

'What were you going to say?' Rhona asked.

'I think we should get some beer too.'

'I was just thinking the same thing.'

24

'And have you told her that?' Amber asked, taking another sip of beer. You'd think she'd not had a sniff of alcohol in years, the way pure elation contorted her face with every taste.

Ted had a handle on the baby, so they'd been afforded a night in the local. Amber was giddy with excitement. Rhona had missed this. It felt like old times: if she closed her eyes she could be in the student union. Amber even had dungarees on. She still lived in the things.

'Course I've not told her. We're not even properly dating. Who says *I love you* when you're not even dating?'

'Might get her to trust you. Finally get you to fourth base.'

Rhona shot her daggers. 'Don't. And I'm not saying *I love you* for sex.'

'You know I didn't mean it like that. Well, why not tell her you're coming back to Glasgow?'

Rhona pulled a face.

'Still not decided?'

'Nope.'

'What's stopping you?'

'I dunno. It just doesn't feel right.'

'You and your gut feelings.'

'Haven't been wrong so far.'

Amber coughed a name into her pint. 'June.'

'Right, well. A minor blip.'

'I'm still friends with her on Facebook, you know.'

'You are not.'

'I am. I never post and we weren't that close at uni. I think she's forgotten I exist. Forever under the radar.' She threw a level hand out to the side and nearly sliced through the neighbouring table's beers. She mouthed a silent *sorry* in their direction.

'Why haven't you mentioned this before? Does she post?'

'You and me kind of drifted apart when you moved south. It didn't feel right for me to drop in your inbox and snitch on your ex.' Amber supped her pint. 'Do you really want to know or will I shut up and we'll forget I ever mentioned it?'

Tough one. 'Will I be happy or sad?'

Amber's face pulled into a manic grin. 'Happy.'

'Okay. Hit me.' Rhona closed her eyes, her hands on her chest, keeping her heart from exploding.

'So, you said you didn't want to go after her for the money, yeah?'

'Yeah.'

'Good. Because she blew it all. Tried to set up another photography biz in Liverpool. Totally bombed. She's working in Starbucks now.'

'Shut. Up.'

'Not a word of a lie.' Amber pulled her phone out her pocket. 'Here, want to see?'

Rhona waved her away. 'No, definitely not. I never want to see her face again.'

Amber took the hint and slipped her phone away. 'Her loss, my gain. It's been brilliant working with you.'

Rhona's chest warmed. This summer *had* been great and it was all thanks to Amber taking a chance on her. 'It's just a shame it has to end.'

Amber reached across the table and placed her hand on Rhona's before giving it a waggle as she pouted. 'I know. It sucks. Just not enough business to go about.'

'It's cool. Everything's booked so far in advance. It's not your fault. I know I could hang about and we could do something in the future, but I need to make foundations sooner. I don't have the funds to last that long.'

'Especially after your grand trip! You excited? Where's first, again?'

'India.'

Amber blew her cheeks out. 'Bloody jealous, pal. I won't lie. Once you have a kid it's hard enough getting a trip to the shops, never mind a six-month holiday.'

'I'm very lucky. Although, I'll need to come back for my nibling.'

'Nib-what now?'

'That's gender neutral for niece or nephew.'

'Ah, the wee bambino. Still don't know what it is?'

'They do. But we're being kept in the dark.'

'Just adds to the excitement.' Amber's face turned serious. 'Promise you'll come see me when you're on your travel break?'

'If I remember.'

'Don't. I would have gone crazy without you.'

'Nonsense.'

'Nuh-uh. In fact, I think I might just lose it while you're away.'

'Don't make me feel bad,' Rhona said, pulling an exaggerated sad face.

'Sorry. It's just, talking to you really helps keep me grounded.' Amber gulped her beer. 'I mean, the booze we drink while you listen helps too.'

'See, you've already found my replacement.'

'I'd better enjoy it while I can.' She rolled her eyes.

'What does that mean?' Rhona scanned the room as she waited for Amber to answer. It was a decent pub with a great view of Kelvingrove Museum, but its industrial finish and quirky decor left it feeling cold. She missed the warmth of the Southside.

Amber took a deep breath. 'Ted's after another baby.'

'Yikes.'

'Ya. I mean, like, I dunno.'

'You're really not keen?'

'See, when we got married I was totally on the *two's a team* wagon: great, great, great. I mean, I'm a single child. I always wanted a sibling.'

'But?'

'Babies. Hard work, man. I'm only just feeling normal again. And I love being back at work.'

Rhona nodded. 'Have you told Ted that?'

'Kinda. I think he forgets work is my little baby too. You've been brilliant keeping it ticking on but I won't have you forever. I've worked too damn hard to let it fold. And it's weddings. You can't truly schedule pregnancy and maternity. Nothing goes to plan. I can't be booking brides in for years to come and wham, up the duff on their big day.'

Rhona couldn't help but laugh. Amber's honesty was what made them so close. 'You can always count on me.'

Amber screwed her face up. 'I know you mean it, but I don't want to hold you back. You might be in Sri Lanka, Australia, Indonesia, A—erm, I think I've ran out of places. You know what I mean. You'll be off, following your heart.'

'That's just for a few months. I'll be settled somewhere by the time you start popping more kids out.'

She lolled her head back, groaning. 'Enough,' she said with a grin. 'So, real talk. If Glasgow isn't calling your name, where is? England again?'

'Nah. I'm done with down south. And I didn't fully discount Glasgow. I just said I wasn't committed.'

'There's a difference?'

'Er, yes. A massive one.'

'But it's on the books? What are you waiting for? A massive billboard asking you to stay?' Amber zoned out, staring at the blank space above Rhona's head.

'Don't you fucking dare. I know Ted has pals in advertising. No, I just . . . something doesn't feel right. I want to say this is home, especially now I know Kirsty, but there's something missing.' She waved her hands in front of her chest. 'Like there's a final puzzle piece and I've not found it yet. Something that's going to tell me where to go.'

Amber made a show of doing a little bow. 'Very mystical and zen.'

'Shut up,' Rhona chided. She didn't expect anyone to understand her way of thinking. The universe always had her back. All she had to do was listen. The problem was, signs and guidance were currently getting lost en route. They were few and far between these days.

Which usually meant they were too close and too big to be seen, screaming blue murder in her face.

She'd meditate properly tomorrow. Clear her head a little.

'Right, right, right,' Amber said, tapping the table. 'Sorry. Very serious now. So, what are your current plans?'

'For when I get back?'

'Yeah.'

'Dunno. Move back in with my parents. Start my own photography business. Not decided on that yet. I'll see how it goes. Travel to see Kirsty, iff she still wants me. That's the placeholder plan. Obviously I'll adjust it as I know more.'

'Good. You need something in the works. I'm all for your way of doing things but you can't leave the country with no safety net.'

'I know. Thanks, Mum.'

Amber scowled. 'I would freak out if I didn't have set plans.'

'Good thing I'm the yin to your yang, then.'

'Have you told Kirsty about your placeholder plans?' She drained the rest of her pint, tipping her head back to get the last dregs.

'Nah, no point. It'll only complicate things if I change direction.'

'Rhona,' Amber whined. 'This girl is gagging for some stability. If you're not going to tell her how you feel, at least let her know she's factored into your future. It doesn't matter how uncertain your plans are; just let her know.'

'You seem very invested in this,' Rhona replied, raising a quizzical eyebrow.

'It's just nice to see you happy. June really fucked you over and you don't deserve that. I really want you guys to work out.'

'Sap.'

'I just don't want you to miss a chance at happiness. Yeah, travelling's good, but you've got the rest of your life to think about. You want to wake up next to someone you love or an empty pillow?'

'An empty pillow with a new view every morning might not be so bad.' She was only joking. There wasn't a view on earth that could beat waking up next to Kirsty. Experiencing both would be the dream. Kirsty had made it abundantly clear the nomadic lifestyle wasn't for her, though.

'You really love her, huh?'

'What makes you say that?'

'Your pupils go all funny when you think about her. Could be the drink though. Speaking of which: it's your round.'

25

'Just say I have food poisoning,' Dani said, swinging her legs over the side of the kitchen counter. It drove Kirsty crazy when she sat there but now wasn't the time for discipline.

'Come on, it'll be fun. Plus, we spent ages on these costumes.'

She'd expected a little kickback about tonight but the dullness in Dani's eyes hinted there was more than hesitation behind her reluctance.

Every year since Kirsty could remember they'd gone to Bar Orama's Halloween party to celebrate Izzy's birthday, which fell on the same day. They were slightly early, given Halloween was a Tuesday this year, but it wouldn't stop Izzy. It just meant she got to celebrate twice, on Saturday and Tuesday. Not a bad deal.

Costumes were a super serious business and Kirsty was glad to see Rhona had taken her warning to heart and was putting some effort in. Or at least, she assumed that was why they'd been left to loiter in the kitchen. She was taking an age.

'We do look good,' Dani grudgingly admitted.

Kirsty was quite chuffed with their final creations. Dani was dressed as a monkey, complete with a long curly tail, held at head height with invisible string. Kirsty was the ringmaster. She'd put her own spin on the outfit, teaming her fitted red jacket with a super short pleated skirt and knee high boots. A top hat completed her look.

She wouldn't usually do a matching outfit with Dani, but this was the first year that she and Ashley hadn't done something together. They were usually the masters of the couple outfit. It was going to be strange seeing them in different gear. The thought was obviously weighing heavy on Dani's shoulders, too.

'Come on, let's get some shots ready. And get your arse off my counter.'

'*Your* counter?' Dani laughed. 'I was sure my name was on the mortgage too. I can put my arse where I want.' She jumped down from the counter and wiggled her bum at Kirsty, her long tail swishing in her sister's face. She gave herself a few good smacks on the arse as she jumped backwards, reversing towards Kirsty as she made monkey noises.

'Ma'am, do you need me to lock this here ruffian up?' Rhona said from the doorway, putting on an American accent.

Kirsty lifted her eyes from Dani and met Rhona's gaze.

Holy fucking shit.

The earth stopped spinning and time ground to halt. Kirsty's breath caught in her throat, her heart on pause.

'Fuck,' Kirsty uttered under her breath.

The look on Rhona's face said she was having similar thoughts at the sight of Kirsty.

Time continued its new pace as Kirsty took Sheriff Rhona in.

Her black skinny jeans were tucked into stylish black cowboy boots. She had on her signature waistcoat, tailored to perfectly hug her in all the right places. Kirsty had seen it before, but with her black shirt and cowboy hat it seemed a million miles away from the smart suit she'd worn to a wedding.

A gold sheriff's badge completed her look, along with what looked like the chain of a pocket watch.

A smile spread across Rhona's face. She bit her bottom lip, struggling to stay in character. She tipped her hat at Kirsty. 'Ma'am.'

Kirsty's legs felt like jelly.

'Rhona, you look absolutely boss!' Dani beamed.

That was one word for it.

'Not bad, eh?' she replied, finally breaking character and kicking a foot out to the side.

Absolutely adorable.

It was a good thing Dani was here or they wouldn't make it out of the flat.

'You like the boots?' Rhona asked, kissing Kirsty on the cheek. 'You look incredible, by the way.'

'Thank you. The boots look awesome. You glad you got them?' They'd been the subject of hot debate this week. Rhona didn't want to buy material stuff she'd only have to store. Kirsty chose not to focus on what that really meant. She was getting better and better at pretending the twenty-seventh of December didn't exist.

'I love them. And I figured they completed the outfit. I had to make my best effort for Izzy.'

Right now would be the ideal time for Dani to fuck off.

Two minutes of peace to kiss Rhona into oblivion was all Kirsty needed.

No such luck.

'Shots, then?' Dani asked, trying to juggle two limes. One hit the floor with a thud.

'Aye, why not? You cut the limes, I'll get the glasses,' Kirsty said, but found herself rooted to the spot, unable to move from Rhona's side.

Desire swelled in her belly, like a fizzy burst of happiness.

Fuck it, Dani would cope.

Rhona's attention flitted between Kirsty's mouth and eyes. She took a step closer as Kirsty brought her hand up, cupping Rhona's jaw and pulling her in.

She could happily forgo the booze tonight. Rhona's kisses got her high enough. If her hands hadn't been on Kirsty's hips there was a good chance she would have floated away.

'Less snogging, more drinking,' Dani scolded.

Kirsty cleared her throat as she pulled away from Rhona. They exchanged a playful look as if caught by a parent or teacher. 'Right, on it.'

She swivelled on her heel and searched the cupboard for the glasses. She had to go on tip-toe to reach them. Rhona helped, or should that be hindered, by slipping a hand under her skirt and giving her bum a squeeze.

Kirsty shot her a look between *don't you dare* and *don't stop*. Dani was still cutting the limes so she took her chance to act out, leaning close to Rhona and keeping her voice to a whisper. 'Careful. This outfit comes with a whip.'

Rhona bit down on her lower lip. Her usually brown eyes were closer to black. She shook her head, the grin she was holding in making her cheekbones more prominent than ever.

'Glasses, as requested,' Kirsty said, lining them up next to Dani.

Rhona leaned one hand on the counter and stood behind Kirsty, peering over her shoulder at the chopping board. 'Tequila?'

There was plenty of room on the other side of Dani. She was in Kirsty's space for a reason: teasing and tempting her to the edge of sanity. It was no surprise her core already felt like it had its own pulse.

'I'm not leaving this flat without a few shots in me,' Dani said, pouring three generous measures.

'You got any beer left or do you want another?' Kirsty asked Rhona. Her hand was back under Kirsty's skirt, her fingers gliding over the lace of her pants on her hip.

Thankfully, Dani was too focused on the booze to have a clue what was happening. Kirsty batted Rhona away, playfully reaching back to grab at her waist.

Rhona's mischievous grin said she was having a great time torturing her.

'Rhona, grab the salt, will you?' Dani asked, passing Kirsty a lime wedge.

Shaker retrieved, they were good to go.

Kirsty held the wedge between finger and thumb, salt sprinkled on the back of her hand. She raised the shot glass with her other hand. 'To Izzy.'

'To keeping it together tonight,' Dani corrected.

Yeah, that sounded about right.

～

'So, did you tell her?' Izzy asked. She was dressed like a sexy clown. There was no end to Izzy's skills when it came to glamming up the mundane.

Kirsty looked across the crowded room to confirm Rhona wasn't within ear shot.

Bar Orama was absolutely hoaching tonight. There was barely room to move, but she and Izzy had carved out a little breathing space near the pinball machine for a chat. Rhona remained with Dani, Hazel, and Trip at a table on the other side of the room.

'The right moment didn't come up.'

Izzy playfully punched her arm. 'Idiot.'

'Hey,' Kirsty chided, rubbing her bicep. 'It's complicated.'

'It's bloody not. I've seen how she's been looking at you all night.'

She couldn't deny that. Kirsty had seen it too.

'I can't just blurt it out in public.'

'You sleep in the same bed.'

She didn't have a good excuse. She'd talked herself out of saying it a thousand times. Just the thought of uttering the words made her clammy.

'What's up?' Ashley asked, breaking free from the throng of people standing between tables. She was dressed like a feminine version of Arthur the Aardvark. Hazel was his best friend, Buster the Rabbit. Annoyingly, they looked damn cute.

'Kirsty's in love with Rhona,' Izzy stated. Kirsty returned her earlier punch. 'Oi. Fact's a fact.'

'Shut up, are you really?' Ashley asked, casting a conspiratorial glance towards their table.

'Everyone stop looking at her, okay? She's going to know we're talking about her.'

'So what? This is so exciting. Although, soon it will just be me and Kim left on the shelf,' Izzy said.

'What about Trip?' Kirsty asked.

'Ach, Trip's got a new girl every week. She hardly counts as single.'

'Is Dani seeing someone?' Ashley asked. Her voice claimed nonchalance but the furrow in her brow was so deep you could farm crops.

Izzy waved her away. 'Please. Dani's never been on the shelf to start with.'

'What's that supposed to mean?'

'Do you think I should tell her tonight?' Kirsty blurted. She would have happily let conversation surrounding her and Rhona die a death but it was better than Izzy waxing lyrical to Ashley about Dani. That ship had sailed, wrecked on the rocks, and was well and truly sunk.

'Course you should,' Ashley said, her eyebrows still knitted.

'Have you said it to Hazel?'

'Of course.' Her brow relaxed and a smile shifted her features to a sunnier mood. 'It has been like, three months since we started dating.'

'That just feels so quick,' Kirsty said. The whole concept was so scary and foreign; a year could have passed and she'd likely feel it equally too soon.

'We said it after two months. I think it's pretty normal.'

'I told Carly I loved her after three weeks,' Izzy said, blasé.

'Yeah, well, you're a hopeless romantic,' Kirsty chuckled. She turned to Ashley. 'Were you not scared?'

'Of what?'

'First time saying it ever is a big deal.'

'First time to Hazel?'

'No,' Kirsty huffed with frustration. 'Like, ever ever.'

'Did you not say it to Travis?'

'He said it to me. I didn't say it back.'

Ashley nodded gently, her eyebrows raised. 'Did not know that. Well then, you know it from the other side. How did that play out?'

Kirsty watched the bartender as he served. His costume effort was minimal but she couldn't blame him: this place was like a sauna. It was bad enough standing about, never mind serving. He'd gone for a T-shirt with the words *error 404: costume not found* printed in bold lettering. He'd shaved his normally bushy beard into a moustache for the occasion though, so props for that.

She didn't think there was any bad blood between them. Like, the immediate aftermath was a bit cringe, but he'd been civil ever since. Still, she felt guilty. She'd had her share of real arsehole moments in the past.

'He was crushed. I wasn't fazed. We're still friends.'

Ashley raised her shoulders as if to say *there you go*. 'Just tell her, then. What's the worst that can happen?'

'Yeah, but the difference is, I avoided Travis like the plague for a month after. I have to share a bed with Rhona.'

'Oh God, yeah. How's that working out?'

Izzy pulled a face and found Kirsty's elbow in her ribs. 'Are you not absolutely demented?' she asked.

'Yes,' Kirsty groaned. 'It's torture.'

'Let's get you another drink,' Izzy said, launching into action. 'Nothing like alcohol to loosen the old tongue. In more ways than one, if you get my drift.' She gave Kirsty a wink as she sauntered to the bar.

Tonight. Progress was happening tonight.

26

'Your rum,' Trip said, placing a round of drinks on the table.

She was dressed as the original Magnum P.I. and Rhona had serious tache envy. Trip looked amazing.

Rhona took a long draw on her drink, trying to calm her jangling insides. Kirsty wasn't even near her and she was driving her crazy.

She looked divine.

Respecting Kirsty's wishes to go slow were paramount, but her iron will was being tested to the absolute maximum this evening.

Trip shifted a shot of Jäger closer to Rhona. 'Bottoms up.'

'Jäger?'

Trip raised her glass in mock salute. 'The one and only.'

Rhona gently pushed it away. 'Nah. Not tonight.'

Dani didn't need to think twice and yanked it close. 'I'll do two.'

'You sure?' Rhona said, trying not to sound patronising.

'Hundred per cent.'

Rhona shrugged. Dani was a grown woman; she could do what she wanted. Although, Kirsty would likely be the one suffering the repercussions tomorrow.

'Why are you not doing shots?' Trip asked as she clinked glasses with Dani and downed the alcohol in one swift motion. Hazel had migrated to join the rest of the group on the other side of the room and the atmosphere had shifted to a whole new hemisphere. Dani was back to sentences, for a start.

'I don't want to get messy tonight. And I definitely don't want to be hungover tomorrow.'

'How come?' Dani asked, doing her second shot.

'I think Kirsty and I need to have a chat.'

Dani's face fell. 'A good chat or a bad chat? You're not leaving, are you?'

Rhona had grown to really like Dani over the last three months. She wasn't the cocky little shit she'd perceived her to be. Peek behind her walls and she was a sensitive wee soul who was fiercely loyal and had a huge heart. Whatever was going on with her and Ashley was killing her and it broke Rhona's heart to see her in pain.

'Good chat. Or at least I'm hoping it will be.'

Dani's shoulders slumped, relaxing at the clarification. 'Thank God. I quite like having someone else in the flat. Halves the moaning Kirsty does at me.'

Rhona gave her a playful kick to the shin under the table. 'You're a messy wee swine.'

'Gives her something to do.'

'Buckle up,' Trip said, her eyes on Ashley and Hazel as they approached.

'I need more shots,' Dani said, leaving in a flash.

Maybe Kirsty should know Dani was nearing car crash

potential. Rhona sucked on her cheek, wondering what to do.

'Hey guys,' Ashley said, taking a seat.

'Having a good time?' Trip asked. Even she sounded fed up with the situation.

Ashley had visited the flat to see Chet this week and for a brief moment Rhona got to experience the real Ashley and Dani. The laughter pealing from Dani's bedroom rarely stopped and when they'd surfaced for air and hung out in the kitchen for a while you could see it wasn't a simple friendship: the body language, the proximity, the way they spoke to each other. Kirsty had simply raised an eyebrow at Rhona and told it was best not to ask.

Ashley and Hazel were as cute as ever, just as Rhona remembered them from Lovefest, but tonight, with Dani? Ashley had barely spoken to her. Sitting opposite the two of them, Rhona needed a jacket to protect from the chill.

Did Hazel know about their past? Rhona would need to ask Kirsty later.

'We are, but probably heading home soon,' Ashley said.

'I've got a PT session tomorrow afternoon,' Hazel informed her, her face sullen.

'Working on a Sunday. No rest for the wicked, eh?' Rhona said, feeling like she needed to bridge the gap.

She twisted in her chair, searching for Dani. It took a second but the monkey tail eventually gave her away. She was at the end of the bar, talking to Kim. It had taken Rhona a hot moment to realise who Kim was dressed as tonight – her pink tank top and denim shorts didn't give much away – but when she spotted the huge watermelon on the bar later on in the night she'd twigged: the girl from Dirty Dancing. It was a good shout; Rhona was sweating in her get-up. Her normally comfy waistcoat was fast becoming a corset.

Dani did a shot before saying something in Kim's ear and another was poured. Kim's stern face said she was near cut-off.

Rhona turned back to the table. 'I'm going to find Kirsty.'

'She's still up the front, by the pinball machine,' Ashley replied.

The crowd was slowly thinning as the night wore on, so it wasn't hard to meander through to Kirsty.

Rhona put a hand on either hip and gave her a squeeze. 'Hey.'

Kirsty's face lit up. 'Hey. You okay?'

'Yeah, it's just. . .' Was this overstepping?

'Uh-huh?'

'Dani's just done four shots in a row.'

'Four?'

'Yeah. She did mine at the table and then went to the bar for more.'

'Fuck.'

'Yep.'

Kirsty's eyes narrowed as she watched her sister at the bar. 'Kim needs to cut her off.'

'I kind of got the impression they've had that chat already.'

'She'll be fine. Thanks for letting me know, though.'

~

DANI WAS NOT FINE.

It hadn't taken long for the alcohol to hit and soon it was obvious she needed to go home. Pronto.

A taxi or Uber was out of the question, so Kirsty and Rhona were forced to walk her back to Shawlands. What was usually a twenty-minute walk had so far taken forty.

Although they had stopped to get bottled water and chips in a bid to soak up some of the booze in Dani's stomach.

Rhona needn't have worried about feeling sober. The icy cold October air was making light work of bringing her round.

'You okay?' she asked Kirsty. She was doing a great job of keeping Dani moving by looping an arm under her and giving her no option but to comply.

'Fucking freezing.'

'Me too.'

'Sorry.'

'Why are you saying sorry?'

'Not exactly the end to the night that I'd envisaged.'

She was going to ask what Kirsty had imagined when Dani suddenly stopped, a hand to her mouth. Rhona stepped back, averting her eyes as Dani chundered all over the pavement. It was all water now, but she didn't didn't need to see it. The sound was enough.

At least there weren't many people still up and around to witness it.

After what felt like an age they were at the flat.

'If you're sick in the close, I'll kill you,' Kirsty growled.

Dani slurred an unintelligible reply.

They only lived on the first floor but hauling Dani up the stairs was like dragging a sack of potatoes, despite them both using a shoulder under each of her arms.

'Dani, you need to work with us here,' Rhona said, trying to keep her cool.

Dani's response was to look her dead in the eye, her stare cold and empty, before her cheeks puffed out and Rhona had water down her front.

There wasn't much left in her, but Rhona's black waistcoat now sported a lovely wet stain.

The growl that came out of Kirsty almost shook the walls. She silently raged, fumbling for the keys in her pocket.

'It's fine, it's just water,' Rhona said, holding on tight to Dani so Kirsty had her hands free,

'It's like living with a child.'

Rhona said nothing.

'Well, not a child, but you know what I mean,' Kirsty said as she kicked the door open and Dani staggered in.

'I'll take her to the bedroom. You get a bucket or something.'

Rhona walked Dani through to her room and deposited her on the bed. She rolled onto her back. 'No, no. Can't have you choking on your sick.' Rhona used her knee for leverage, but as soon as she had Dani in position she rolled right back.

'No. Not comfy,' she mumbled.

Kirsty appeared in the doorway. 'I'll need to get that monkey suit off. There's sick in the fur.' She gave Dani a whack on the arm. 'You're a fucking idiot.' She was fuming, but love still hugged her words.

Rhona would be the same with Michael. She'd do anything for that annoying wee git.

'I'll get her a glass of water, then I'm going to have a quick shower. It's not soaked through my shirt, but I still feel minging.'

Kirsty looked like she was going to be sick herself. 'Don't.'

'Guys, don't fight,' Dani slurred, her voice hazy.

'We're not fighting. We're just discussing how much of a nuisance you are.'

'Where's Chet?' She tried to sit up and nearly toppled over.

'He's on the dresser, staring at your drunk ass,' Kirsty jibed. The cat really didn't look impressed. Rhona had to suppress a laugh. She gave Kirsty a kiss on the cheek and left.

∽

Rhona froze, half the buttons of her shirt undone, as Kirsty entered the kitchen.

'Sorry, I thought—I was just going to shove this straight in the machine,' she said, sensing Kirsty's hesitation.

She held the balled-up monkey costume aloft. 'Great minds. I feel minging after trying to wrestle this thing off her.'

'She okay?' Rhona's fingers were still frozen on the button, unable to move or complete their task.

'She'll be fine. Probably feel like death tomorrow, but she'll be fine.' Kirsty shoved the costume in the machine with a thump. 'Let's not be hard on her tomorrow, yeah? I mean, I'm mad as hell right now, but she's going through a lot.'

Rhona nodded. 'Yeah, sure. I won't mention it.'

'What's happening here?' Kirsty asked, her eyes going to Rhona's hands.

She hadn't bothered to put any lights on and the faint moonlight illuminating the room perfectly highlighted Kirsty's features. There wasn't another person on earth who could look so good, even after wrestling a drunk monkey.

'This is going in the wash, then I'm going in the shower.'

Kirsty nodded, her eyes glinting. Without breaking eye contact she began to undo the gold buttons of her ringmaster coat.

Rhona watched in wonder as they popped open to

reveal Kirsty's bra and bare stomach. As she slipped the coat off and into the machine Rhona thought for sure her heart was going to hammer so hard it would launch out of her chest.

'Do you need a hand?' Kirsty asked.

Rhona's clit throbbed. She shook her head but the memo didn't reach her mouth. 'Yes, please.'

She listened to the sound of Kirsty's gentle breathing as her fingers relieved Rhona's of their hold on the button. They made light work of the rest. She had to remind herself that oxygen was a necessity as Kirsty slipped her hands under her shirt and guided it off her shoulders, her fingers tracing Rhona's arms. Her skin was electric, every hair standing to attention.

The shirt went in the wash.

If Rhona hadn't felt so damn manky she would have wrapped her arms around Kirsty without hesitation, but the cold air tickling her skin only served as a constant reminder of how sweaty and horrid she'd felt this evening. Now wasn't the time: she needed to wash to fully enjoy the moment. They'd waited so long; it had to be perfect.

She watched as Kirsty gulped, her eyes trailing the length of Rhona, taking her in like there would be an exam the next day.

'Shower?' Kirsty asked.

27

The harsh lighting of the bathroom made her wince, but with a view like Rhona there was no way she was keeping them closed a second longer.

She watched as Rhona leaned into the shower cubicle, turning the faucet on.

Kirsty had never been so vulnerable.

Which wasn't a surprise, given she was standing in her bra and a skirt that suddenly felt way too short.

She didn't quite know what to do with herself.

The idea had seemed great on impulse, but now she was acting it out, not so much. Her courage waned with every passing second.

She stepped closer, the temptation to touch her making Kirsty tremble.

'I don't know what to do with my hands,' Kirsty said with a quiet chuckle as her hand hovered over Rhona's side. This was unusual. She'd never been so nervous before sex.

But then she'd never experienced a build-up quite like this.

Rhona leaned forward, pulling Kirsty close, and kissed her. She smiled, breaking contact. 'Let's get clean.'

Kirsty watched in awe as Rhona undid the top button of her jeans and shimmied them to the floor.

The assignment was clear and there was no rush. They'd waited this long: why not take their time?

Kirsty locked eyes with Rhona as she unzipped her skirt before letting it fall to the floor. She kicked it aside.

The less clothes she had on, the less vulnerable she felt. Rhona's loving gaze wrapped around her like the steam pouring from the shower. Her goosebumps were gone. Warmth enveloped her.

Still, her smile faltered a little as she unclasped her bra. She held it in place. 'Together.'

Rhona didn't say a word. Instead, she reached round and mirrored Kirsty. Her breath staggered as Rhona let the bra fall to the ground, revealing her breasts and stiff nipples.

Kirsty had thought her clit was hard before, but it stiffened further as heat pooled between her legs, desire building low in her belly.

She let her own bra fall and sensed Rhona holding back, the urge to touch now a screaming voice in both their heads.

'You're perfect,' Rhona said, her voice so breathy it was almost inaudible over the shower.

'So are you.'

Kirsty couldn't hang about any longer. She slipped her pants off and stepped into the shower.

She watched Rhona do the same through the fogged-up glass and Kirsty greeted her with a bottle of shower gel, skooshing a dollop into her hand.

Kirsty's head spun as she watched Rhona rub the gel over her body, lathering her breasts and letting the suds run over her stomach down to the perfect patch of black hair between her legs. She stepped in, letting the jet of water wash her clean, and Kirsty could wait no more.

The heat of her flesh against Kirsty's sent a shiver down her spine, the goosebumps back in force. Hands were everywhere, taking in each curve and valley. Kirsty didn't know where to touch first.

She hadn't planned on getting her hair wet, but before she knew it they were under the shower head and Rhona had her pressed against the wall.

Her hand cupped Kirsty's breast, her thumb circling her nipple as she bit her neck. Kirsty groaned.

'Touch me,' Kirsty managed, her hands gripping Rhona's taut stomach.

She was done taking her time. Now speed was the only option.

Rhona, true to form, was more intent on teasing her.

She brushed the back of her hand down Kirsty's stomach, bringing it to a halt above Kirsty's centre.

'Are you sure?'

'Yes.'

The throbbing between Kirsty's legs was almost unbearable.

Rhona traced her other hand downward and grabbed Kirsty's bum, pulling her up. Kirsty wrapped her legs around her waist, steadying them against the wall. The ceramic tiles were cold on her skin.

She'd never been with a woman strong enough to do this. The way Rhona's breasts pressed into her own made her heart skip a beat.

It was a good thing she was craving speed, because there was no way she could last long once Rhona touched her.

With a final check they weren't in danger of slipping, Rhona guided a hand between them. A lion would be proud of the growl Kirsty made when Rhona's fingers made contact, skirting over her wet core before sliding inside her.

Kirsty tilted her head back and closed her eyes, revelling in the heady sensation of every thrust.

Rhona used her own hips to get purchase, pushing behind her hand to go deeper. As predicted, Kirsty's orgasm was already stoking, euphoria building with each passing second.

'Don't stop,' she panted.

'Never.'

Rhona's thumb joined the action, massaging her clit, and that was it. Kirsty was completely undone.

'Fuck,' she cried, her eyes screwing tighter.

Rhona kept going, drawing the orgasm out.

It was a good job Rhona was holding her against the wall, because she was pretty certain she had no bones left when she finally caught her breath.

'Wow,' Rhona said and Kirsty could feel the pull of her lips as she smiled against her neck.

'That was quick,' Kirsty replied, almost apologetic.

'Three months of pent-up frustration will do that.' She kissed Kirsty as she slid her fingers free. 'I found it hot.'

She could already feel round two brewing, but first there was another itch to satisfy.

Kirsty dropped her feet to the floor, surprised to find they could support her.

Rhona didn't take much encouragement to swap places and Kirsty gently backed her into the corner of the shower cubicle.

'Now it's my turn to have some fun,' she said, running a single finger down Rhona's chest, between her breasts, and finally stopping at her belly button.

A wicked smile spread over Rhona's face as Kirsty dropped to her knees, her face now level with her centre.

She kissed just above Rhona's pubic hair while running a hand up the back of her leg. She felt Rhona's muscles tense as she reached her thigh, anticipation heightening every touch.

With a gentle pat she lifted Rhona's leg over her shoulder, exposing her core. Kirsty's heart raced at the sight, the pulse between her legs still riding high from her own orgasm.

Cupping Rhona's bum she edged her closer, her tongue running her length and finding her hardened clit.

Her knees already ached a little from the hard floor of the shower but something told her she needn't worry: this wouldn't take long.

Rhona's hips arched as she circled her tongue over the hard nub before gently sucking.

A low guttural moan confirmed she was going in the right direction.

Shifting into a better position she gently slid two fingers into Rhona's wet centre, keeping rhythm with her tongue.

She could do this forever, but sadly it wasn't to be. Rhona's internal walls tightened, her hips bucking as she came.

Rhona's hand gripped the back of Kirsty's head, pulling her closer as the orgasm rippled through her muscles.

Her hand relaxed, signalling for Kirsty to stop.

Kirsty panted against her core, physically and mentally exhausted. Her chest ached, the effort of holding everything together for so long taking its toll. This moment, though, this exact point in time, so tiny you could balance it on a pinhead: for a split second, everything was perfect and Kirsty had never felt so happy.

'You okay?' Rhona asked, her hand stroking Kirsty's temple.

She used Rhona's hips for leverage and support, her own legs shaky as she stood. 'I'm good. Just savouring the moment.'

Rhona pulled her in for a kiss. 'Fancy savouring it further in bed?'

'Try and stop me.'

28

Kirsty pressed her face against Rhona's chest as she woke up.

They'd slept like this all night – Kirsty's arm and leg draped over her, Rhona's arm snaked under her neck, resting on her back – and although she desperately needed to pee she'd found herself staring at Kirsty for the last half hour, unable to tear herself away.

Even asleep, she was gorgeous.

'You awake?' Kirsty asked, her voice groggy.

'Yep.' Rhona kissed the top of her head.

The feeling of Kirsty's bare skin against hers was a pure hit of dopamine. They'd spooned plenty of times in the last week, but without clothes it was next level.

'You sleep okay?' Kirsty asked, rising onto her forearm to make eye contact with Rhona.

'Amazing. You?'

'Yeah. I should probably check on Dani. What time is it?' She scrunched an eye up as she spoke. Rhona had never seen anything cuter.

'It's nearly one.'

'One?!'

'You late for something?' Rhona chuckled.

Kirsty collapsed back onto her chest, her free hand quickly finding one of Rhona's breasts. 'I'm not going anywhere with these boobs in my bed.'

'I do need to pee though. Sorry.'

'Can you leave them here?' She gave a little squeeze for good measure.

'You check on Dani and I'll pee. Me and my boobs will meet you back here.'

Rhona grabbed her pyjamas and pulled them on before padding through the bathroom. It felt like a different place to where they'd had sex last night. The memory was already saved in her mind as flawless, every detail exact: the bathroom was near heavenly.

This morning it looked a little worse for wear.

She gathered up their clothes after she'd peed and beelined for the washing machine, putting a cycle on.

Doesn't matter how fantastic life is: adulthood chugs on regardless.

She filled a glass with water and wandered back to the bedroom, only to find it empty. She chapped on Dani's door and got the okay to enter.

Dani looked like death itself.

'That better be for me,' she said, her voice so husky you could grate cheese on it.

'It wasn't, but you can have it if you want,' Rhona said, placing the glass on Dani's bedside table.

She launched onto the double bed, slotting in beside Kirsty, purposely having a wee bounce as she got comfy.

'Don't, don't,' Dani pleaded, a hand on her stomach.

Kirsty chuckled, using the mattress for leverage as she

added a few bounces of her own. 'What's up? Not feeling good?'

Her cheeks pooched and Kirsty stilled, taking the hint.

'Can I get you anything?' Rhona asked, resting her chin on Kirsty's shoulder as she studied Dani.

Her face was drained and her hair matted. Nicer things had been spotted coming out of woods and inspiring folklore.

'I probably just need some food, then I'll be fine.'

'You paying?' Rhona asked.

Dani groaned.

'Do you remember spewing on Rhona?' Kirsty asked.

Dani clamped two hands over her face. 'You're kidding. Did I really?'

'Yep.'

'Here or at the pub? I don't remember leaving.'

'Here.'

'Thank fuck.' There was a pause before an eye peeked out between her fingers. 'Sorry, Rhona.'

'It's cool. You missed my boots, that's the main thing.'

'Did Ashley see me like that?'

'She'd left long before then,' Kirsty replied.

Dani flung two hands to the ceiling and winced as if movement hurt. 'There is a God.'

'So, food's on you, yeah?' Rhona asked.

Dani fumbled for her phone and flung it onto the bed by Kirsty. 'Knock yourselves out.'

∽

A FEW WEEKS LATER, Rhona parked her car outside her brother's bungalow in the Edinburgh suburb of Ravelston. She'd always liked Michael's house, but the area was far too suburban for her liking. She preferred being close to the action. No one wants to hop on a bus if they fancy grabbing a coffee. The closer her fingers were to the pulse of the city the better.

It was good to stand after the drive. It shouldn't have taken long, but an accident just before Linlithgow had brought traffic to a standstill, adding a chunk of time. She rolled her neck, loosening her muscles.

A neighbour was in his drive, washing the car. He raised his hand as a hello, and Rhona returned a nod and a smile.

'Here to see Michael?' he shouted, far too cheery and awake for a Saturday morning. God, she needed more coffee.

She almost replied with a joke – *brown skin gave me away, eh?* – but he didn't seem the type to get her humour. She played it safe instead. 'He's gone crazy in IKEA. Needs me to do the hard work putting it together.'

He gave a knowing nod. 'Have fun!'

She grabbed her duffel bag from the boot and creaked the wrought iron gate open. The garden looked good: in summer the borders would be full of flowers and fauna, but it was all asleep just now, the soil weed-free and neat. The lawn was pristine.

Who would care for it when the baby came?

Maybe she could nip through and mow it for them now and again. Wouldn't be hard. And it would be a great excuse to see her nibling.

Or she could move to Edinburgh.

Nope. That definitely felt wrong. Like putting on someone else's trainers – right size and shape, but the fit was all weird and uncomfortable.

Glasgow was fast becoming an anchor point, with Kirsty the beacon in its centre.

Rhona unzipped the pocket of her bag and rummaged for her keys. Nothing. *Shit.* She'd left them at home.

She knocked on the door and waited, the chilly winter air nipping at her cheeks.

She'd still not told Kirsty that she loved her and it was getting harder to contain by the day. The thing was, when did they officially start? How soon was too soon? Technically they'd only been official for a few weeks. Way too soon for the L-word.

The door opened and Charlene enveloped her in a hug.

'Rhona!' she beamed, still squeezing her tight. 'It's been ages.'

'It has been, eh?' she said, breaking free. 'I've missed you.'

'You too. Come in, come in.'

She moved aside and Rhona finally got out of the cold. With the door closed, she dropped her bag to the ground, taking Charlene's hands in her own and stepping back to admire her. 'Look at you! A proper bump and everything. You look amazing.' She'd always been incredibly petite and only came up to Rhona's shoulder, which only made the growing baby bump look more pronounced. From the front it wasn't too obvious, but from the side it looked like she was smuggling a watermelon.

Charlene blushed. 'Thank you. Slowly getting used to it all.'

'And what about me?' Michael said, appearing in the hall.

Rhona gave his head a shove before pulling him into a tight hug. 'You're the same scruffy arsehole I know and love.'

'Cup of tea?' Charlene asked, on her way to the kitchen.

'Coffee if you have it, please.'

'No probs. I'll get that and join you in a bit. You'd better start now. We can catch up while we work.'

'Is there a lot?' Rhona asked. She knew they'd bought a few things, but Charlene's tone hinted she might be in for a shock.

'Erm, quite a bit, yeah,' Michael replied with a cringe.

He wasn't bloody lying. The entire far wall was lined with flat-pack boxes, ready and waiting to be assembled. 'Holy shit.'

'For small people, babies need a heck of a lot of stuff.'

CRIB DONE, Rhona now worked on the changing table while Charlene tackled a chest of drawers. Michael was sorting the drawers for both units.

'So, that's our news,' Charlene said, having filled Rhona in on the last few months – promotions, car trouble, and neighbourhood scandal. 'What's happening with you?'

Rhona whacked two pieces together: a dowel not playing games and refusing to go in the hole. *If in doubt, give it a whack. Never fails.*

'Not much. Weddings have pretty much dried up, but I've been taking work for engagement shoots and a few other random jobs.'

'As long as you're busy,' Charlene soothed.

'How's Niall?' Michael asked.

Heat flushed Rhona's cheeks. She hadn't told Michael or her parents she was moving in with Kirsty. It all felt kind of messy and she wasn't sure if staying was the right thing to do, certain it would be nothing but torture and she'd soon move home.

He lifted his eyes from the screw he was tightening. 'Your silence is noted. You haven't murdered him, have you?'

'It was close,' Rhona said, getting to her knees to put more weight on the unit. The dowels were causing real issues. 'I moved out a while ago.'

'You did? Shit, sorry. I must have totally forgotten.'

Rhona stood, her thighs aching. She gave them a shake as she arched her back with a satisfying crack. 'Don't worry, I didn't tell you.'

She didn't have to look to know Charlene and Michael were exchanging glances.

'It was complicated,' she said, getting back to work.

'Complicated,' Michael repeated like he'd just heard the word for the first time. 'So, where are you now?'

'Shawlands. Actually, that reminds me. I brought you guys scones. Best scones you've ever tasted. Don't let me leave with them.'

'Where's Shawlands?' Charlene asked. 'And thank you for the scones. This baby is making me ravenous.'

'It's in the south of Glasgow,' Rhona said, opting to sit on the floor, legs straddling the changing station. Just the top to go now.

'On your own?' Michael asked, clearly picking up on her reluctance.

'I, erm, I'm kind of seeing someone.'

'There you go. Jesus, Rhona. It's like pulling teeth with you sometimes,' he joked, throwing a spare dowel and hitting her in the head.

'You know I don't like talking about relationship stuff.' She didn't. It put her stomach in knots.

'So like Dad sometimes,' Michael said with a grin. He turned to Charlene. 'Babe, can you move these out of the way? I could at least be doing dowels on the wardrobe unit then.'

Rhona wondered if she should help. Charlene was more

than capable, but being pregnant and all it felt right to ask. But they had their routine down and she didn't want to offend. She kept shtum.

'So, what's her name?' Charlene asked as she moved the drawers.

'Kirsty.' Rhona kept her eyes on the pile of screws she was sorting into size order.

'Kirsty, nice. Serious then?' Charlene enquired as she sat back on the ground. 'Must be, to move in together.'

'You've kept that a good secret,' Michael added. 'You've been in Glasgow since February. Been going on that long?'

'Since . . .' Rhona hummed and hawed. They met in August. But that didn't count. They also had their failed date then, but you could hardly declare that a starting point. Second kiss? Nah. Kirsty had dragged her feet after it. The third? Probably. God, what a roller coaster it had been. 'Last month,' she finally settled on.

'And you've already moved in together?' Charlene blurted.

'I was living with her before we got together.'

'Ah,' Michael said, seemingly understanding.

'Like I said, it's complicated.'

'She's not, like, married or something?' Michael asked, leaning over the flat panel and positioning a line of screws.

Rhona shot him a steely glare that could bore a hole through him quicker than the screwdriver she was currently wielding. 'Yes, Michael. I'm currently living with my lover, her husband, and their eight children,' she said, her voice deadpan.

He laughed. 'Alright. Just asking.'

'So, you're not the bit on the side. Why's it complicated?' Charlene asked, getting to her feet and moving her completed piece to the side with a shove of her hip. Only a dozen or so more boxes to go.

'Ugh. It's me that's causing the issues.'

'No change there.'

Rhona ignored her brother and carried on. 'She's worried I'm not coming back, or whatever, after I go travelling.'

'But you are, yeah?' Charlene asked, grappling with a box.

Rhona sprung to her feet. 'No heavy lifting, missus.' She waddled the box over to Charlene's area. 'I am coming back, yeah. I just don't know if I want to commit to Glasgow.'

Michael made a noise somewhere between a cough and a groan.

'Yes?' Rhona asked, towering over him, hands on hips.

'Hmm?' he said, sucking on his lips, flashing her huge doe eyes.

'Spit it out, man.' She picked up one of his completed drawers and walked it back to her unit.

'This is so typically you.'

'How come?' she nearly shouted.

'With relationships you fall faster than a cannonball, but with everything else, you're a commitment-phobe through and through.'

'Am not.'

'Are so.'

'Am not.'

'Are so.'

'I cannot wait to have children,' Charlene sighed to no one in particular.

'Give an example,' Rhona commanded. She already knew what he was going to say. *Indecisive* would be her chosen word. She had no trouble committing. It was deciding on what to commit to that was the issue.

'University. How long did you hum and haw about that?'

'Big decision.'

'Manchester.'

'Serious repercussions.'

'What car to get.'

'Not to be taken lightly.'

'June's engagement ring.'

'Thanks for bringing that up—'

'Sorry.'

'—but again. Big decision.'

'Right, look, that was wrong of me to mention, but my point is: you'd sooner commit to a tattoo than pick somewhere to live. When it comes to stuff like this you get all weird.'

'I am not weird.'

'Guys,' Charlene interjected. She was going to nail this parenting shit.

'Okay, not weird. But it's like,' he stopped what he was doing and locked eyes with Rhona. 'You're fine when it's your heart – you can listen to that no bother. But as soon as you get your head involved you're a spiralling mess.'

'Charming.' She pulled a face.

'Lead with your heart, not your head. Being happy doesn't need to be complicated.'

'You make it sound so easy,' Rhona said with a huff.

He was right, but she wasn't going to admit that.

She would love to just go with her gut, but her head wouldn't allow it. It had to expand every possibility, poke holes and find faults, problem solve. She liked to think it made for calculated conclusions, but really it just tied her in knots, overcomplicating everything.

Realistically, she knew no plan was perfect, but the thought of choosing wrong terrified her. Some choices had repercussions for years, if not a lifetime. There was no point rushing into something if it wasn't concrete in her mind.

'The best pace is your own pace,' Charlene said, giving Rhona a half smile. 'When you're ready to make a decision you'll do just that. Can we have a scone now? It's all I've thought about since you mentioned them.'

Rhona laughed. 'Three scones coming right up. But jam and butter? Butter and jam? Butter *or* jam? How ever will I decide?' she said dramatically, leaving behind a chuckling Michael and Charlene.

29

Sleet battered the window as Kirsty nuzzled into Rhona's chest. December brought relentless shifts at work and she was absolutely done. But still, she wasn't ready to sleep.

Rhona's skin against hers as they held each other after sex was too good to waste.

'How long do you think we've been dating?' Rhona mumbled into Kirsty's hair.

Tough question. 'Depends on what you count as the start.'

'Exactly. Like, when's our anniversary?'

'Already planning my present?'

'I'm just hoping I've not missed it,' Rhona said with a chuckle. She traced lazy shapes on Kirsty's back, each pass of her fingers like a shot of happiness to her heart.

'First date doesn't count. I think maybe, when you moved in?'

'Are we decided on that?'

'You think it was another time?'

'No, no. Just making sure we're agreed.'

'So, middle of October. We've been together nearly two months,' Kirsty said.

'But I've known you for five.'

'Correct. Gone quick, hasn't it?'

'Too quick.'

Where was this going? The countdown to the twenty-seventh forever loomed. She'd even gifted Dani the advent calendar Mum got her. It felt like a countdown to Rhona leaving, not Christmas. There was no way she could enjoy the chocolate.

The air was heavy, silence suddenly all consuming, like TV static.

She could feel the beat of Rhona's heart as it drummed hard on her ribs. Her fingers stopped skimming Kirsty's back.

Oh God.

Kirsty stilled, bracing for something horrible.

'I love you,' Rhona said, her voice quiet.

Kirsty had to rewind and play the moment again, just to be sure she had heard correctly.

She raised herself to look Rhona in the eye. She looked scared. Where had this insecurity come from? Kirsty's heart clenched at the thought of her putting doubt in Rhona's head.

'I love you too.' Simple words, but they were like bullets, more powerful than Kirsty could imagine. It was like a building had been sat on her chest and she was suddenly free. She wanted to gasp air and stretch her limbs.

Tears rimmed Rhona's eyes. She gulped before speaking. 'I've been wanting to say that for a while.'

'Me too.' Kirsty kissed her.

The atmosphere was charged. Rhona might as well have just proposed, for how Kirsty felt. This was monumental.

She should get a plaque above the bed. *On this day, in this spot, Kirsty Hamilton said 'I love you' to Rhona Devi.*

What now? She'd never done this before.

A parade, national holiday, maybe a statue? Any of them felt suitably fitting.

Rhona grinned. 'It feels so good to have that out there.'

'We should have a proper date,' Kirsty said, giving Rhona another kiss. 'I'm off on Sunday. Want to do something on Saturday night?'

'That would be nice. We've not actually had a proper date. Never one we've seen through to the end, anyway.'

A new sentence stuck in Kirsty's throat. She couldn't sit on this one for as long. Time was running out. 'Does this mean you'll come back to Glasgow?'

Rhona's eyes broke contact for a split second. It was enough for Kirsty to guess what was coming.

'Let's not talk about it,' she said, slumping back to Rhona's chest. She didn't want to tarnish the moment they'd just shared.

It was too late, though. 'No, we'll need to talk about it sooner or later. We should chat now.'

'You're still not decided, then.'

'I just need time.'

'That's the one thing we don't have right now. What's holding you back?'

Rhona's muscles stiffened. 'It just doesn't feel right. Something's missing. I can't explain it.'

Kirsty forced herself up again. 'So basically, I'm not enough.'

'I didn't say that.'

'You're not denying it, though.'

Rhona rolled her eyes. 'Don't.'

'Excuse me?'

'Don't pick a fight where there isn't one.'

Kirsty scoffed. 'One minute you're saying you love me, the next you're debating moving to Sri Lanka.'

'Now you're really reaching.'

Anger seared through Kirsty like pure heat. Being naked was completely the wrong option. Being near Rhona was completely the wrong option.

She pulled herself free and grabbed her pyjamas, yanking them on.

'Kirsty,' Rhona pleaded, sitting up.

She stomped to the kitchen and didn't even have a glass out before Rhona's footsteps followed. She ignored her and turned the tap on.

She kept her back to the room as she took a slow sip of water. Her hands trembled; tears fogged her vision.

She could never have a happy moment. There always had to be something to balance it out. The higher the high, the lower the low.

Rhona's arms wrapped around her waist and her head settled on Kirsty's shoulder.

'I'm coming back to Scotland. That's not up for debate. And you're the reason for that. I didn't say because I didn't want to freak you out.'

'Why would I freak out?'

'You've never been in a relationship. It's a huge step: to be the reason someone moves. I didn't want you to think I was coming on too strong or being too much.'

It was only then that Kirsty realised she'd been holding her breath. She relaxed, putting the glass down.

'Why not Glasgow, then?' Her voice was quiet but she might as well have shouted the question into the silent room.

'It might be. I just don't want to be rushed into a decision.'

Kirsty barked with laughter. 'Rushed?'

Even Rhona had to laugh. 'Okay. Rushed isn't the right word. Just . . . be patient with me.'

'Patient? You think I've been anything but patient?' She spun to face Rhona. 'All I ever fucking do is wait, Rhona. You've had me living in limbo for weeks.'

'Me?'

'Yes.'

'You're the one who didn't want to take things further. And I respected that.'

Kirsty groaned, pushing past Rhona to pace in the dark kitchen. 'I didn't want to take things further because I don't have a clue what this is.' She gestured to the empty space between them.

'Why can't you just enjoy what we have?'

'Because,' Kirsty almost shouted before remembering Dani was asleep. 'All I ever think about is the fact you're leaving and you might not come back.'

'But I am coming back.'

Kirsty wanted to scream and stamp her feet. Rhona just wasn't getting it. She rubbed at her temple, wearing out the wooden floor of the kitchen as she walked back and forth. Rhona didn't budge from leaning on the counter. 'So, I'm not enough. What's missing? What's going to magically make you call somewhere home?'

Rhona crossed her arms. Even in the darkness she could see tears rimming her eyes. The last thing she wanted to do was upset Rhona, but she needed to know. It was now or never.

'I don't know, Kirsty,' Rhona said through gritted teeth. 'I wish I had the answers but I don't. I didn't move to Glasgow to fall in love. I moved here to make money and leave.'

'Apologies for the inconvenience.'

'I didn't mean it like that.' Rhona rubbed at her eyes, scrunching them closed as she thought. 'I'm no good at making decisions.'

'Well, let me make the decision for you. Come back to Glasgow. We can be happy.'

'And what if that's wrong? What if I'm no good? You hardly know me.'

'Well, I'll get to know you. That's the point.'

Quiet descended. Kirsty stepped closer to Rhona but she turned away, attempting to hide the tears that stained her face.

Kirsty willed her voice to calm. 'What's the worst that can happen? You move to Glasgow and we don't work out? Is that what's worrying you?'

'Kirsty,' Rhona huffed. 'I don't have a straight answer for you. Something isn't right. That's all I can say.'

'So, that's it? Will you know by the time you leave, or are you just going to swan off and leave me waiting until you decide to come back?'

'I'll know by the time I leave.'

Kirsty pretended to look at the clock on the wall above the breakfast bar. 'So, what time does divine intervention hit? Because I've known you five months and you're still no closer to making a decision. What's going to change in the next few weeks?'

Rhona chewed on her cheek, still unable to look at Kirsty.

'You're going to leave and I'll still be none the wiser, aren't you?' When Rhona said nothing she repeated herself. 'Aren't you?'

'Night, Kirsty.' Her voice was monotone, a glaring full stop on the conversation.

Kirsty's quiet chuckle rang through the room, the noise remaining in the air as if echoing, mocking them. She turned to leave, but not before making one final point. 'Do us all a favour and stop being so fucking selfish.'

30

Rhona lay on the sofa, taking a break from her computer. She'd done a family portrait shoot yesterday. Work was still coming; it was just going in tangents to what she'd expected from her life.

She finally understood Kirsty's craving for stability. It would be great to have weddings booked for when she returned. It had been comforting to look at her diary with June and pretty much know her cash flow for the next twelve months. Now, she looked at her diary and flipped between *Will I even be a photographer?* and *How will I find the work?*

She'd done okay so far with finding stuff, but it was bloody exhausting. Her nerves were constantly on edge:; you couldn't plan one week to the next sometimes.

As for her other worry: would she end up like June and have to admit defeat? A guaranteed pay cheque was looking more tempting by the day.

She'd shelved the idea of travelling and working. It might work for Tibs the cat, but she didn't have a Kirsty.

Things were still somewhat frosty between them, even a

week after their fight. Kirsty's words rang in Rhona's ears, hitting a nerve. She was right. But Rhona was too stubborn to admit it.

This trip was meant to be a luxury, a reward for getting through all that shit with June. Now it felt like a massive thorn in her side.

She hated Kirsty being mad at her.

The problem was: how the heck could she fix things?

Her phone buzzed against the coffee table. Amber. She hit the silence button, not in the mood to talk.

For the first time in a long time, Rhona was feeling down right melancholy.

She contemplated going to bed and giving into the spiralling doom. These photos weren't due for another week anyway.

Her phone buzzed again. Weird. Pocket dial?

Rhona stared out of the window, her view of the opposite roof framed by grey sky. It was too cold for snow, but there was something in the air. Probably rain, knowing Glasgow. Certainly not the right weather for a walk. Although, she could. Get a wee takeaway coffee from Kirsty, clear her head in the fresh air.

As soon as her phone stopped rumbling against the wooden veneer it started again. Rhona sat up, her heart stuttering. Was something wrong? Amber never did this.

Her hand trembled as she picked up the phone, her stomach already twisting itself into a knot.

'Amber?' Her voice was unsure, as if a paramedic might be more likely to answer than her friend. Why would they call her, though?!

'Rhona!' Amber squealed, high on excitement. *Okay. Not in danger – good.* 'Thank God you answered. I was about to lose hope.'

'You okay?'

'Good question. How quickly can you be in town? Browns, to be exact. You know where that is? Off George Square?'

She could hear the sound of traffic in the background and the occasional roar of a passing bus engine drowned Amber out.

'What's going on?' There was a pause. Rhona checked her phone, still connected. 'Amber?'

'Hey, sorry! Just giving a drink order through the window.'

'What's going on?' Rhona asked again, more stern. She was in no mood for a stupid drunken phonecall that went in circles.

'Sorry, sorry. My mind is *scattered*. I thought this was a friendly meeting.' She dropped her voice and Rhona had to strain to listen, narrowing her eyes as if that might turn up the volume. 'I'm with Abigail Conti.'

Rhona just about dropped the fucking phone.

Abigail Conti was a renowned wedding planner. Not just in Glasgow. Not just in Scotland. And not just the UK. She was big. Like, big with a capital B. If you wanted a high-end wedding, you went to Abigail. It wasn't all celebrities; the money-laden hoi polloi were her main bread and butter. The kind that thought ninety for a car was cheap.

'How do you know her?' Rhona hissed. Abi had nearly a million followers on TikTok and a fair amount on her other social media, too. She wasn't the type of woman you just sent a message to or bumped into when doing your Tesco shop. Her PAs probably had PAs.

'She's followed my Instagram for years. We've spoken on and off for a while now.'

'You kept that quiet.'

'I hardly thought it would come to anything.'

'Still, get you hobnobbing with the wedding elite. You're not the woman I thought I knew,' Rhona joked, giddy with excitement.

'Right, listen. She needs you down here now. I thought this was a friendly thing but it's gone sideways. She loves your stuff. This could be massive, Rhona.'

Rhona's stomach twisted for a whole new reason.

'Me?'

'Well, us. But you're part of the package.'

'There's a package?'

'If you hop a taxi you can be here in thirty mins, yeah?'

'Probably yeah.'

'Thank fuck. I'm shitting myself.'

Rhona's stomach was doing equally impressive flips.

'Right, I'd better go. She's got the champagne out. Be quick, or I'm going to be steaming and God knows what I'll agree to.'

'Just make sure she signs a cheque at least.'

༄

Thirty minutes later, Rhona was sitting in a taxi, currently stopped at the lights near Trongate. Her leg wouldn't stop bouncing.

Her nerves were so wound up they'd developed their own nerves, which in turn had wound tighter.

She had no idea what this meeting was about, or if it would even come to anything, but this was massive.

She'd had no time to text Kirsty but there was too much to explain: it would be better done face to face anyway. No matter the outcome, this needed celebrating. She'd grab some prosecco on the way home.

The taxi turned into George Square and came to a halt. Adrenaline made up ninety-nine per cent of Rhona's body now. She was almost vibrating with nerves and anticipation.

She hopped out and ran-walked to the stone canopy outside Browns, taking a second to make sure her top and coat were just as they should be. She'd stuck with the messy bun her hair was in: there was no time for styling the untamable.

Heat blasted out as she opened the door and the bottom of Rhona's stomach about escaped with it. *Abi is just a woman, a person like me. Nothing to be scared of.*

Amber sprung to her feet on the other side of the opulent restaurant and signalled Rhona over with a little wave.

Abi turned to face her with an award-winning smile. This was really happening. She looked just like her photos: shoulder-length brown wavy hair, brown eyes, and a pearly white smile. Her short-sleeved shirt was nothing special, but on her it wouldn't be out of place on the cover of *Vogue*.

Rhona's legs felt like jelly as she walked through the bar area of the art deco-styled restaurant. This place was swish. It had a real ladies-who-lunch feel about it. Rhona felt like a sore thumb: less than an hour ago she was lounging on her sofa in a pair of manky joggers.

Time to put on a show.

She turned her smile to full beam. 'Abigail, hi. I'm Rhona,' she said, extending a hand for Abigail to shake. She returned it: nice and firm.

'Please, call me Abi.'

Amber was quiet, a half-drunk glass of fizz held in front of her lips. Presumably without it she would spill a thousand excited sentences in Rhona's direction.

Rhona folded her coat and hung it over the back of her

chair before sitting.

'So,' Abi said, giving Rhona a moment to get comfy. 'Before I start, glass of fizz?'

Rhona nodded. 'Are we celebrating something?' she asked with a coy smile and quick glance at Amber.

'Hopefully,' Abi said, with an equally cheeky grin. 'And any excuse to drink at lunchtime, eh?'

'I'll drink to that,' Rhona replied, taking a sip. Did that make sense? Didn't matter. She'd said it now. God, alcohol was a good shout. Even one sip was taking the edge off the jangling bag of nerves she currently was.

'Did Amber tell you what we've been chatting about?' Abi asked.

'Not really. Apart from that you like our work.'

'You won a Masters of Wedding Photography award for your work, didn't you?'

She'd done her research; this woman was serious. A fresh wave of adrenaline pumped through Rhona's veins. 'I did. But the company I was associated with then, I have nothing to do with it now.'

'Don't worry. I've already separated the wheat from the chaff. It's your work I'm interested in. Not your unscrupulous ex.'

Rhona gulped, trying to free the words caught in her throat. It didn't work.

She continued, 'Your work this summer was also amazing. I wouldn't be surprised if you won another. Your photos at Loch Earn blew me away.'

'Thank you.' Heat radiated from Rhona's cheeks. She didn't know what else to say.

'I'll cut to the chase,' Abi said, filling the silence. Amber was literally on the edge of her seat. 'Our client base is growing and I've had to let one of my current team go. I'm looking to hire new photographers on a freelance basis, and add them to our repertoire. You'll get a small team on location. Now, I've already discussed the logistics with Amber. This is where you come in.'

Rhona's eyes felt like saucers. Was this real life?

'What do you need me to do?' Rhona asked.

Amber chipped in. 'I've explained about my family commitments and what that might entail in the future. Plus, I already have bookings for next year. Which is where you come in. Although, Abi knows about your plans to travel this month.'

They had been busy. Rhona nodded, dying to know what Abi was going to ask of her.

'As you can imagine, we get a lot of clients who require their dream day to be abroad. The location wedding will never fall out of fashion. They can range from Iceland to Morocco: anywhere, when it comes to my clients.'

'Nice.' It was all Rhona could manage. Every other word had fallen out her of head.

'Equally, a huge draw for our clients is having a dream Highland wedding. We're talking proper remote, lochside affairs. Particularly popular with our American clients, those ones.'

'I can imagine,' Rhona said, putting two and two together and hopefully getting the same answer as Abi.

Abi's phone vibrated against the marble table, making Rhona jump.

She looked at the name and scrunched her face up before turning her attention to the photographers. 'Sorry, guys. I'd better take this.' She answered the call as she got up, disappearing to a quiet section of the restaurant.

Amber turned to Rhona so quickly it was a surprise she didn't get whiplash. 'Pal! Can you believe it?'

'I don't quite know what I'm meant to be believing yet.'

Amber grabbed Rhona's hand, squeezing it tight. 'She's going to ask you to do the location weddings.' She relaxed back in her chair, a smile wider than the Clyde plastering her face. 'Me and you, the dream team, back together again.'

'Me? Why does she want me?'

'Because you're amazing! We're amazing! You know the shoot I did at Glengarry Hotel? She said it was some of the best wedding photography she's ever seen.'

'Shut up.'

'I swear,' Amber said, a hand over her heart. Her face turned serious as she leaned closer to Rhona. 'I know you're still undecided about what you want to do in the future, so don't feel you need to answer today. If you don't want to do it, I'm sure Abi and I can work something out.'

'You're going to take her offer?'

'Hell, yes! I've heard rumours about how much she pays. I can still do my own stuff too. We're not exclusive to her books.'

Interesting. Very interesting.

Rhona and Amber sat up straight as Abi made her way back to the table. 'Sorry, ladies. Work emergency.'

'Don't worry about it,' Rhona said, waving her hand in the air as if to dismiss the thought.

'So, where was I?'

'In the middle of describing my dream job, by the sounds of it,' Rhona said, unable to help herself.

Abi's grin returned. 'I'm glad you think so. A lot of people are put off by the travel. My wife and I have two kids, so I totally get it. But I think you and Amber complement each other beautifully. It sounds like something you'd like to discuss further, then?'

Rhona only just stopped herself from making a smart

remark. 'Yes, definitely, I'd love that.'

Abi's features softened, like a weight had been lifted. 'Fantastic. Are you free this weekend?'

'I could definitely manage a meeting this weekend.'

Amber and Rhona exchanged looks. Amber nodded in agreement.

'Brilliant,' Abi said, that conspiratorial smile quirking her lips again. 'What about a little more than a meeting, Rhona? You're away soon, so your passport's valid, yes?'

'Yes?' Rhona replied, the short word lasting a lifetime longer than usual.

'Are you free this afternoon to fill out some paperwork? We can have a proper meeting to discuss future plans, of course. I'll have my PA arrange it for next week.'

'Yes,' Rhona replied again. Why did it feel like she was being backed into a corner?

'Okay. And one final question: how do you feel about going to Tuscany tonight? I'm a photographer short for a project and up shit creek without a paddle.'

'Tuscany?' Rhona spluttered.

'I know it's really short notice, but it's only until Sunday.'

'Tuscany? Until Sunday?'

Abi nodded. 'Sorry, I know. I'm clutching at straws.' She took Rhona's hand in her own. 'I wouldn't usually throw someone in at the deep end, but I know you can handle it.'

Not the worst corner to be backed into by any means. She wasn't doing anything. How could she say no? 'I'm sure I can manage that, yeah.'

Rhona gulped. Her throat was dry and her mouth wet all at the same time. This was crazy, once in a lifetime stuff.

'Fantastic. Let's finish off this bottle, then we can take a walk to my office.'

Ask and you shall receive. She couldn't wait to tell Kirsty.

31

'It's not, though, is it?' Kirsty asked Dani as she made a latte.

'How?'

'Because how can it be self-sabotage? It's self-preservation.'

'Same thing.'

Kirsty rolled her eyes. 'Completely different.'

'You're the expert now?' Dani said with a chuckle.

'I know more than you.'

Today had been absolutely manic. Christmas shoppers were out in force and if Kirsty never saw another hot chocolate again it would be too soon. Which was too bad, because her next order was for four of the blasted things. It was so busy that Tara had been drafted to work behind the counter, taking orders and barking them at Dani for takeaways. Kirsty was left to tend to the more relaxed table orders. She was beat, though, and bed was calling. She couldn't wait to snuggle into Rhona. No matter how hard the day was, at least she had Rhona to go home to.

Things still weren't right between them and Kirsty was

starting to wonder if Dani was right. Not that she would ever admit that to her sister.

Rhona says *I love you* and Kirsty finds a way to ruin a special moment they could never get back? Classic. Not to mention the wedge she'd firmly slotted between them. Sounded like sabotage to her. What the fuck was wrong with her head?

'You need to make it up to her before she goes,' Dani said, lining up a row of five takeaway cups. The till was bulging today: Mum would be ecstatic.

'There's nothing to make up. It was . . .' She paused, choosing her words. 'A mutual disagreement.'

'Aye. Caused by you.'

'I might have instigated it, but it was only what we were both thinking. You can't *cause* a fight by stating the truth. That's hardly fair.'

'You're hardly fair.'

'What's that supposed to mean?'

'Dunno. I'm focusing on this mocha.'

Kirsty bumped her hip into Dani's. It was good to talk to someone that got it. She might be a complete wind-up merchant, but she knew what Kirsty was going through and never judged. Anyone else might label her crazy.

The queue showed no hint of dwindling and they still had a few hours to go. 'Want to get a takeaway tonight?' she asked Dani.

'What? On a school day? Surely Kirsty Jane Hamilton isn't deviating from her week's meal plan?'

'Shut up. You want one or not?'

'Of course. As if I can be fucked cooking tonight. Will I text Rhona?'

'Yeah, go for it.' Kirsty ducked to the milk fridge, hiding the smile taking over her face. Rhona and Dani were firm friends now. In fact, they'd been bouldering a few times with Trip, which must have been a sight to see. She wasn't sure she'd ever seen Trip jog to cross the road, never mind do actual sport. Regardless of prowess, the trio were hanging out a lot and it was doing Dani good. She'd even caught Rhona teaching Dani how to meditate. Sometimes she felt like she'd slipped into the twilight zone.

Another check appeared on the bar for her. Three hot chocolates and a cappuccino. At least it offered a little variety.

She'd just locked the coffee machine's group head into position when a familiar voice called her name.

Rhona.

Greetings were overcome by confusion when Kirsty spotted what she was wearing. 'You're awful fancy. What's going on?'

Rhona's smile was instant: so strong it hit her eyes first and Kirsty's face about ached just looking at her. 'You're never going to believe what's happened!' She scanned the counter. 'It's busy here, how do I get round to you? Get out the way?'

'Through the kitchen,' Kirsty said, pointing in the door's general direction. She was on the back foot, with not a clue what was going on.

It took her a while, and for a brief moment Kirsty wondered if she'd got lost on the way, but eventually Rhona appeared at her side.

She looked amazing. But she also looked very, very, out of place. These days she was usually found in joggers, not her best coat and a top usually reserved for high-end weddings. It even looked like she'd polished her boots.

Rhona gave her side a squeeze, aware Kirsty wasn't up for full-blown PDAs in front of a queue.

'So, what's going on?' Kirsty asked with a nervous chuckle.

'Urgh, I don't even know where to start.' She reminded Kirsty of the toys they would get as little kids. Wee springy things that you'd push down and eventually they would explode into the sky, inevitably conking someone on the head. She was wired, with restrained energy waiting to burst out of her.

'Start with why you look like you're off to the Ritz,' Kirsty joked, pouring her three hot chocs.

Rhona looked at her clothes like she'd not been the one to dress herself. 'I had a meeting.'

'A meeting? You never said.'

'It was super last minute. Like, actual last minute. Amber called me and said I had to get to Browns ASAP.'

'Ah, Browns. That explains the get-up.'

'You know it?'

'Yep. Super fancy. So who were you meeting there? Wedding client?'

Rhona looked at her watch. 'I'll need to explain the details later; I don't have much time. But yeah, kind of.'

Nerves gripped Kirsty. Something felt off. She was happy Rhona was happy, but a subtext loomed over the conversation and Kirsty didn't like it one bit.

'Where you off to?'

Rhona looked at the queue and back at her watch. Her grin returned with force. 'So, it wasn't a client. It was a wedding planner. Like, the biggest in the business. And she wants to hire me!' Kirsty was surprised Rhona didn't bounce on the spot.

'That's amazing!' she replied, still certain there was a *but* on the way.

'She loves my work and wants me and Amber to go freelance for her.'

'Oh my God,' Kirsty exclaimed. This was good news.

'Amber will handle the more local stuff and I'll do the things further away, the ones abroad. I'll get to go somewhere new every week in peak season. This is amazing, isn't it? I can't believe this is really happening.' Rhona held her fingers to her temple, the other hand on Kirsty's hip as if she needed to steady herself.

So, there was the *but*. Rhona was so wrapped up in the news that she maybe hadn't factored in reality, and Kirsty really couldn't blame her for that. But if she was in a different country every week, how was she planning on seeing her? What was the point of a girlfriend if they were only home a few months of the year?

'Lucky you,' Kirsty said, trying to sound upbeat. They could have a chat this evening: surely Rhona wouldn't take a job that meant they could never see each other? 'What we doing to celebrate tonight, then?'

Rhona pulled a face, a full-on cringe. *Great.* Kirsty braced herself further.

'We'll need to hold off on the champagne. She needs me to go to Tuscany in —' Rhona checked her watch again. 'Well, I need to be at the airport in an hour, so I'll need to leave soon.'

'Tuscany?' Kirsty stuttered. 'Like, in Italy?'

Dani leaned back, making eye contact with Rhona. 'Tonight?'

'Yep,' Rhona said, her smile still on full. 'It's crazy. I don't think my mind's caught up with it all yet.'

'Tuscany, tonight?' Kirsty repeated, just to be one hundred per cent certain she'd understood.

'Back on Sunday,' Rhona said, pumping her eyebrows. 'So, not long.'

Kirsty didn't know what to say. It was like having advisers on her shoulders. One was saying she should be happy, jumping for joy with Rhona. This was her dream. But on the other shoulder, a voice was telling her to stamp her feet and cry, say it wasn't fair. Did Rhona even think about her, or was that it? Kirsty was forgotten, a better offer received?

She decided to fall in the middle. 'Cool,' she said, not managing to conjure even an ounce of enthusiasm. 'I guess you'd better get ready then.'

'You don't seem that happy about this.'

Kirsty shrugged, fairly certain the voice campaigning for tears was on the way to victory. 'Just busy and tired.'

Rhona's shoulders slumped, her features following suit. 'You finish at seven, yeah?' she asked, stroking the back of Kirsty's arm with her thumb. 'I'll phone you when I get to Tuscany.'

Kirsty nodded, forcing a half smile. 'That would be nice.'

Rhona stole a glance at Dani. The atmosphere was leaden. Get a lump of coal and you could make diamonds in quick time. *Fuck.*

'I'd better go,' Rhona said, uncertainty lacing her words. She kissed Kirsty's cheek.

'Be safe.' Kirsty didn't recognise her own voice; the words were quiet, timid.

Another check appeared on the counter and Rhona slipped through the kitchen door. The exit was on the other side of the café, but she stole a glance as she passed the window, locking eyes with Kirsty, her face a picture of confusion and hurt.

'What was that about?' Dani asked, her voice like a foghorn.

Tara turned to face them as the queue moved down. 'Kirsty.'

'What?'

'You couldn't have been more icy if we put you in the freezer,' Dani chided.

Kirsty didn't feel like talking. She focused on making her drinks instead. She tensed her jaw, all too aware of the tears that were forming.

'You need a minute?' Dani asked out the corner of her mouth.

Kirsty froze, weighing up if she could make it through the kitchen without crying. She couldn't be bothered with Mum's questions. Well meaning or not.

'We'll be fine for ten minutes,' Dani offered when Kirsty still hadn't moved.

She nodded, her teeth still clamped together, and set down the half-finished latte.

Kirsty chewed on her bottom lip as she pushed open the swinging door to the kitchen. She kept to the left, knowing Mum would probably be at the right-hand hot plates.

The room was a mile wide and her legs heavy. Finally, she made it to the office. With the door closed she sat in the chair, staring blankly at the wall and pulling at her bottom lip with a trembling hand. Only when she was certain no one had followed her did she let the tears fall.

32

The last two days had been chaos. Mainly the good kind.

Yesterday had been a manic dash to the airport, where she'd been caught up in introductions and making a good first impression. They were a brilliant team. Her photography assistant, Liam, was a particularly good laugh. They had gelled straight away, which was fortunate seeing as they were soon to be working with each other for the foreseeable. She'd thought the Hamilton-Bough wedding had been a whirlwind, but this was a full-blown tornado. There was so much to learn. Even at normal speed it would have been a lot to take in.

The buzz was amazing, though, and Rhona was more than a little pleased with herself for stepping into the role with relative ease.

Now it was nearing midnight, and although she was shattered, adrenaline was keeping her mind awake.

She gave up staring at the ceiling and grabbed her hoodie from the side of the bed.

It was bloody freezing.

She'd made it to Florence airport late in the evening only to be whisked away to the venue: a beautiful medieval castle in the middle of the Tuscan countryside. It was like nowhere Rhona had ever attended before. Take away her camera and she could have stepped back in time, or into a fairy tale.

The impressive castle was perched on a hill, surrounded by trees, and Rhona wished it was warmer so she could venture out onto the balcony. She settled for the armchair next to it, admiring the darkness surrounding her. The stars twinkled overhead, more than she'd even experienced in her life. It made her insides feel strange as her brain tried to compute the unfathomable. She was a tiny drop in a big, big ocean.

The bride and groom were investment bankers from London and Rhona thought she'd done them proud. It was hard to know what they expected without meeting them prior, but Liam had done a grand job of filling her in on the way over.

She looked at her phone and sighed. Conversation with Kirsty had been weak. She hadn't had a chance to call and text messages were getting shorter as the hours wore on. By the time Kirsty went to bed, they were at one-word answers.

Rhona thought she'd be happy.

Yes, she might be away a bit more than expected but, Abi said most jobs would be in the Highlands; maybe one in four to a foreign venue. She was a wedding photographer: Kirsty couldn't expect her to be home at weekends regardless of where she was.

But maybe that wasn't why she was angry.

Rhona hadn't actually pressed for specifics or even asked if Kirsty was mad. She was reading between the lines. Seeing issues that maybe weren't there.

Her response hadn't been what Rhona had played out in her head, though. Kirsty couldn't have been less interested if she tried.

Maybe that was it. She'd hit the same roadblock June had. Just eight years quicker.

What am I doing wrong?

Rhona fired off a quick text, telling Kirsty how much she missed her.

A cackle of laughter floated through the stone walls. She wished Kirsty was here. They could be cosied up, Kirsty on her lap, right now, admiring the night sky together. The memory of them dancing under the stars floated to the front of her mind. She wanted that moment back, not this icy chill that stood between them.

She hated the thought of Kirsty being mad at her. The notion sat heavy in her stomach, dragging her down. The niggle had taken the edge off the entire day. She should be riding a high: instead it was like someone was grabbing at her ankle, trying to pull her under. Tomorrow's plane would be lucky to take off with the added weight she bore on her shoulders.

She texted Dani, hoping she was up to her usual nocturnal antics and could put her mind at rest. They were an hour behind Italy; there was a good chance she'd still be awake.

If she'd known Abi's team a little better it would have been comforting to offload, get an outside perspective. She didn't want their first impression of her to be the lesbian with relationship issues, though. Thankfully, it had been such a manic turnaround that there had hardly been any time for personal chat other than the basics.

Rhona's phone illuminated the dark room: Dani's reply lit up her lock screen.

What's up? x
Is Kirsty mad at me? X
Do you want me to be truthful? X
That's a yes then. Why? X

Three dots bounced on the screen, signalling Dani was typing. Rhona watched with bated breath. This was a long one.

She thinks she'll never see you if you're in a different country every week which is fair enough if it's true but I don't think you'd be so excited if that was right? I said she needed to talk to you but she's been a right sad sack. X

Fuck. Well that explained a lot.

I was in a rush. I obviously didn't explain myself very well x
So it's not true? X
Of course not x

First she gets upset thinking Rhona wasn't coming back to Glasgow, then Kirsty thinks she's taken a job where she wouldn't even be in the country most of the time. No wonder she wasn't chatty.

Is she still awake? X Rhona asked, hoping Dani might get the hint and go wake her up. She needed to speak to her now, clear the air. What if she'd sat on this so long she'd mentally broken up with her and Rhona would return to packed bags and a goodbye?

She took a faltering deep breath.

She went to bed ages ago. Sorry x
No worries x

Rhona stared out the window, the stars fuzzy dots as tears clouded her vision.

Maybe she just wasn't cut out for a relationship.

∾

'You okay?' Liam asked as he plonked himself into the hard airport seat in the departure lounge. 'You've been super quiet.'

'Yeah, just tired,' Rhona lied.

Kirsty's reply to her text had been cutting: *Guess we'd better get used to that x*

Rhona hadn't even bothered to reply. The rest of the morning passed without further communication and Rhona was bracing herself for a difficult conversation when she got home. Or back to Kirsty's. Whatever you wanted to call it now.

Liam produced a roll of Munchies and tore off the top piece of foil, pointing the packet in Rhona's direction.

She took a chocolate and flashed him a smile.

He stared straight ahead as he chewed. He was only in his early twenties, but the age gap with Rhona wasn't noticeable. He was a hard worker and professional to a T. It was easy to see why Abi had hired him.

He ran a hand over his bleached buzzcut. 'You know, if we're going to be working together, it might be nice to be honest from the start.'

Rhona smiled despite herself. 'Very astute.'

'I'm nothing if not observant. So, what's really wrong?'

Rhona let out a pained huff. 'My girlfriend's mad at me. I think we're going to break up.'

Liam's face turned sullen as he swivelled to face her, the huge fluffy coat on his lap spilling over them both. 'Why do you think that?'

'She's mad at me and communication has never been our forté. I think this is the final straw. I don't exactly have a good track record when it comes to relationships.'

'Meaning?'

'It's complicated. My ex and I didn't part on good terms either.'

'Does anyone break up because things are good?'

'Fair point,' she replied. She watched an elderly couple pass, the guy laden with bags and the woman carrying a small purse. 'It's complicated. Really complicated. So now I'm looking back at that relationship wondering what I did wrong, so I can try and make this one work. Does that make sense?'

Liam righted his position as he thought, facing himself straight on again. 'Not really,' he laughed.

Anyone else and she would have gotten snappy. She wasn't in the mood for talking. After this she wouldn't see him until February, though. She couldn't leave on a bad note. 'I just don't want to repeat past mistakes, that's what I'm saying.'

'And what were the mistakes, if you don't mind me asking?' He popped another chocolate in his mouth.

Rhona slumped forward, leaning her chin on her hand. 'I don't have a clue. I mean, I'm not saying I'm perfect, but I must have done something wrong.'

Liam chewed. 'Why, though? Sometimes people are just arseholes. You don't need to have done anything wrong. Everyone has their own issues. It sounds like you're putting the burden on yourself. What if it was all on her?'

Rhona scrunched her face up. He could have a point, but it didn't help her solve things with Kirsty. 'Regardless, the issue with Kirsty is all my fault.'

Liam offered her another chocolate. She shook her head. He ate another. 'You want my opinion?'

'Not really,' she joked.

'Whatever,' he said with a wave of his hand. 'I think you're overthinking things. Go buy her some perfume or whatever. Have a chat when you get in. I bet it's not as bad as you think.'

Rhona looked at her watch. She had thirty minutes to spare: a walk around duty-free wouldn't hurt anyone. She left her bags with Liam and had a wander.

Her brother's earlier advice rang in her ears. She was thinking with her head, not her heart, making everything more complicated than it needed to be. She stopped, spying a shop just past a fancy clothing outlet. She knew what to get Kirsty. Hopefully it wasn't too late to win her heart back.

33

Kirsty flicked through the TV channels. It wasn't that the choices were bad; it was just nothing was holding her attention. All her mind could think about was Rhona.

This wasn't sabotage, or whatever Dani wanted to label it. She loved Rhona but there was no point in having a relationship if they never saw each other.

She was dreading the chat they'd need to have when she got home. She'd almost switched shifts with Dani so she could be at work all day and put off the inevitable.

The front door clicked open and Kirsty closed her eyes, pushing her head hard into the cushion.

She thought back to her stupid watch analogy and pictured her heart now – tightly wound in bubble wrap, ready for what was coming.

'Hello?' Rhona called, unsure if the flat was empty.

'Hey,' Kirsty replied, her voice as flat as she felt.

Kirsty didn't move as Rhona's footsteps neared. She did open her eyes, though. She didn't want to look weird.

Rhona crouched at the side of the sofa and kissed the

top of her head. She didn't look herself. Her sparkle was gone, her eyes sullen. 'Hey,' she said, with a pitiful smile.

This didn't bode well.

Kirsty felt her bottom lip wobble and she fought to hold everything in, but she was like an overflowing coffee cup – there was no chance of containing how she felt.

'Hey, what's wrong?' Rhona asked, springing to her side and scooping Kirsty into a hug.

She listened to Rhona's heart, counting each beat in a bid to level her emotions. She closed her eyes, scrunching the tears away as the TV chattered in the background, some nonsense about cattle farming that she'd inadvertently left on.

There were a thousand things she wanted to say, a whole Rolodex of questions, but she eventually settled on: 'I missed you.' She should have said that this morning instead of being a brat.

'Enough to cry?' Rhona asked the top of Kirsty's head. She stroked her hair, her nose buried deep in Kirsty's wavy locks. She felt Rhona's other hand lift from her back and the TV clicked off. 'Sorry, I don't want to see cows getting hurt.'

For some stupid, unknown reason, that was what broke Kirsty, and a sob broke free from her carefully constructed confines.

'Hey, whoa, what's wrong?' Rhona asked again.

'We're going to break up, aren't we?' Kirsty asked, her breath hitching.

'Is that what you want?' Rhona's hand stilled on Kirsty's back and she could feel the aggressive thump of Rhona's heart against her ribs.

Tears dammed further conversation and Kirsty found herself incapable of speaking unless she wanted to become an absolute wreck. She opted to shake her head instead.

They sat like that for an age and Kirsty wondered if they would ever talk again. It wouldn't be a bad thing. She'd happily never utter another word if it meant living in Rhona's arms.

'Dani thinks you've maybe got the wrong end of the stick,' Rhona said, her voice hoarse.

'Me?'

'Yeah. It's my fault. I was in a rush and excited and thinking about a thousand other things. This new job: I won't be abroad all the time. A bit, yeah, I won't lie about that. But for the most part it will be jobs in the Highlands.'

'Yeah?' Kirsty waited for the other shoe to fall. There was always a *but*.

'I can be based anywhere, I guess, as long as I'm within driving distance of the airports. But—'

Kirsty tensed, preparing herself for a fresh blow.

'What's wrong?'

'You're going to say something I don't want to hear.'

Rhona sighed. 'Sit up, let me look at you.'

Kirsty rose, pawing at her eyes, well aware she probably looked a state. Rhona switched positions, pulling Kirsty's legs over hers and settling in.

Rhona tilted her head, her dark eyes swallowing Kirsty whole. 'I was going to say,' Rhona continued, grabbing Kirsty by the hips and pulling her closer. 'That I'd rather be based here. In Glasgow. That sound okay?'

Kirsty felt like she'd just been handed the moon and the stars. 'I'd like that.'

Rhona's smile was too cute but Kirsty felt like there was still more she wanted to say. There might be a *but* yet. She hated this scepticism more than anything else in the world, but it was part of her and if she was ever going to love Rhona properly she needed to learn to love the whole of herself, too. She couldn't wait for a lifetime of Rhona proving her pessimism wrong.

'I think it would make the most sense for me to move back in here,' she said, looking sheepish. Kirsty's chest split with happiness again but her poker face held. Rhona continued, 'I know it's a big ask. But I think it makes the most sense, while I'm trying to find my own place. Rather than travelling for viewings and everything, you know.'

Buts could be good too, it would seem. 'That makes perfect sense, yes.'

The sparkle was creeping back into Rhona's eyes. 'Good. So, you'll save me a spot in your bed while I'm away?'

'I'll try not to forget you. Promise.'

'Actually,' Rhona said, looking rather coy. 'I had foreseen this problem. And I think I've found a solution.'

'Oh, really?'

She reached for her duffel bag at the end of the sofa, leaning over Kirsty's knee and wiggling her fingers in its direction. 'Urgh, I can't reach it. Can you?'

Kirsty reached back, dragging it closer. 'Jesus, that's heavy.'

'Don't worry: no one you know. Right, close your eyes.'

Kirsty wiggled free of Rhona's hands and scooted closer, placing a leg on either side of Rhona's hips, wanting to make sure she wasn't going anywhere. After a quick shimmy to get comfy she closed her eyes, sucking on her top lip to hide how awkward she felt.

'Okay, now hands out.'

She listened as the duffel was unzipped and the clink of what sounded like a glass bottle rang through the room as Rhona placed something on the coffee table.

'No peeking,' Rhona said.

'There will be if you don't hurry up.'

Rhona gave her a playful shove. 'Steady, or I might book an Airbnb instead.'

Kirsty mimed zipping her lips before holding her hands out again. Something light but sizeable was placed in her palms.

She opened her eyes to find a box in her hands and a bottle of champagne on the table.

Her heart stuttered to breakneck speed, nought to one hundred in a split second. That had better not be an engagement ring.

'Open it,' Rhona urged.

Kirsty's hands shook as she creaked the box open.

'Oh my God,' she blurted.

'Do you like it?'

Kirsty was gobsmacked. Nestled inside was a beautiful silver watch.

'Rhona, this is Gucci. It must have cost a fortune.'

'I couldn't quite afford a Rolex but I thought it was nice. You can wear it while I'm away. Not quite wearing your heart on your sleeve. More like my heart on your wrist? You do remember saying that thing about watches, yeah?'

Kirsty leaned forward, pulling Rhona in for a kiss. 'Of course I remember.'

'I just wanted you to know that no matter where I go, I'll come back.'

'You should have brought me a boomerang, not a watch.'

'Now there's an idea. Here gimme that back,' she joked, swiping at the box.

Kirsty snapped it shut, holding it over her head, out of reach. Rhona pivoted forward, pressing herself against Kirsty. Her eyes drifted to Chet in the armchair opposite. 'Fancy going somewhere Chet's not watching?'

34

Kirsty straddled Rhona on their bed, her hips grinding against Rhona's, in rhythm with their mouths as they kissed.

Rhona couldn't believe her luck.

'I really missed you,' she said between kisses. So much had gone wrong due to lack of communication; now she wanted to say everything she was thinking, just to be sure Kirsty didn't miss something important or get things skewed.

'I missed you too,' Kirsty said, pushing harder against Rhona's core.

She stilled as Rhona snagged her gaze. 'I love you.'

'I love you too.' They held steady for a moment, time suspended. Kirsty kicked into gear, as if remembering what they were actually doing. 'Now, get this top off.'

Rhona held her arms up, letting Kirsty relieve her of the clothing before doing the same for her.

Her boobs were perfectly level with Rhona's face. She kissed each one gently, following the swell of the bra's lace cups.

'I'm so glad I got dumped and Amber offered me a job,' Rhona mumbled into Kirsty's breasts.

'And my mum made me do that stupid Lovefest thing.'

'Ever hear from Ross?'

Kirsty arched her back, pulling away from Rhona with a devilish grin. 'Don't ever mention him again. Especially when we're in bed.' She tapped Rhona's nose with a finger before trailing it down and pulling at her bottom lip.

'Sorry,' Rhona said, taking Kirsty's finger in her mouth and sucking. She flicked her tongue across its tip.

Kirsty groaned, her hips finding purchase again. Rhona held her steady, rocking against her, dying to take her joggers off but wanting this to last as long as possible.

She released Kirsty's finger and leaned forward for a kiss. Desire built in her core, a wave of want rippling through her with every sway of Kirsty's hips.

Their lips parted and Kirsty's tongue found hers.

Two years ago she was probably sitting on her kitchen floor, bawling her eyes out. Now she was about to be fucked by the love of her life.

Patience was a wondrous thing.

Rhona ran a hand up Kirsty's back, tracing the line of her spine until she reached the clasp of her bra. With a flick, her breasts were free and Rhona felt the weight of them against her own.

Kirsty shimmied free, throwing the bra to the floor. Rhona groaned at how good Kirsty looked: temptation was running rampant inside, screaming for her to fully undress Kirsty and take her right now.

Instead, she ran her hands up the curve of Kirsty's torso until they found her chest, each palm the perfect size to cup her breasts, Rhona's thumbs circling a nipple each.

Kirsty undid Rhona's bra and slid it off one arm at a

time, Rhona unwilling to fully concede her grasp on Kirsty's boobs.

'You're so hot,' Kirsty moaned breathlessly as their mouths connected again.

She'd spent today's plane ride worrying she'd never experience this again. Her chest ached with the realisation she'd not have Kirsty for six weeks. She wasn't wishing her trip away but her focus had shifted.

And it shifted again when Kirsty dipped her head to Rhona's neck, 'You working tomorrow?' she asked, her breath floating over Rhona's skin.

'No.'

Rhona felt her smile before teeth lightly nipped at her skin and Kirsty sucked and kissed the bare expanse.

Heat flooded between her legs and every kiss pushed her closer to the edge.

She slid her hands down Kirsty's sides and under the hem of her joggers, using her bum to pull her closer. She had no idea what her next move would be, only that she wanted all of Kirsty now, in every way possible. And even that wouldn't be enough.

Kirsty drew back, and after an awkward dance, her joggers were on the floor.

Rhona let her eyes wander, hoping to commit the image to memory. You could travel the world and never see anything so beautiful. And here she was: Rhona's to enjoy, right here, in her bed, all to herself.

She ran the back of her hand down Kirsty's thigh and her muscles stiffened to Rhona's touch, pleading for her to take things further. She traced the inside of Kirsty's leg, skirting her thumb along the crease between hip and core, before resting her palm on top of Kirsty's leg.

Kirsty smiled between kisses. 'You're just teasing me now.'

'Never.'

She let her hand hover lower again, her fingers flitting over the hair between Kirsty's legs.

'Rhona,' Kirsty moaned. It was a ticking-off and a command all in one.

She'd tortured Kirsty and herself enough. Rhona snaked her hand between Kirsty's thighs and into the wetness of her core.

'God, you feel so good,' she groaned, sliding two fingers inside her.

Kirsty responded by thrusting her hips, riding Rhona's fingers and pushing hard against her hand.

'Fuck,' Kirsty cried, breaking their kiss to straighten herself and get better purchase.

She could feel Kirsty was close and she wanted this to last as long as possible, so she slowly pulled out her fingers, shifting them into a V-shape, running them the length of her core.

Kirsty laughed under her breath, pleased with the change of tactic.

All of Kirsty was hard, responding to every touch as Rhona teased the pleasure out. Rhona's fingers massaged her with long, purposeful strokes, building Kirsty's climax.

Sensing Kirsty could take no more, Rhona slid her fingers back in and brought her free hand to the front, using her thumb to massage Kirsty's hard clit.

Her breathing became more ragged the closer she got and it wasn't long before Kirsty let out a splintered cry, her internal walls clamping hard around Rhona's fingers. She stilled, panting hard as she collapsed forward, her head on Rhona's shoulder.

'Wow,' she huffed.

Rhona held her by the hips, savouring the post-orgasm rush that shrouded the room.

Composure finally returning, Kirsty nibbled her collarbone. 'You've got way too many clothes on.'

'You'd better help out, then.'

Rhona lifted her hips and Kirsty pulled her trousers and pants off, slotting a thigh between her legs and pressing hard against Rhona's core.

She was already so wet.

Kirsty's kisses only added to the pulse that was forming between her legs.

She tasted like coffee, which was perfectly apt for Kirsty. Rhona could never drink another cup without thinking of her. No matter the continent she was on, no matter what kind it was, coffee would be Kirsty. And much like the drink, Rhona could happily enjoy a cup of Kirsty every day. She was the perfect pick-me-up in the morning. And if she had too much, Rhona would be awake all night.

Kirsty shifted, pulling them onto their sides, the kiss never faltering.

'Stay there,' she said, using a hand on Rhona's thigh for leverage as she turned. Soon they were top to toe, Kirsty nestled between her legs, her tongue quickly finding Rhona's core.

Rhona gasped, the pleasure instant, her body already on edge.

With Kirsty's centre so close it felt rude not to return the favour. She encouraged Kirsty's leg onto her shoulder, creating a lazy sixty-nine as her mouth sucked and stroked Kirsty's clit.

She drove her tongue harder, sweeping its length, mirroring what Kirsty was doing.

Rhona closed her eyes, wanting to remember exactly how it felt, the way Kirsty's tongue glided over her, bringing her closer with every swoop. Kirsty groaned and the vibration against her clit sent a shockwave through Rhona's body.

Pleasure pulsed through her and soon it was impossible for Rhona to hold it any longer: she was in freefall, tumbling into oblivion like she'd jumped from a plane without a parachute.

She bucked her hips, her muscles spasming as she came.

Kirsty followed soon after.

Hot breath on her core as Kirsty laughed woke Rhona from a daze and she rolled on to her back, absolutely spent. Kirsty traced a finger along her ankle and up her foot. 'Something to remember me by, when you're off enjoying the world.'

'I'll certainly never forget that.'

Kirsty kissed the top of her foot. 'And I've still got another nine days to top that.'

Rhona grinned.

35

Kirsty twisted round, slotting between Rhona's arm and her side. She rested her head on Rhona's chest, kissing her skin as she got comfy.

They'd be warmer under the duvet but she didn't want to move: every second with Rhona was precious.

'I knew this would happen as soon as I saw you at Lovefest,' Rhona said dreamily.

'Oh, you did, did you?' Kirsty joked as her finger followed an imaginary line across the top of Rhona's breast.

Rhona chuckled. 'Well, kind of. A room full of people and I couldn't help but look at you. It was like you were the only person there.'

'Your photos would prove otherwise.'

Rhona playfully prodded her back. 'Hey, let me be sappy.'

'Okay, okay. Sorry.'

'Do you not remember me from that night?'

'Course I do. I came home and told Dani I'd met an absolute fox of a woman.'

'Romantic.'

'I told her about you as well.'

That earned a tickle attack. Kirsty panted, her giggles still ringing in the air. 'No, no, no. Time out, time out.' Rhona pulled her back into an embrace, their legs intertwined.

'Well, then, Mrs Romantic, you've still not taken me on a proper date. Are you really going to leave me hanging until February?'

'I'd better fix that, stat, eh?' Rhona said, giving Kirsty's shoulder a squeeze.

'I'm working every day until Christmas now. When do you go to Queensferry?'

'Christmas Eve, so Sunday.'

Kirsty clicked her tongue against the roof of her mouth. 'Doesn't leave a lot of time.'

Rhona raised herself up on her forearm. 'We could go now, if you're keen?'

'Now?'

'Yeah, let's make the most of our last day off together.'

∽

BAR ORAMA WAS BASICALLY DEAD, which wasn't a surprise given how minging the weather was. Not to mention it being the last proper Sunday before Christmas. Everyone was either cosy inside or manically shopping.

'Grab a booth; I'll get you a rum,' Kirsty said to Rhona, intent on picking up their last attempt at a date and actually finishing it.

Travis stopped wiping down the bar as she approached, flipping the towel over his shoulder and greeting her with a warm smile.

'Didn't think I'd be seeing you this side of Christmas,' he said.

'Rhona's away soon; we're trying to make the most of my day off. Only one I've got before she heads off.'

'That sucks.'

'Tell me about it.' She ordered their drinks and watched Travis as he made them with careful precision.

He was a good guy. He just hadn't been the right guy for Kirsty.

'You on your own today?' she asked as he set down her white wine.

'Aye. Well, Kev's in the back and Kim's starting at four.'

Kirsty nodded. Her intentions hovered between them, the words playing hard to get. She cleared her throat quietly. 'I'm sorry for being an arsehole when we were together.'

Travis's face twisted with confusion. He was speechless for a second, as if having to compute what he'd heard. 'Where did that come from?'

'Just been contemplating my life choices the past few months. You didn't deserve to be treated that way.'

He nodded, his lips pursed. 'Let's consider it water under the bridge. We were both different back then.'

Kirsty stepped round the side of the bar, holding her arms out. 'A hug, for old time's sake?'

Travis gripped her like a bear and she was sure a few vertebrae popped. 'Now, go sit.' He ushered her with a mischievous grin. 'Your drinks are getting warm.'

'What was that about?' Rhona asked as Kirsty slid into the booth beside her.

'Just strengthening some bridges. Making them fireproof.'

Rhona pulled a face. 'I won't ask.' She sipped her rum.

'So, you coming to North Queensferry on Boxing Day, yeah?'

'That's the plan. I'm shitting myself, to be honest.'

'How so?'

'I'll be meeting your entire family. Talk about going in at the deep end.'

Rhona smirked. 'Hmm. Imagine. I should invite my cousins too. A few members of the extended family. Aunties. Uncles. Track down a few creepy family friends...'

'Alright, alright. I'd forgotten about the wedding. I should have known then that you planned on sticking around. No one would endure my family if they didn't plan on playing the long game.'

'They weren't that bad.'

'You have to say that.'

Rhona smiled into her rum as she drank. 'It'll go quick, you know.'

'Boxing Day?'

'No, you goose. The six weeks I'm away. You probably won't even notice I'm gone.'

'I doubt that. Although, I'll be able to starfish in bed again.'

'See? Already finding the positives.'

Kirsty had to keep reminding herself that she'd only known Rhona since August. It was strange to think that this time last year she didn't even know she existed: now her world was tipped upside down and the thought of not seeing her made her chest ache.

She took Rhona's hand over the table. Her watch caught her eye and whatever witty comeback had been brewing was lost.

'I want you to live in the moment when you're away, but will you message me, just whenever you get the chance?'

Rhona gave her hand a squeeze. 'Of course. And photos, if there's good enough internet.'

'I just need to know you're okay. Travelling alone is dangerous. The occasional check-in would be nice.'

'I promise you'll hear from me. I still wish you could come.'

Kirsty shook her head. 'This is your thing. Although,' she pulled out her phone and quickly bashed a website address into her browser before turning it towards Rhona. 'I found this company you can hire camper vans from and they plan a route for you. We could do Europe, or at least a bit of it, in the summer if you're keen?'

Rhona's instant smile said she was onto a winner. 'If you're there, I don't mind where we go.'

Six weeks. She could do this. A temporary blip before the rest of their lives. Yikes, that was a big thought. Excitement raced in her veins, nothing else.

'How about another round of drinks then we head back to bed?'

'Sounds perfect,' Rhona replied with a grin.

SEVEN WEEKS LATER

Rhona finally spotted her bag on the luggage carousel. It was almost as if they'd made hers last on purpose.

She scooped it up and hauled it onto her back, the weight of it making her stagger slightly. Six weeks of hauling it around India and she still wasn't used to it.

India was beyond her wildest dreams. She'd started in Varanasi then bussed it to Rishikesh, and from there she took a detour to visit relatives.

Punjab was amazing. She'd met with family who greeted her with open arms, despite not seeing her for near on twenty-five years. She'd visited Amritsar's Golden Temple, eaten like a queen more times than she cared to count, seen the real Punjab on a walking tour with 'Uncle' Tanvir, and experienced the breathtaking gardens at Virasat-e-Khalsa.

Then it was off to Delhi, Jaipur, Pushkar, a few other places, then Ahmedabad, before finally, Mumbai.

She'd seen stepwells and temples, Gandhi's home, and camels roaming freely; she'd white water rafted, seen handcrafted leather more intricate than she could have ever imagined, and bazaar markets she would never forget. She'd sat on a hill and watched the sun set, thinking there could never be anywhere more perfect, only to be proven wrong the next day.

It was all she wanted and more.

But standing in the baggage reclaim area, she couldn't help but be excited. There was no post-holiday depression here.

Rhona was watching the flat-screen view of the waiting area and there, in the top right hand corner, was Kirsty.

She was a tiny blip on the huge screen, but Rhona could see her knee was bouncing as she scrolled on her phone.

They'd texted every day Rhona had service, so Kirsty was well aware of how her adventure had gone. Still she couldn't wait to show her pictures and recount stories in bed tonight.

Her bones ached with how much she missed her.

With a final deep breath, she passed through the automatic doors, following the corridor round until the doors to the waiting area were finally in sight.

She clocked Kirsty straight away, but it took her a moment to see Rhona.

Then all bets were off.

If her bag had weighed less she would have matched Kirsty's speed, but she was more concerned about getting the blasted thing off so she could get a better grip on Kirsty. It dropped to the floor just as Kirsty leapt full speed into her arms.

The world slowed to a halt, the airport vanishing around them.

Rhona held tight, as if her life depended on it.

'I missed you,' Kirsty said into her neck before kissing Rhona.

God, those lips. Rhona's legs went weak, which was an

issue; they were the only thing keeping her and Kirsty upright.

Kirsty pulled back and Rhona was left looking like a sad puppy. She dropped to the ground before kissing Rhona again, putting a smile back on her face.

'Come on, let's go, before I get done for indecent exposure.'

Rhona's eyes widened. 'You've really missed me, eh?' she joked.

She picked her bag up off the ground and heaved it back on. Kirsty took her hand and led her off.

'Your car's not far.'

'You get on okay with it?'

'Yes,' Kirsty boomed, clearly impressed. 'I didn't realise how much I missed driving. Dani's been using it too. I hope you don't mind.'

'Course not. That's why I added her to the insurance as well.' Rhona kissed Kirsty's hand and got a kiss on the lips in return, making her awkwardly stumble. The sooner this bag was gone the better.

'You've not missed much,' Kirsty said, swinging their clasped hands.

'No?'

'Nah. Izzy went on a disaster of a date. More on that later. Ashley and Hazel are still together. Dani's become some fucking mediation mogul. Oh, and,' she took a breath. 'My sister's up the duff.'

'You're kidding.'

'Hand on heart,' she replied, doing exactly that.

'Just to be clear: Kat, not Dani?'

'Can you imagine? Good God. Yes, Kat. Thank the stars.'

'This is amazing! Both of us aunties in the same year. Dani excited?'

'Over the moon.'

'I bet your mum is too.'

Kirsty rolled her eyes. 'Just a bit. Takes the pressure off me, finally.'

'I didn't realise there was pressure.' They passed through the automatic doors leading outside and the Scottish air hit Rhona like a punch in the face. Jesus, it was cold. She wished she'd put on more than just a T-shirt.

'Don't worry, still don't want children. I haven't gone baby crazy in your absence.'

'Good, or I'd be right back on a plane,' she jibed.

Kirsty stole another kiss while they waited to cross the road.

'Erm, do you know? I think that's literally it. It's been boring as fuck without you here.'

'Good to know I'm the instigator of your entertainment.'

'Always.'

Finally, they were at the car. Rhona dumped her bag in the boot before getting into the passenger side. It was super surreal not to be driving *her* car but after her mammoth journey home she didn't have the headspace or legs for it.

Kirsty put an arm around her headrest and leaned over for a proper kiss. Not one where half an airport waiting room was watching.

Despite the chilly Scottish air making every hair on her body stand to attention, Rhona could have melted right there. She brought a hand up to Kirsty's jaw, cupping it, and pulled her closer.

She moaned as Kirsty's tongue slipped between her parted lips.

The door to the car in the next bay opened and Rhona jumped a mile at the sound.

Kirsty sniggered. 'Come on, let's get home.'

'Do you want to have a bath together?' Rhona asked, halfway up the close stairs.

'Now?' Kirsty asked, fishing her door key out.

'Yeah. I feel minging from the plane.'

'Maybe later.'

Rhona huffed under her breath. She was sluggish and dirty from travelling but the urge to get Kirsty naked was strong. A bath had felt like a good compromise.

'Dump your bag here,' Kirsty said, tilting her head to the hall floor and extending a hand. 'Then follow me.'

Intriguing. Rhona took her hand and let herself be led. When she reached the kitchen door she just about jumped a mile.

'Surprise!' chorused a group of familiar faces.

Kirsty hugged her from the side, planting a kiss on her cheek. 'I'd wanted you to myself for the night but they said they couldn't wait.'

Dani bounded over, giving Rhona a hug an anaconda would be jealous of. 'Do you like your sign? I made it,' she beamed.

A banner hung on the far wall with huge handpainted letters declaring WELCOME BACK RHONA. Or at least most of it: she'd misjudged the space and only gotten half of the final A to fit.

'It's brilliant,' Rhona said, her thundering heart making words tough.

Tears pricked at her eyes, the sheer volume of love in the room coaxing them to the surface.

Soon she was surrounded by the whole gang – Izzy, Kim, Trip, Ashley, and even Hazel – all wanting to hear about her adventures and see pictures.

A beer was thrust into her hand by Trip. 'Good to have you home, pal.'

Rhona's face cracked into an unbreakable smile when Kim gave her a hug as Izzy simultaneously *cheers*ed her.

She snagged Kirsty's gaze on the other side of the room as she grabbed a drink. She smiled, her eyes saying she felt the same way Rhona did.

Everything had clicked into place. All roads led here. She was exactly where she was meant to be. She was home.

LEAVE ME A REVIEW?

Will you leave me a review?

I hope you enjoyed Love Detour. If you have a moment I would really appreciate an honest review on Amazon and / or Goodreads. Reviews help me grow as an author and help new readers know what to expect. The more people that take a chance on my books, the more books I can write. It doesn't need to be anything fancy, a few words will do. Thank you.

~

Allie McDermid is a lesbian romance author. Her debut novel, Love Charade, was published in July 2022.

Born and raised in Perth, Allie now lives in Glasgow with her ever-growing gang of cats. She is partial to a good scone.

ALSO BY ALLIE MCDERMID

Want to know what happened at the first ever Lovefest?

LOVE CHARADE

Holly Taylor didn't expect to return to Glasgow. And she certainly didn't expect her parents to enter her into a dating competition on her first day home.

Jen Berkley is happily single. Having vowed to never date again after her horror ex broke her heart, no one is more surprised when her best friend convinces her to take part in a dating contest.

Jen wants to win the money. Holly wants to regain the trust of her parents. Will they get what their hearts desire or will the charade fool no one?

Set in Glasgow and full of Scottish charm as well as lashings of delicious desire, smouldering sexual tension and even a few laughs, buy Love Charade today and find out if some things just can't be faked...

ALSO BY ALLIE MCDERMID

Need to know more? Enjoy year three of Lovefest, today!

LOVE MAGNET

Gemma Anderson is new to lesbian dating. Recently divorced and looking for love, the annual dating festival is a last resort after a string of failed matches.

Steph Campbell has long come to terms with being perpetually single, so working in her bar during the most loved-up season of the year, she hardly expects to encounter a match.

Gemma is letting her head rule her heart. Steph is content to just be friends. Will they find a way to put their differences aside?

Book three in the Lovefest series is filled with slow-burn romance, lashings of spice, and a sassy granny who kills it with one-liners. Buy Love Magnet today and discover if opposites really do attract.

Printed in Great Britain
by Amazon